See Dan Run

A Caper

P.R. Steele

Also by Author

The Money Run

Cover design: P.R. Steele   Interior design: Amy Ruiz Fritz
Editor: Sue Clark

ISBN: 13: 978-0996028721

DEDICATION

This book is dedicated to my wife, Gail, to our children Troy, Jennifer and Mike, David and Leigh, Jason, and to our grandchildren – Little Bit, Hankster, Charley, Mae, the Big Fella, Moe, Cameron, and Nathan.

ACKNOWLEDGMENTS

First to Sue Clark for believing this story was exciting, encouraging me not to give up writing all together, and showing me how to be a better writer.

Second, to Amy Ruiz Fritz for all her technical help in getting this book put together. Her email is amy@social-assistant.net if you need technical help with your book.

All the critique groups for helping point out many of the flaws.

JC for always smiling and finding the little mistakes.

The real people in the book who were in the Marine Corps with me. You've made my life a hoot. Guys…it's been a hell of a party and I'm glad we shared it.

And to those who I've pissed off or offended, let me apologize. We all know I've got flaws.

And mistakes in writing belong to me.

Now, everybody, I have a favor to ask. Please go to the website, amazon.com, and leave a candid review. As Elvis would've said, "Thank you. Thank you very much."

Richard Steele

What if one stole twenty million dollars from the military payroll?

His biggest concern would be getting caught. If that happened, his five Marine Corps combat brothers would also suffer.

CHAPTER ONE

April 7, 1972, on a cargo ship off the coast of Washington State.

Dan Burton leaned forward in the pilot seat of the new Bell Jet Ranger helicopter preparing for takeoff from the ship. His stomach was upset, not from anything he ate, but from what he suspected. The same two guys had again hidden duffel bags in the cargo space, as they had a few weeks before. The bags weren't filled with art objects. Dan figured they contained drugs, which meant no way in hell would he have anything to do with them, let alone transporting them.

If he were caught flying Ken's drugs, even unbeknownst to him, Dan would have messed up his entire future as well as five of his combat brothers. Dan had vowed to protect them at any cost.

The ship deck beneath the helicopter rolled up and crashed down. The angry waves pitched the ship, mirroring his state of mind.

Dan had never, on any of his missions in Vietnam, overlooked the pre-start check list, yet the first item, "Check Battery Switch," still remained untouched. Dan wrapped his thoughts around having a come-to-Jesus meeting with his employer, Ken, who owned the duffels and the helo.

He rubbed his temples. If the Feds put me under a microscope about flying drugs, they'll find out about the money. And everything was going good until now when Dan was bringing some of the money back that he'd deposited in Switzerland. How could he have missed all the signs that Ken was transporting drugs? Damn it. When they caught Ken, Dan would be in deep shit.

It'd blow his fellow Marines, Jack Higgins, Joe Hegidio, and Charles Pogany's cover. And it could expose Dennis Lee and John Ludwig's participation in the heist. They weren't the ones who took the payroll money from the military in Okinawa, really and truly.

That money had been sitting in six different accounts in Switzerland, and Dan had figured out how to move some of it back to the States. How could he have been so stupid?

Well, Ken, I'm through with you, you lying bastard. Today's my last day, and before we get back you're going to tell anybody who asks that I knew nothing about the drugs.

Ken yanked the copilot's door open and moved his slender, a bit shorter than Dan's, body into the seat. "Hey, Buddy, let's get going."

Dan flinched. "Shit, you startled me."

"Sorry about that." Ken smoothed his shiny black hair.

Dan engaged the starter. "Ken, we're having a talk, and no more putting it off. It involves way more than just my concerns." The turbine spooled up.

"Okay, but let's get this thing out of here."

Dan remained silent until the aircraft rounded the peninsula and the skyline of Seattle appeared. Today Dan took the direct route with the Bremerton ferry crossing the Sound.

As the helo approached the ferry's wake, Dan said,

"Okay, Ken, I saw those guys last week slip some duffels in the luggage compartment, just like today. Then they closed up the engine compartment. So, what's that all about?"

"I've told you and told you. I don't want to pay foreign excise tax in Taiwan on artwork and what not. That's all. Honest."

"Bull...shit. So, you won't mind me taking a look see when we..."

"Like hell you are. You're not touching those duffels. End of conversation." Ken poked his index finger at Dan. "You need to remember something. I'm the boss. Got it?"

Knowing Ken's fear of flying, Dan nodded his head and rolled the helo into a steep turn to Ken's side.

"Stop it, damn it. You idiot. What the hell are you doing?"

"If this idiot doesn't get some answers pretty quick...well." Dan took all the power off the aircraft and pushed the nose over as they began an autorotation. The aircraft fell like a brick. "So what's in the bags?"

"Stop it, stop it, you goddamn maniac," Ken yelled.

They passed through five hundred feet as the water grew closer.

Dan leveled off and started a gentle climb. "You may be the boss alright, but I'm not hanging my ass out hauling your illegal bullshit drugs. And, I'm checking out those duffels."

Ken wiped his forehead and tried to catch his breath. "You're crazy. That little ditty did it. We're through."

"Fine with me, but..."

The helicopter shook and the low engine oil pressure light illuminated, along with several lights on the caution panel. Dan couldn't believe his eyes. The engine oil pressure gauge read zero.

"Aw, shit." Dan checked their position over Puget Sound.

Ken clutched the dashboard. "What was that?"

"We're out of engine oil. Zip. Nada." Dan tapped the engine oil gauge.

"Bullshit. This thing is brand new," Ken yelled.

"I double checked everything when we shut down on the boat. But wait. What about that guy closing the engine compartment, Ken?"

The engine low oil pressure light had been illuminated for the last nine to ten seconds. Now the engine ran without any oil. Dan didn't have to be told that all the oil had streamed along the airframe.

Dan cleared his mind as he keyed the radio mic. "SeaTac, this is November two four zero niner tango declaring an emergency. We're nine to ten miles on your two zero six at five hundred feet heading one one zero to our base ops helo pad, squawking seventy-six hundred."

"Ah-h-h, roger, zero niner tango. Say emergency and intentions," Seattle tower replied.

"We've lost engine oil pressure, and are nine miles out of home base. Looks like we're going to have to put it in the water. Will keep you advised."

"Roger, zero niner tango. We have a visual. You're trailing a lot of smoke. We'll scramble rescue aircraft."

"Roger, SeaTac. I've got my hands full."

"What the hell do you mean, put it in the water?" Ken yelled over the intercom.

"Means, if the engine quits, we're in deep shit. We'll be making a liquid landing." Dan nursed the helo toward their home base a little north of Tacoma.

Dan babied the aircraft as he tried to gain altitude. The higher they were, the further they could auto rotate, but he didn't want to change the power setting and strain the ailing engine. Either he would make their base helicopter pad or they were in trouble.

"Are we going to make it?" Ken wrung his hands.

"Probably not. Technically...the turbine should've

already quit. If we go down, stay in the bird until the rotors stop."

"You're serious."

"Hell, yes, I'm serious. If we get out of here and make it into the water, the hypothermia will kill you before you know it. The life vests won't protect us from the cold. So keep moving. This water temperature gives you about a five-minute life expectancy."

"Look, there's the pad. I can see it. Can't we glide or whatever?"

"No. At this altitude, we'll make…maybe a quarter to a half a mile in the autorotation. We're still five miles out. You can't swim that far."

Ken started crossing himself and fiddling with his life vest.

"Don't inflate that inside," Dan shouted.

"Why not?"

"It's too bulky inflated, and there's a good chance you'll puncture it getting out."

The conversation died. They approached three miles. Dan nursed the helo to eight-hundred-and-fifty feet. The silence in the cockpit was louder than the engine.

After a minute or so, Dan keyed the radio. "SeaTac, zero niner tango is approaching feet-dry and the pad is in sight. Thanks for the following, and I'll call when clear and on the deck." Dan began the transition to land.

"Roger that, zero niner tango. Glad you're there. Thanks for the call. The Coast Guard was just launching. I'll call them back."

"Roger that and thanks again." Dan reduced the power and pulled the nose up.

Only a hundred yards away from the landing spot, Dan's altitude was high and airspeed fast enough to safely auto rotate, if necessary.

By a miracle, the turbine power plant had held together. The helicopter began to shudder making the normal transition to a no-hover landing. At last, Dan began feeling a bit more comfortable as he guided the aircraft to the helo spot.

They made it, and what a good piece of luck. "Thank you, Lord."

As he radioed SeaTac tower, Dan glanced at Ken unbuckling his seat and waving at his limo driver who had parked the limo well off to the side of their helo pad. Dan glanced out at Ken's body guard, Ron. What's up with him? Ron was pointing at something and waving toward the limo.

While Dan shutdown the aircraft, Ken bolted out, grabbed the bags from the luggage compartment, and ran toward the limo.

Most aviators say bad things happen in threes. Dan stepped out of the cockpit, opened the engine cowling, stood on a platform and noticed a safety wire to the engine oil drain plug was missing. Dan rubbed oil between his fingers. The engine oil drain-plug had fallen out. Dan figured the guy he saw closing the compartment door out on the ship had cut the wire so the loosened plug would fall out. Number one bad thing confirmed.

Ken was taking the bags. Bad thing number two was now a fact. The bags had to be full of drugs.

Dan couldn't miss the two dark Mercedes 450 sedans racing across the tarmac from the left side of the aircraft and the painted helo spot. The Mercedes have to be druggies inside. So, that's why Ron was trying to get Ken's attention. Bad thing number three had just arrived.

Dan didn't need his Marine Corps training to tell him something was wrong.

The lead, dark-green Mercedes, skidded sideways, stopping close to the front and to the right of the helicopter, protecting the occupants from Ken and Ron. The second vehicle, a black Mercedes, slid sideways about ten yards to the right and behind the green one. In total, six men pulled automatic weapons and opened fire on Ken and Ron.

Without a moment of hesitation, Dan leapt from the aircraft and ran at the nearest shooter who was using the black Mercedes as a shield. Dan was behind the drug guy in full stride when he hit him in the back. The impact knocked the attacker down making him drop his weapon. Still dazed, the guy reached for his 9mm pistol from his shoulder holster, but Dan was ahead of him. With the adrenaline pumping, Dan kicked him in the face, knocking him unconscious. He grabbed the Browning 9mm, slid back the bolt chambering a round, and shot the next closest gunman in the knee. Then Dan opened up on the next shooter with two shots to the upper right torso.

The four occupants in the lead Mercedes had Ken and Ron pinned down and they appeared to be moving in for the kill. Dan started shooting at them from his vantage point, hitting one of the assailants in the leg.

As soon as the others realized they were being attacked from the rear, two of them started shooting at Dan. Then all four concentrated on him. They had automatic AK-47's against his single 9mm. He jumped into the safety of the bulletproof Mercedes, regretting he didn't grab the AK-47 instead of the pistol. Dan slammed the door, put the car in gear, and burned rubber toward the four remaining drug guys. The car became a weapon.

Dan accelerated toward them, but the car suffered multiple hits on the bulletproof windshield. The onslaught took its toll and the windshield gave way as he ran into one of the men. He swerved around the front of the second Mercedes. Dan came to a sliding halt between the remaining bad guys and Ken's limo.

Taking cover by lying down on the seat, he opened the passenger door, and crawled out behind the car. Lying on the ground he felt exposed between the shooters and Ken's limo.

Damn it, he thought, because all he had was an empty 9mm. The first man who Dan shot came to and limped his way to the other shooters behind the first Mercedes. Ken and Ron kept returning fire. Just as Dan thought it might become a stalemate, one of the attackers pointed a rocket propelled grenade at him. Dan ran toward the limo as the smoking RPG spiraled toward the Mercedes. His world went spinning out of control as the percussion from the explosion blew him into the air like a rag doll. Dan's world turned black.

CHAPTER TWO

Minor scrapes and bruises covered most of Dan's body. The most serious wound turned out to be a dislocated right shoulder. The good news was the force of the explosion blew him across the concrete helo pad, and then about fifteen yards into the tall grass. He didn't need all the scrapes he got from rolling past the helo pad.

Hearing voices, Dan couldn't make out anything being said. He tried to get up, but realized his right arm was wrapped to his abdomen.

Dan's thoughts were clouded and confused. He had a hard time opening his eyes, struggling to clear his mind. I must be in Vietnam, he decided, mumbling something about "How's Jack and Roadhawg? Are they all right?"

Dan blinked his eyes trying to focus on the person peering down at him, when he realized he was in a hospital. "Christy? Are they okay?"

His fiancé, Christy Abbott, was standing beside his bed holding his hand. "Honey, I'm here," she said.

"I thought I was in Vietnam." Shit, why am I crying? I must look like a blubbering idiot.

Rivulets of mascara ran down Christy's Sally Fields-like

face. She leaned over and kissed his forehead. "Dan, Honey, it's me, Christy. You're okay. Can you hear me?"

"Where are we?"

"We're here in Seattle. You're not in Vietnam."

"I'm where? Seattle? Okay. I remember. What's going on?"

She kept holding his hand, "You're too hard-headed to be hurt very much. Just relax, Dan, and try to be still. Everything's fine."

An approaching nurse said, "Let me see how he's doing. How's your shoulder feeling?"

"It hurts." Dan winced as he tried to move. "Even my hurts hurt."

"Well, you check out just fine. I'll be right back." The nurse smiled as she left.

"How's Ken?" Dan said to Christy.

"He's fine. He's on his way over." Christy rubbed Dan's forearm.

Dan closed his eyes, gathering his thoughts. "I don't think they were trying to kill me. I think they were going for Ken. And he's just fine?"

Christy nodded her head.

"Do you remember what we'd suspected last night?" He looked around the room. "Ken hauling drugs?"

Christy leaned down and whispered in his ear. "Honey." Christy glanced behind her. "It'd probably be better if we don't talk about anything in here. But I think I'm thinking what you're thinking." She frowned.

"Holy shit, man," Ken bellowed as he walked in. The cuffs on his bell bottom pants made him look like a taller Sonny Bono. His psychedelic shirt would make even Sonny put on sunglasses. "I know you're a great Vietnam Marine Corps hero and all. But man, you were a one man wrecking crew. If it wasn't for you, I'd be toast. I owe you, my man. Many thanks."

"You son-of-a-bitch. You're higher than a kite. Those

guys were a drug deal gone bad," Dan said. "Or something close to it. I never knew. If I had, I would've never hauled drugs. Ever. I'm through with you, understand?"

"Hey, man, don't go gettin' all pissed off. Those guys are some really bad asses. We knocked the hell out of them today, buddy." He winked at Dan.

"Where do you get the we?" Dan's head began to hurt. "If you ain't noticed, I didn't come out of that crap smellin' like a rose."

"Come on, man." Ken ignored Dan's attitude. "They've got the guy in custody you knee-capped. Plus, the guy you made a hood ornament outta. He was the head honcho's brother. The other one you took down was his personal body guard. You knocked the bejeezus out of their little operation."

"You seem to know an awful lot about them. By God," Dan hissed in pain as he tried to sit up, "you're in with them, aren't you? I told you no drugs when we started the flying service. And I..." Dan stopped as a couple of men in suits walked in.

"Good afternoon. Are you Ken Anderson?" One of the suits said.

Ken stood about six foot even with a wiry build, yet he stood about a couple inches taller than either of the two gents. He raised his hand and straightened his slick, black hair as he smiled.

"Well, sir, that'd depend on who's askin'." Ken smirked, wiping his Fu Manchu mustache.

"I'm FBI Special Agent Thomason and this is Special Agent Riley. We'd like to ask you and Mr. Burton some questions." Thomason removed his sun glasses.

Ken, never missing a stride, replied, "Why, gents, I'd be glad to. Why don't you give me your cards?" He reached for his business cards. "And I'll have my attorney set up a meeting at our mutual convince. And, you can see, Mr. Burton's in no condition to speak to anyone right now."

They made no move to share their cards.

"Excuse me. You gents do have some sort of identification, don't you?" Ken said.

Thomason handed Ken a card. "Contact us by noon tomorrow." He frowned at Ken and then at Dan. He and Riley left with an air of authority.

"What's that all about?" Christy looked first at Dan and then Ken.

Before Dan could speak, Ken started. "It's the Feds being Feds. Some bad guys get shot up and the Feds can't take the credit, so they have to be a pain in the ass." He held up his hands appearing to be lost, and shrugged his shoulders.

"By God." Dan grimaced through his pain. "Those drug guys were waiting for us in case their loosened oil plug didn't work."

"Ken." Christy cut in. "Why don't we let Dan get some rest? I'll stay here and tell him good night."

Ken nodded, winked at Dan, waved good-bye, then sauntered out.

Christy, still holding Dan's hand, said, "What we talked about…is it a fact?"

"Christy, it's everything we feared. John and Ken are knee deep in it. The shootout was most likely a drug deal gone bad. The black Mercedes guys weren't with the welcome wagon lady. I'm worried, and I…" Dan stopped as the nurse walked in.

"Okay, boys and girls," the nurse announced. "We need to let Wyatt Earp here get some rest. Let me take your temp and give you this pill to help you sleep." She shook the thermometer and placed it in Dan's mouth.

Christy leaned over and kissed Dan's forehead. "I'll see you in the morning. Oh, yeah, I called Jack and Joe and they're on their way up."

The nurse checked his temperature, gave him some pills, and left.

After the room emptied, Dan tried to figure out just how much trouble he'd brought on the other three Marines. He could tell Ken wanted to talk to him, one-on-one. And, so did the Feds, but not to pin a medal on him.

John Abbott and Ken Anderson owned the helicopter. Among other things, the new air ambulance service flew charter flights and that's how Dan came to fly for Ken. John Abbott was Christy's ex, and at first he seemed okay with Dan and Christy's engagement. John was living with a new found love. And yet, at the same time Ken's bevy of women kept John busy. John screwed the leftovers of Ken's women anytime he wanted. He was being a typical male whore dog.

Lying there in bed with the effects of the drug to help him sleep, his last thoughts concerned the suits. Two nights before, he'd called his Marine Corps combat brothers, Jack and Joe, otherwise known as Roadhawg, around the six of them, and talked at length about his concerns with the offshore flights. Dan realized he needed to be worried.

The Feds were on to him.

P.R. STEELE

CHAPTER THREE

The next morning, Dan managed to get out of bed, even though he knew his nurse would pitch a fit. Now, at least, his senses were working. He recognized the familiar smells and sounds on the ward. Stretching let him know where the aches and pains were and what wasn't working. He slipped back into the bed and yawned as Christy walked in.

She held her finger in front of her lips, checked out the room, and then walked over to Dan. She whispered in his ear, "Those FBI guys stopped me last night in the parking lot as I walked to my car."

Dan nodded.

Christy leaned back to check Dan's expression, then whispered. "They wanted to know if I'd be an informant against you and told me in no uncertain terms what would happen if I didn't."

Dan nodded again as she stood. She winked, then spoke out loud. "Look, here're the clothes I brought you. Oh, by the way, how are you feeling?"

Dan smiled. "I feel fine, mighty fine in fact. You know me, a Redneck,. . .white socks and Blue Ribbon beer. I bleed one hundred percent American. Matter of fact, I feel like a one-ten plugged into a two-twenty outlet, and the next woman I take on will light up like a pinball machine with a payoff in silver dollars."

"Dream on. You're a mess, Dan Burton. We'll get you home and let you get rested up…" She acted startled as Thompson and Riley walked in.

"Good morning, Mr. Burton. Ma'am." Special agent Riley grinned. "We just checked with the doctor, and he said you're scheduled to check out of here today."

"That sounds Jim dandy. Glad to hear that."

"Today is Wednesday. We're meeting with Mr. Anderson and his attorney on Friday at nine-thirty in his office. We'd like to have you there." Riley raised his eyebrows. "Do you see any conflict?"

"No, sir. I see no conflict." Dan yawned.

"Well, good. We'll see you then." Thompson rubbed his chin, and looked at Christy. "Ma'am."

After the two agents left, Dan sat up. "Honey, if you'd hand me my clothes, I'm ready to get out of here."

Moving slower than his grandpa, Dan changed. He made it over to Christy and said in a low voice. "Those two are up to no good."

Dan favored his paternal Apache grandpa. A body builder's muscular frame, no facial hair and his dark complexion came from his paternal Mexican Grandma. Dan's black hair matched his eyes. He spoke Spanish as a second language, thanks to his Grandma who raised him after his mother died during child birth.

Christy nodded. He asked her if she'd heard from Jack and Roadhawg.

She lowered her voice. "They arrived last night. They're going to rent a place somewhere north of here after they get another car."

"When will Jack contact us?"

"Six tonight at the Seven Eleven phone booth." Christy had a home in Gig Harbor, and had given Jack the number of a payphone near there.

"That's good, Baby. You've done real good." He hugged her. "But, I think I've screwed it up for all of us."

"Quit it. Go feel sorry for somebody else. It could've happened to anyone. Nobody's blaming you. So, stop it." She kissed him, and squeezed his max gluten.

Dan's release happened before lunch. Christy drove, crossing the Tacoma Narrows Bridge over Puget Sound to Gig Harbor. She exhaled. "Don't turn around, but I think we're being followed by a tuna boat of a Ford."

"Good. That answers that."

"Yep. They wouldn't be following us over the shootout, would they?"

"Well, it looks like we're going to have to switch to plan B." Dan sighed.

After the two of them arrived at Christy's house, Dan contacted the other three of the six involved in the missing military payroll from Okinawa. They were ready to drop everything and disappear, just as Jack and Roadhawg had vanished two days before.

Thompson and Riley hadn't asked Dan any questions about the shootout. Dan surmised his association with Ken and the drugs was the problem, and if so, that would put all six of them in jeopardy. He knew if the Feds found him guilty, the other five Marines would sure as hell be in the same fix.

A four door, dark blue Ford Galaxy with black wall tires, and small hub caps was parked down the street. Not in plain sight, but too obvious for Christy and Dan not to notice.

A little before six, Christy and Dan walked out of the house and got into her car. She dropped him off at the Safeway store, and as planned the tail stayed on Dan.

The phone rang just as she entered the phone booth.

"Christy?"

"Yes."

"This is Jack. What's happening?"

She brought him up to date. Jack told her he and Roadhawg had rented a vacation rental in Poulsbo on the water. They'd set up a meeting for the next day in Bremerton about thirty minutes north of Gig Harbor. Jack told her they'd bought a 1964 Chevy wagon as a safe disposable car. "Oh, by the way, how's Dan?"

"Typical Dan, worrying about everything."

Christy picked up Dan at Safeway along with the tail. She told Dan about the plans for the meeting the next morning.

"Dan, how are you going to lose the boys behind us tomorrow?"

She laughed when he told her.

The next morning, Dan got into his flashy 1957 Corvette with the top off. He headed toward McChord Air Force Base, near Tacoma, all the while making sure the Feds were in trail behind him. Being in the Reserves, the 'Vette was stickered for passage onto any military base. Getting in line for the gate guard, Dan fished out his military ID. The Ford Galaxy followed two cars behind.

Dan spoke to the armed guard. "I want to alert you to a possible problem."

"Sir?" the sentry said as he handed back Dan's ID card.

"Don't look now, but two cars behind me is a Ford. I noticed one of the men passing a pistol to the other one. I think you'd better call a backup. Maybe question the car behind me, so you don't alert them until some help arrives."

Speaking into his walkie-talkie, the guard called for backup. To Dan, he said, "Thank you for the heads up, sir."

Dan drove onto the base. In his rearview mirror he saw the sentry taking his time with the car in front of the Feds. Out of their sight, Dan drove into the officer's club parking lot. The keys were under the driver's floor mat in a four door, faded-brown, 1963 Plymouth Valiant. Dan smiled as he got into his disposable car.

He turned the key and nothing. He banged the steering wheel, jumped out, opened the hood and reconnected the battery. The battery would go dead if he left the battery cables attached because of an unknown short. He slammed the hood, and jumped in the car, then slammed the driver's door, and stepped on the accelerator twice.

Dan turned and looked at the approach to the parking lot to make sure the FBI agent's car was not in sight. He turned the key as the old six cylinder came to life. The Valiant ran smooth as silk as he drove off the base under a brimmed hat and a fu-manchu mustache. Dan smiled at Riley and another agent being frisked by a well-armed security backup team.

Dan walked into the bus station in Bremerton. His alarm went off. He didn't recognize a soul. Where could they be? He began to walk around the depot.

Dan jumped as Roadhawg poked him in the back. "Hey, Sailor, wanna have a good time?

Jack spoke. "Looking for trouble, Marine?"

"Where the hell did you come from?" Dan hugged Jack and then Roadhawg, both wearing tie-dyed shirts and desert boots.

Joe belched. "We've been waiting on your late ass. But let's get out of here and chew the fat." Roadhawg cut up with Dan as they headed out.

"Glad to see you boys wised up and got a nice wagon." Dan admired the Chevy as they got in.

Jack started the wagon then Dan said, "First of all, guys, I feel like hell because I've brought everyone into my mess."

"Danny, my boy," Jack grinned. "This just spices it up, and come on. We knew it would be a matter of time."

"Yeah, but..." Dan began.

"Don't 'yeah, but,' us. We all know Bedford's still stirring the pot. I heard after he got kicked out of the Corps, some dumb butt in the CIA got him hired with the FBI," Roadhawg said.

Dan shook his head. "You've got to be kidding. Bedford steals the payroll, we take it from him, and he gets a government job?"

"Alright, girls. Enough." Jack held up his index finger. "Danny, tell us about tomorrow."

Dan went over the time and place for the meeting at Ken's attorney's office. They decided to go to Seattle and check out the location. As the ferry took them from Bremerton, they began their plans. All the options and contingencies they could come up with were settled. By three that afternoon, they'd finalized their plans. They'd taken the time, well Jack had, on the ferry from Seattle back to Bremerton, to go over everything again and again. After they got off the ferry, they took Dan to their rental property, isolated and on the water outside of Poulsbo.

"Girls, this place is way cool. I like it a whole lot." Dan surveyed the trees covering the three isolated acres. "And, you told the rental agent that friends would be visiting, so no big deal if extra people show up?"

Jack nodded.

"Fantastic." Dan put his hands in the hip pockets of his Levi's.

When it was time to leave, they drove Dan back to his Valiant in Bremerton. Forty-five minutes later, he parked it in the Bachelor Officer's Quarters (BOQ) at McChord. The last thing he wanted was for the Feds to make the Valiant. What they didn't know was paramount.

Dan hitched a ride back to the O'Club where the '57 Vette waited along with a four door plain Jane Ford down the block with what looked like two Feds in the front seat.

Without a lot of fanfare, Dan got into the Vette and led the way back to Christy's. He parked in the garage, saw her car, walked in the house, and yelled, "Lucy, I'm home."

Her two boys, Allen and Jason, age six and eight, ran down the stairs and attacked him.

Christy's mom, Grace, came out of the kitchen and smiled at the ruckus. "She took my car to run back to the office. Something got screwed up on one of her escrow deals." Grace looked at her watch. "She said she'd be back in about fifteen minutes."

Dan played with the boys and helped with their chores.

"Hey, Grace, come over here." Dan was looking through the crack in the living room curtains. "They're still there."

Grace just nodded her head. "Christy told me the FBI was watching you, Dan. Are they going to cause trouble?"

"Yep, I think we can bank on it."

P.R. STEELE

CHAPTER FOUR

The next morning, the cool morning breeze off the water did little to sooth Dan's nerves. Jack and Dan were in a taxi in a parking lot off the water in downtown Seattle. He twisted his mouth as his mind raced through all the contingencies.

Man, there were just too many things that could go wrong.

Dan listened as Jack went over the plans with the cab driver. Their getaway vehicle would be the taxi, and for the right price the driver was more than willing to drive them.

Dan adjusted his short-sleeved polo shirt with a shoulder movement, and looked for lint on his slacks. He rolled his head as he eased out of the cab. He leaned on the roof. His full blooded Apache grandfather taught him an ancestral ritual of looking toward the morning sun with his eyes closed to sooth his tensions. Now he envisioned the events with clarity. Dan felt the connection with his grandfather assuring him he'd be okay. Inner peace took over.

I'm ready.

"Okay, Jackson. It's about ten minutes to show time. Let's go." Dan slapped the roof of the taxi, climbed back in and closed the door.

"Our check list is good. Same with the walkie-talkies. And, if I'm not sitting out front, circle the block counter clockwise. We'll be on the move if we're not in the loading zone," Jack said.

"I'm good with that. When I'm alone, I'll let you know what's happening." Dan held up his walkie-talkie.

As per Jack's plan, the taxi dropped Dan off two blocks from the attorney's address. The briefcase felt strange to Dan, but his leather, soft soled, hard heeled loafers felt like track shoes. He sighed as he walked to the elevator. Second floor suite two-ten. Here we go. The elevator doors opened. He almost laughed out loud. Yea, though I walk through the valley of the shadow of death, I will fear no evil, because I'm the meanest mother in the valley. I'm ready for you bastards.

He opened the glass door to the office.

The receptionist glanced up from her oversized oak desk. No other people were waiting. The room felt cold. His leather heels clicked off the marble-like floor as he walked to her desk. "Dan Burton for my nine o'clock with Mr. Jones."

"Yes, they're expecting you." She stood and motioned. "This way."

Dan followed her through a door, down a hall to a conference room. Her heels echoed in unison with Dan's hard leather heels. She ushered him in and said, "Please make yourself comfortable. Mr. Jones and Ken Anderson will be with you in a few minutes."

Dan stood looking out the conference room windows. The sun sparkled off the bright blue of Puget Sound. Dan tried to relax. To think a few days ago I almost bought the farm out there. He wiped a bit of perspiration from his chin as he took the gun fighter's seat at the mahogany conference table. As he glanced around the room he noticed several paintings on the walls.

That Picasso doesn't look like a reproduction, and I'll be damned...is that a Monet? Jones's law practice must be generating a hell of a lot of revenue if he can afford those?

Voices in the hallway announced Ken and Jones's entrance.

"Mr. Burton, good morning," Bob Jones began. "We'll be meeting with some FBI agents and some of their legal folks. I'll show them in."

"Yeah," Ken smirked. "The same two bozos, Riley and Thomason, plus several other bozos toting briefcases."

"Okay, for the last time," Jones pointed to Ken, "you're not to say one single word. Understood?"

"You worry too much, Bob," Ken shot back.

Jones shook his head, and turned toward Dan. "I'll be representing you and Ken unless there's a conflict of interest. If that's the case, I'll advise you that I can't represent you. But I don't foresee it."

Dan nodded. In his mind he no longer worked for Ken

"Don't answer them or say anything until I say it's okay."

"Yes, sir." Dan shifted on the wooden chair.

"See how easy it can be?" Jones glared at Ken. Then he pushed the intercom button and asked the secretary to show in the FBI agents.

After they were seated, the conversation bounced around between the legal folks and Bob Jones who did most of the talking. The language got heated about joint representation.

"Gentlemen, would you excuse me. It appears I need to speak with my clients in private." Jones ignored the opposing attorneys.

The issues on the table left no questions in Dan's mind. The FBI wanted him, not Ken, and for something other than the shoot-out. Dan followed Jones and Ken down the hall and into a smaller conference room.

"Dan, would you wait in here while I talk with Ken?" Jones opened a door to a small conference room.

"Sure," Dan said. Jones left, closing the door. Dan listened to their footsteps as they walked down the hall. Good. He approached the window and slid it open with ease. The fire escape was at least three windows away, but the window opened above the alley. The alley led to the street around the corner from the taxi zone in front of the building. Dan inhaled, smiled, and shut the window.

All right, the distance is at least twelve to fourteen feet to the ground. That's doable if I drop down to the street. Dan tiptoed to the door and peeked out into the hall. The stairs were nowhere in sight. He closed the door. Then he opened his brief case, took out the walkie-talkie, switched it on and pressed the transmit button twice. He received a double click from Jack who remained in the taxi.

"X-ray, this is Zulu," Dan said.

"Zulu, I have you five by," Jack answered.

Dan transmitted in a whisper. "X-ray...I'm the primary. The first option is not looking good. I'm going to go recon." He'd just told Jack the fire escape was not an option. And, Dan needed to locate the stairway.

"Roger. We're stationary," Jack said.

"Roger, I'll be back." Jack ended with a double clicked letting Dan know he copied Dan's last transmission.

Dan knew he had to check out some other options. He went to the door and peeked out to make sure nobody was in the hall. He tiptoed as quiet as a mouse down the hall, glad he'd worn soft soled shoes. He smiled thinking some quiet heels would've been nice.

He made it to the corner and ducked around it. About fifty feet to the end of the hallway was an exit marked "Stairs." He could hear Jones and Ken talking in a room as he passed.

"Go to hell," Ken yelled.

"Listen, and listen good. I told you to take care of him."

"You don't call all the shots. Now, you listen. I said I won't."

"Damn it, you will, or you'll be next. You've screwed up for the last time..."

Dan couldn't make out all of what Jones was saying as he kept moving toward the exit.

He approached the exit door and exhaled as he looked back down the hall, still vacant. Dan sighed in relief. The exit door was unlocked. He eased the door open to check out the stairs, then started back to where he needed to be waiting. All of a sudden, Bob Jones stepped out from the room where he and Ken had been arguing.

Ah-h-h, damn it. Dan came to a halt. Jones walked down the hallway.

Damn it, damn it. He's headed toward my room.

"Hey, Mr. Jones," Dan said.

Jones spun around. "What are you doing out here?"

"Where's the pisser? I've gotta piss like an Arabian race horse. I thought it was down this way." Dan tilted his head and raised both palms.

"Well, it's just around the corner at the other end of the hall. Come on, I'll show you."

Ah-h-h, double damn it. Dan worried about the lie, as he walked beside Jones. "Well, what's going on?" Dan continued to take the initiative.

"Well, Dan, it appears there's a conflict of interest..."

Dan cut him off. "What? How's that?"

"I'm not at liberty to tell you what the FBI has going. You're definitely going to need your own representation." Jones began to swagger.

Once in the men's room, Dan pressed the issue. "When did they tell you this?" He figured Jones hadn't been talking to the Feds, because the Feds were waiting further down the hall.

"Well, that's not important. What's important is you

need to wait in the smaller conference room while I go get them. They'll talk with you." He stood in front of the urinal beside Dan.

"Okay, then, I'll meet you all in the conference room."

Dan was ready to make his escape, if he could ditch Jones.

"I'll walk you back." Jones made it sound more like an order than an offer, as they walked to the sinks.

Jones ushered Dan into the conference room. Dan knew he had very little time. He listened to Jones's shoes clicking down the hall past the men's room. Dan hurried to a window, opened it, and took off his loafers. I hate these noisy heels.

With his shoes in one hand and briefcase in the other, he ran to the door, peeked out and watched until Jones walked into the other conference room. A secretary approached from the opposite direction.

I'll be hanged. I've got maybe ten to twenty seconds head start, if I'm lucky. Well, here goes nothing. He stepped into the hallway in his socks holding on to the shoes.

The secretary continued toward him. He smiled at her, and tilted his head. "New shoes and I've already got blisters."

She stopped. "I can get you some band aids, if you'd like."

"No, that's alright. Thanks anyway," Dan said over his shoulder. He turned the corner, and began to sprint as he heard a door open. He figured Jones and the agents were headed toward his empty conference room.

He flew down the stairs. He fell down on the slick floor in the lobby, still in his socks. He jumped up, slipped on his loafers, then trying to look care free, walked outside.

The taxi parking spot was empty. No taxi. No Jack. Dan began to run clockwise around the building. As he crossed the alley, Jones yelled down from the open window.

"Hey, there he goes."

CHAPTER FIVE

Dan stood for a moment at the first corner, looking for the taxi. Thomason and Riley ran out of the building and spotted him. Dan sprinted to the next corner increasing the distance from the FBI agents. Down the block at the next corner, Jack sat in the cab at the light waiting to turn left. Dan ran across the street to the opposite side and jumped in as the light turned green.

"Go. Go. Go," Jack yelled to the driver. The cab tires squealed as they accelerated toward the bay. "Damn it. They saw us. Oh, shit, they're flashing their badges, and an agency car's pulling up. Here they come," Jack shouted.

Dan fished out his walkie-talkie, and transmitted. "Whiskey, this is X-ray. Do you copy? Over." He shook his head as the set remained silent.

The taxi had more than a block on the Feds. When the cabbie caught a red light, he turned right closing on the bay. Dan tried contacting Roadhawg as the taxi began losing ground in front of the Feds. Jack pushed twenty dollar bills in the driver's shirt pocket, and kept Dan and the driver abreast of their pursuers. At last Roadhawg answered.

"X-ray, this is Whiskey. I've got you loud and clear. Say,

your position, over."

Dan sighed. "Whiskey, we're about one mike out, over." Dan just told him they were less than a minute away.

"Roger that. We're turnin' and burnin'. I've got clearance to depart on your arrival, over." Dan and Jack smiled at each other. Dan checked the FBI vehicle's position. He scowled as it drew ever closer.

The cabbie, as pre-briefed, drove out to the jet ranger on the landing spot. Jack shoved a fist full of twenties at him. The heliport was vacant except for an Air Ambulance helo waiting for the passengers. Dan and Jack sprinted to the helo. Dan jumped into the co-pilot's seat and Jack in the passenger compartment. Both put on their head sets. "Well, it's about by God time you two slugs showed up. I was getting' bored," Roadhawg drawled as he pointed to the approaching agency car.

Dan yelled. "Let's go."

Without looking at Dan, Roadhawg lifted the helicopter into a fifteen-foot hover. Riley and Thompson jumped out of their car, battling the rotor wash. Roadhawg pointed to a plastic briefcase on the ground below where the helicopter had lifted off. They could see Riley jog over and pick it up.

Roadhawg gave Riley and Thompson a two finger Cub Scout salute and then waved goodbye as he air taxied backwards over the water and took off.

Their rapid departure was for show.

Dan yelled, "What was that all about?"

Roadhawg handed Dan a piece of paper. "Danny, this is a copy of what I left Riley and Thomason.

> *See Dan Run.*
> *Run Dan Run.*
> *Run Run Run.*

What we don't understand is this...Simply put, why aren't you after the original thieves? You know we want to tell you who took it and give back what you want. Our new attorney, point of contact, will be Steven Mitchell.

Over the intercom, Roadhawg said, "I wanted them to know we're way, way ahead of them."

"We don't need to piss them off," Dan said after he read the note.

Jack took it from Dan and read it. "Damn it, Roadhawg. We all need to be on the same page. And we've never even given Mitchell his retainer yet. What the hell are you thinking?"

"First of all, if they're pissed off, that's good. Because when they're pissed, they're not thinking clear." Not missing a beat, Roadhawg transmitted to SeaTac approach. "SeaTac, uniform two zero five eight niner is off Seattle heliport feet wet, parallel the shore heading south at five hundred or less, over."

"Ah-h, roger, eight niner. You're clear."

"Roger that," Roadhawg answered and double clicked the transmit button letting approach control know he understood.

Jack broke the silence. "Alright Danny, what happened?"

Dan filled them in, but he stopped to make sure he got it clear about what bothered him.

"So," Roadhawg thought out loud, "Jones was chewing out Ken about taking care of someone. And that he'd do it now. Doesn't sound like the good kind of taking care of? So, who do you think he was talking about?"

"It sounded like it was me. But then, I think he said he'd already taken care of it or them. Whatever. I was moving away and trying to not get caught."

Jack brought them back to the moment. "Okay, so far so good. We now know they're after us and we suspect it's about Okinawa. And we're fixing to disappear like a fart in a whirlwind. A couple days of R & R solidifying our plans,

31

and then poof. We'll be gone."

Dan pointed to the oil pressure gauge. "Well, that's all fine and good, but this thing was to have over thirty minutes of running the engine on the ground before it was flown again."

Roadhawg hugged the shore line as a precaution. He said, "Dan, quit being a worry wart. I ran it for over thirty minutes to make sure the engine's okay, and then flew another fifteen up here to pick you girls up. And, I had it turning another twenty minutes or so. It'll be fine."

"Yeah, but check out the oil temp." Dan tapped the gauge as it hovered just below the redline.

In the distance, the wind sock appeared marking the helicopter landing pad where Dan used to work. As they approached, the landing site looked clear. Dan wiped perspiration from his forehead. He looked around to make sure their rental car was parked where they'd left it. The operations building looked deserted as Roadhawg hovered to land. Dan smiled.

"Well, girls," Jack said, "it looks all quiet and I don't see anyone following us. So let's get this thing on deck while it's still in one piece.

Dan laughed. "Well, by God, us three Rednecks' luck just held out. I feel better that this baby made it back here for us." Dan gave the two thumbs up as Roadhawg sat the helicopter on the landing spot.

"I'll meet you two in the car. Let's haul ass." Jack stayed behind as the other two hurried to the rental car. Jack made sure they left nothing behind in the helicopter.

CHAPTER SIX

Riley and Thomason returned to Jones's law office, walked to the receptionist and asked for Mr. Jones. After a call to his secretary, his assistant walked out and inquired about what they wanted.

They presented their identifications and told the secretary they were there to see Mr. Jones. She left to get Jones. When Jones stepped into the waiting room, the Federal Agents handed him the warrant for Ken's arrest.

"This is highly unusual in light of everything," Jones said.

"We wanted to arrest both Mister Ken Anderson and Mister Daniel Burton. But, if we find any hint of aid or obstruction from you in regard to Mr. Burton's escape, we'll have a warrant with your name on it in a New York minute." Riley snarled.

"First, gentlemen, let me assure both of you, I had no knowledge of Mr. Burton's flight. But this is," he waved the warrant, "ridiculous."

"We don't think John Abbott's murder is ridiculous," Thomason said.

"What? John's dead?" Jones glanced at the warrant.

"Yeah," Thompson said. "Let's go get your client." Riley nodded in agreement.

The FBI agents followed Jones to a conference room. Ken sat at the large round conference table. Jones pointed his finger and said, "Not one word. Not one single solitary word, Ken. Do you hear me?"

Ken nodded.

Jones shook the warrant at the FBI agents and began. "They're on a fishing expedition, and this warrant is charging you for the murder of John Abbott. I know this is a shock, Ken, and unbelievable, but the warrant is for real."

Ken opened his mouth as Jones shook the warrant at him and yelled. "Not a word."

"Mr. Anderson, you're under arrest for the murder of John Abbott." Riley reached for Ken's hands, cuffed them, and read him his rights.

Jones pushed the intercom and shouted, "Martha, get me Matthew Griffin over at Justice and have him find out about bail."

Jones smirked because Dan had run. They were charging Ken Anderson with John Abbott's murder and Dan looked guiltier than hell.

Then to Ken, Jones said, "I'll have you out in less than a couple of hours. This is all bullshit, and Ken, don't even give them your name until I get there."

Back to Riley and Thomason, Jones said, "You're not to have a single word with my client until I'm in his presence. Do you understand me?"

The two agents seemed to ignore Jones, who smirked as he walked to his office thinking how easy everything had proceeded.

At Ken's air operations, Jack, Roadhawg, and Dan left the deserted parking lot in the rental car.

"So far so good." Roadhawg bragged.

Looking off into the distance, Dan said. "That's what

they heard the optimist say passing the eighty-eighth floor after he'd jumped off the Empire State Building."

"Come on, Danny, lighten up. It went off like clockwork. The plan was perfect." Jack tried to reassure Dan as he drove into the shopping center's parking lot where the three of them had left one of their disposable cars. The car they were driving was rented in a fake name. Again, they left it in a parking space and the three drove off unnoticed in the Chevy wagon.

After an hour or so, and about sixty miles north, Dan parked at the rental house by the shore in Poulsbo. The road leading to the water covered over a half mile in either direction with tall Sisku pines growing along its shores.

"Lord, this place is quiet." Jack looked at the house. "I could stay here a long time."

"Or until the Feds show up," Roadhawg teased.

"Only us three, and Christy and Ellen know where we are." Dan closed the car door. Ellen was Jack's wife and was on her way to meet up with them.

"Christy should've called or been here a couple of hours ago." Jack looked around. "Let's get something to eat and work on plan B."

Roadhawg belched. "Ah now, that was at least an eight point five or a nine point oh."

"Girls, I don't see Christy's car. She should've been here waiting for us," Dan said.

"Maybe something came up with her boys," Jack said.

"No. Something's wrong." Dan began to pace. "She was going to leave the office at nine-thirty, and be waiting here. This isn't good."

P.R. STEELE

CHAPTER SEVEN

Noon came and went, but still no sign of Christy. Dan sat on the back porch in the shade looking south all the way to Tacoma. Something was wrong. He felt it deep in his gut, and his gut never lied. The breeze off the water cooled everything except his nerves. The sun crept behind the Olympic Mountain Range between them and the Pacific Ocean.

Dan jumped up from this chair when he heard a car approaching. Jack and Roadhawg walked out the front door as an old '64 Ford approached. Dan could see Jack trotting toward Ellen as she got out of the wagon. Damn it, Christy should've been here by now.

"Hey, baby," Jack shouted, "Outta all the gin joints in all the towns in all the world, you drive into mine." The Casablanca line brought a smile to Dan's face as he went to the front yard. She'd driven up from L.A. three days behind Jack and spent the night in Medford, Oregon.

During Jack and Ellen's lengthy embrace, Roadhawg teased them. "You two are embarrassing me. Go get a room."

With both arms wrapped around her, and still locked in

the embrace, Jack gave Roadhawg the finger.

"Real cute, Jack. Real cute. Jack just gave me the finger again, Ellen," Roadhawg tattled.

Ellen nodded her head and hugged Jack all the tighter. After a moment, they broke the embrace. Jack helped her with the luggage, food, and other items she'd brought. Once inside, the mood changed because of Christy's absence. They couldn't risk calling her house because the line might be tapped. Dan walked out past the curve in the drive and out of sight beyond the forested lane. He jogged back.

Once inside Dan said, "My gut's telling me something's happened to Christy. She's too punctual, you know what I mean?" He looked at Jack, and then Ellen.

Jack said, "What if Ellen drove down to Christy's?"

"She might be recognized," Dan said.

"So she could say she knows nothing about anything. I know they're most likely looking for Roadhawg and me, along with Dan, now," Jack said.

"It's what, about forty-five minutes to an hour down there?" Ellen said.

"Maybe." Dan rubbed his temples.

"If there's a problem, I could call you all from a phone booth in Gig Harbor."

"Ellen, you've just driven eight or so hours. That's asking a bunch," Dan said.

"Hey, how about this? We drive into Bremerton, pick up a couple more disposable cars. Ellen could drive down to Christy's and call us at the phone booth at the bus station. We've got the number right here." Roadhawg reached for the tablet that had most of their clandestine information.

They settled on times for the call, back-up times, and code phrases if Ellen was being followed or the authorities were close by.

Jack glanced at her. "Guys, I think it's a good plan. The

Feds might be looking for me, but they've got no reason to detain me. For that matter, the same goes for Ellen."

She nodded in agreement and looked at her wrist watch. "Come on, let's go. It's almost three."

Jack and Ellen got into her station wagon along with Dan and Roadhawg. Ellen and Jack went over the plans for that evening several times. Once in Bremerton, Ellen drove to a parked rental car that they'd left earlier. Jack, Dan, and Roadhawg climbed in the rental and took off. Ellen left for Gig Harbor.

The guys bought a newspaper and circled several used cars listed that met their criteria. After two calls, they drove to the first address. They put on the disguises they'd brought and wore sun glasses as an added precaution. Jack got out around the corner and walked to the seller's house. Out front, he looked the car over, and then knocked on the front door.

"Sir, I'm the one that called about the Chevy." Jack pointed his finger at the car.

"Well, I've got the keys. Want to take 'er for a spin?" the guy said.

He told Jack he'd retired from the Navy and wanted to live close to the base in Bremerton. "How'd you get here?"

"Hitched a ride with a guy from the unit." Jack fibbed about being in the Navy and hitching a ride. They took the Chevy for a test drive.

While Jack drove to check out the car, the owner talked. "Well, she's only got forty-two thousand miles, and for a sixty-five, she's barely broke in."

Jack chuckled to himself as he drove past Dan and Roadhawg in their parked car.

When they got back to the seller's house, Jack began the negotiation. "She runs good, and seems well kept. I gotta tell you, she's probably worth every cent you're asking, but what's your bottom dollar?"

"The ad said six seventy-five, but I'll take six-and-and-a-quarter. I got the title in the house."

Jack knew not to pay the asking price. He felt people might remember. "Would you take six cash right now?"

"Well, seein's as how we're both in the Navy, you got a deal." He stuck out his hand and they shook on the sale.

Jack paid him with twenties and fifties. He didn't want to be flashing big bills. Their throw-away cars had to be four-doors or wagons, nothing flashy or attention getting. Those were easy to acquire, easier to go undetected and even easier to sell.

The plan was for Roadhawg to follow the same routine and buy another old car. He found a '62 Cadillac. They left the Chevy in a shopping center parking lot.

Dan checked his watch. They still had twenty-five minutes until the call from Ellen.

The three of them piled into Roadhawg's `62 Caddy and headed to the bus depot. Jack stretched out in the back seat. "Lord, I could sleep here, no sweat."

"I think I'll need a couple of deck hands to help me launch and dock this yacht," Roadhawg joked from behind the steering wheel as he played with all the gadgets. "Hey, Danny boy, come on. Admit it. This baby's got it all, and everything works."

Dan looked at Roadhawg and winked. "Roadhawg, you done good."

"I wish we had some news about Christy., Roadhawg said in reply. "I hope everything's okay. But my gut tells me something ain't right."

"By God, I hate to admit it, but I agree." Dan checked his watch again.

Jack leaned into the front seat. "Let's not worry about it until we know something, deal? I'll go stand by the phone. We've got a couple of minutes."

Jack walked to the phone booth outside the bus depot. Dan hit the phone booth with his fist. Jack tried to reason with him, but Dan shoved Jack away and began to pace. At six sharp the phone rang. Jack answered. Dan, standing by the car, hustled to the phone booth and stood by Jack. The Roadhawg followed Dan.

Jack gave him a thumbs up as he listened to Ellen. "Okay, I've got it. We'll see you all in about an hour. Bye." Jack hung up, then the three of them hurried back to the Caddy.

"There's been some bad news," Jack began. "Christy's ex-husband, it's John Abbott, isn't it?"

Dan nodded.

"Somebody murdered him this morning, and that's given the Feds reason to suspect you." Jack pointed to Dan.

"Ellen said the boys are upset, and Christy and her mom have a lot on their plate. And get this. The Feds, have named Roadhawg and me," Jack nudged his arm, "as possible accomplices."

"Somebody killed John Abbott? Christy's ex?" Dan said?

"Yeah. His murder gave the Feds all the excuses they needed to plaster our pictures all over the news."

"I don't think the ol' lady who sold me the Caddy was coherent enough to make anything out about me. Besides we all have damn good disguises on." Roadhawg looked at Jack.

"Yeah, I agree." Jack rubbed his Fu Manchu beard. "I'm sorry, Dan. El also told me Christy has been questioned at her house." Jack held up both hands giving the quote signs. "She said the boys are upset, and she and her mom have had a lot on their plate."

"What the hell." Roadhawg raised his voice. "You'd said her ex was heavy into the drug dealing with Ken. Think it had anything to do with the shootout and you?"

"I don't believe in coincidences," Dan said. "I knew something had to have gone bad for her not to come."

"Here's the deal." Jack said, "They're being watched.

Ellen said they'll slip out and try to make sure they're not being followed and meet us here at the bus depot. We'll stake it out and if they're clear, we'll pick them up and beat feet." Jack glanced at his two buddies.

"Okay, the truth is, they'll be followed so we'll go with the plans we have for that," Dan said.

"They'll call at seven forty-five and hope to be here between eight-thirty and nine."

"Well, the plot thickens," Roadhawg mumbled as they got back in the Caddy.

Dan said, "Did Ellen confirm the plan when they'll get here?"

"Yep. She said ten minutes, in then out." Jack looked from Dan to Roadhawg.

The plan was for Ellen and Christy to wait two to three minutes after they arrived at the depot, walk in the front of the depot, into the ladies room, change clothes, and then out the back of the bus station. If they're being watched, that would be the best shot for losing the FBI tails. Each would get into a different taxi.

"Well, all this has made me hungry. Let's go eat." Roadhawg started the Caddy.

"Danny, you're awfully quiet. Are you okay?" Jack ignored Roadhawg.

"Yeah, Jack, I mean, Christy's long over her ex, but he's the father of the boys, and ah-h…"

"Still gotta be tough for her, you know?" Jack sighed. "And I'm sure the Feds are probably giving her a hard time."

"I can't believe the douche bags are trying to hang it on us." Roadhawg stopped at a traffic light. "I guess it worked when we ditched them, 'cause the Feds are acting stupid. It gave them an excuse to try to hang it on us. I'm still starvin'."

"We're in deep shit with our pictures in the news. It'll change everything. Glad we went with all of us wearing disguises," Dan said.

Leaving the stop light, Roadhawg said, "Well, we need a little bit of planning on the pick up tonight. Do you think it'll be safe to stay at the place we have rented?"

"You all did wear the disguises, didn't you?" Dan said.

Jack answered. "Nope. We weren't even suspects or whatever then. I think we'll be okay for tonight. But we outta beat feet tomorrow. They've really got nothing on Roadhawg and me. It's your ass they're after." Jack pointed toward Dan.

"*Au, contraire*, buzzard breath. Aiding and abetting, and if they've put me in the loop for the money run, you can bet your candy-asses they're after you, also."

"Well, if they get us both, you'll have to spring us. I'm just saying, let's be extra careful that the three of us aren't arrested at the same time." Jack grinned.

Roadhawg said, "I'll amen to that."

"So let's get out of here." Dan sounded depressed.

"Come on, could we go grab a bite and stew over things? The clock's ticking and we've got less than two hours." Roadhawg drove into the shopping center parking lot in front of a McDonalds. He took Jack and Dan's orders and got out.

"Hurry up. Ellen doesn't poke around," Jack said.

"Yes, mother, I'm hurrying. Six burgers, three fries, and Cokes?" Roadhawg grumbled as he left the guys and hurried toward the front door.

Dan watched Roadhawg walk away. Damn it, this is all my fault. Now, we're wanted and on the run.

A plain four door sedan pulled into the McDonalds. Dan's thoughts froze. Oh, Shit.

CHAPTER EIGHT

Ellen saw the two FBI cars parked out in front of Christy's when she arrived. She drove up the driveway, parked the car and walked to the house. When Christy answered the door, she smiled and stepped outside.

"How can they be suspects...Jack, Roadhawg, and Dan?"

"I think they're looking for any excuse to get warrants for their arrest," Christy answered. "They said my ex was murdered around seven this morning. I mean the time of death doesn't match up. They've got nothing on the guys." She wiped the corners of her eyes.

"Christy, how are you doing? I mean about all of this?"

"We've been separated two...almost three years now. He was into drugs, women, and anything illegal. I got over him a long time ago. I mean it's hard to believe, but the boys..."

Ellen heard Christy's voice breaking up. "How are they doing?"

"They haven't seen him since Christmas. They're upset, but they're more worried about where Dan is. They miss him so much."

Ellen checked her watch. "I've got to call them in eight to ten minutes. If it's okay, I'll just excuse myself and go make the call."

"Okay. You know where my bedroom is. Just use that phone. Where are the guys?"

"Out of town. They'll leave just after we hang up."

"Cool. Let's go in. I'll introduce you to the pain-in-the-ass agents." Christy rolled her eyes.

Once inside, Christy led the way to the kitchen/dining room where the agents were seated around the table.

"Agents Thomason and Riley." Christy pointed them out.

"This is Ellen Higgins. Jack Higgins wife."

"Ma'am" agent Thomason interrupted, "we're looking for your husband. Do you know where he is?"

"No, I don't. I just arrived from California. Why are you looking for Jack?"

"Ellen, they think he, Dan, and Roadhawg had something to do with my ex's murder."

Ellen looked at the agents. "Are you all insane?"

"We want to talk to them to clear this up. That's all. They aided Mr. Burton in avoiding us serving him with a warrant for his arrest." Agent Riley pulled a sheet of folded paper out of his suit coat pocket.

"Let me get this straight," Ellen pounded her finger on the table. "Dan isn't under arrest, and you want Jack and Roadhawg for...what? I'm not answering to anymore of this nonsense."

"Mrs. Higgins, we can arrest you," Thomason said.

"Bull crap. Christy, I've got to use the ladies room." Ellen turned and left. She closed the door as she entered the bedroom. She dialed the pay phone number where Jack waited.

"Yes," Jack answered the pay phone outside of Bremerton.

"They have a warrant for Dan's arrest, and claim to have

warrants for you, too. They think you all are involved. Christy's fine, so are the boys. They're most likely tracing this, so bye for now. I'll check in later." She hung up.

A Plain Jane FBI-looking car caused Jack to freeze when he left the phone booth, but the car was an elderly couple looking for a parking space. It appeared that Roadhawg had the same thought about the elderly couple because he drove his Cadillac past Jack. Jack trotted away from the phone booth down the street and around the corner, making sure nobody was watching until he was out of sight. He jumped into the driver's seat of the throw away '65 Ford parked on the side street. He drove to their rendezvous parked and jumped into Roadhawg's Cadillac that was waiting for him.

Jack relayed the information to Dan and Roadhawg. They remained silent.

Everything was set. The only thing new was a slight change of plans. They needed to solicit two young women to assist in the switch at the bus station. They arranged for a taxi to be waiting out in front of the bus station and one out the back by the parked buses.

An hour and a half later, each of them was in place, waiting for Ellen's phone call.

At seven forty-five, Ellen excused herself to go to the bathroom. She entered Christy's bedroom and called Jack at the phone booth. After a brief contact, they were ready.

Ellen walked into the dining room. She smiled at Grace who had been making dinner in the kitchen.

Grace, on cue, said, "Christy, why don't you and Ellen get out of here and take a break. I'll entertain these guys."

"Good idea, Grace. Come on Christy," Ellen said.

"Ah, where do you two think you're going?" Agent Riley said.

"For a ride, if it's any of your business." Ellen said

glowered at him.

"Listen, we know you called your husband a while ago and told him everything that's going on…"

Ellen cut him off. "Listen, yourself. Nobody's under arrest. We haven't broken any laws. It's still the United States of America, and we're leaving. Come on Christy."

Agents Thomason and Riley trotted after them. Ellen noticed two more agents sitting in another dark sedan in front of the house. Both agency cars fell in behind Ellen and Christy in Christy's Mustang.

Once in Bremerton, as planned, Ellen drove toward the bus station. About a half a mile away, Christy pressed the transmit button on her walkie-talkie. "Lone Ranger this is Tonto."

Ellen drove into the parking lot at the bus depot.

Before Ellen got out, she took the shopping bag with their disguises, from the back seat. She and Christy entered the bus depot as the two agency cars pulled in. Thomason and Riley hurried out of their car and followed.

Christy clicked her walkie-talkie twice. Dan clicked back twice. She'd just told him two agents were following them and Dan let her know he received the message. Jack and Roadhawg listened on their sets.

After the women entered the station, they headed toward the ladies room. Ellen whispered, "Hey Christy, see that long haired dead beat bum sitting there?"

"Yeah."

"That's your fiancé." Ellen giggled.

Not even looking twice, Christy answered. "I'd never have picked him out."

"Well, here we go," Ellen said as they walked into the ladies room.

"Are you here for the change?" Ellen asked the woman resembling Christy. The pair of women waiting there had been paid earlier to change clothes with Christy and Ellen.

"Yes," one woman answered. According to the plan Ellen handed the look-alike her blouse, slacks and sunglasses. Then the woman changed into them and walked out. The second woman stayed behind.

A taxi with the meter running waited outside for the first departing decoy. The second set of agents followed the other woman who left the ladies room moments later dressed in Christie's clothes.

"See ya, girl," Ellen said to Christy as she was next to walk out of the restroom.

Riley and Thomason were standing close to the entrance of the bus depot. Riley elbowed his partner. They recognized Ellen right away. Riley hurried after her. She walked out the entrance of the bus depot on the opposite side of the building. Another taxi was parked with the out of service flag up as planned. Thomason paced, inside, still glued to the ladies room entrance.

Once outside the depot, Ellen hurried to the waiting taxi, opened the door, jumped in, and said. "Is the meter running?" The password the cabbie was waiting for. The cabbie almost burned rubber leaving Riley running after them. Ellen turned back. Riley had stopped and was talking on his walkie-talkie. She knew he must've told the other two agents to pick him up as he chased the fleeing cab.

At the corner, the cab turned and Ellen caught a glimpse of Riley waving to the approaching agents. Two blocks down, Ellen's taxi made a sharp right, and fifty feet later stopped beside a '65 Chevrolet. Ellen jumped out and onto the back floor board, as planned. The cab had moved down the street as the agency car sped around the corner almost hitting an old looking man driving a '65 Chevrolet toward them.

Ellen watched the agents disappear around the corner

chasing the cab. "You can get up here. It's all clear," Jack said.

Climbing over the seat, Ellen giggled, "It worked. "

Dan watched Thomason as Christy's look-alike walked into the doorway of the bathroom and turned to go back into the ladies room. Then an elderly lady shuffled out wearing a grey wig, a frumpy dress, baggy hose, and clumpy shoes. It appeared to Dan that Thomason had dismissed the old lady trying to see if the Christy decoy was coming out. The long haired old geezer and the frumpy old lady walked out of the bus station arm and arm. Down the street, Roadhawg waited in his `65 Cadillac for them. The elderly couple got in.

Roadhawg keyed his walkie-talkie. "Tonto, the Lone Ranger is clear."

Jack, Ellen and Roadhawg met up in the shopping center where the Chevy wagon was parked. Then Jack and Ellen dressed as the old couple got in their wagon. They drove off with the Cadillac following them. Roadhawg stayed behind watching for tails as planned.

"I can't believe it worked so well." Ellen hugged Jack.

"Yes, it did, didn't it? Well, see that Chinese restaurant?"

"Yeah?"

"I've got to run in there for a minute."

"What for?"

"Well, when we all get back to the place, I figured we'd be hungry, and we've got nothing fixed. So, I took the chance that it'd go this way, and I ordered a boat load of Chinese takeout."

"That sounds really good, but hurry. I worry that they'll be scouring the neighborhood."

"One," Jack held up his index finger, "they don't know the car, and two, they aren't looking for this face." He pointed at his disguise, as the dark clouds opened up obscuring the windshield. Damn it I hope this isn't a bad omen.

Ellen grabbed his arm and said, "Wait until this rain lets up."

"I'll be just a minute."

"Oh, shit." Ellen ducked down. "That looks like one of the Feds."

"I'll be right back. Stay out of sight."

"Jack, it's them," she whispered.

Jack froze

CHAPTER NINE

Much to Jack's relief, the FBI drove through the strip mall parking lot, and moved on. Jack hurried inside. How much longer were they going to take to bag his Chinese take-out? Chills ran through his body. And it wasn't even cold.

When Jack and Ellen arrived at the hideout, outside Poulsbo, tension ran high.

Dan asked Jack and Roadhawg if they'd worn disguises when they rented the place they were in.

"No." Jack said, "We weren't even under the radar at that time. So, I've been thinking on the way here tonight. We need to leave ASAP. I saw nice motels or whatever over in Edmonds the other day."

"Yeah." Roadhawg joined in. "We can scoot over to Kingston. Jack and I did it when we first got here. There are lots of motels on Interstate five. We shouldn't raise any flags if we're careful."

Christy looked at Ellen. "We're all packed."

"So are we," Ellen said.

Dan put another envelope addressed to Agents Riley and Thompson on the table.

They left within five minutes in three vehicles.

Roadhawg inhaled more than his share of Chinese on the way out the door. The rest took theirs to eat on the way to Kingston. The trip to the motels for the night was hurried.

The next morning, the five of them met in a corner booth at a local diner. They made plans in a corner booth. Dan left for a few minutes to make a phone call from a phone booth outside.

Dan hung up the phone and walked back to their table. "I like this attorney guy, Steve Mitchell. He's good and he's expensive, but I think he'll be worth every penny."

"Yeah, but does he have the balls to take on the Feds?" Roadhawg adjusted the black baseball cap he wore all the time now.

"I think he's going to have fun screwing with them." Dan finished with his notes from the call and handed them to Jack and Roadhawg to copy the information.

"Steve Mitchell's phone number will be our new point of contact if our other plans fall through."

Jack kept his eyes on the papers.

"Okay." Roadhawg glanced up from his notes. "And he knows he'll represent all of us?"

"Yes. But mostly me, if and when the time comes," Dan said.

Christy held Dan's hand. "After you drop me off at the attorney's, I'll give him the retainer." She held up an envelope Dan had given her earlier. "Afterwards I'll take a cab to the ferry and go back over to Bremerton and pick up the rental we left there last night. Then go straight back to Gig Harbor."

"Well, I guess we're outta here, then." Roadhawg got up from the booth.

"We'll see you there in a couple of days. Be careful." Ellen stood and hugged Jack.

Christy wiped a trace of a tear as she held Dan. "I know I'll see you this weekend. It's just…that there's so much going on between now and then."

Dan wrapped both arms around her and held her extra tight. He whispered, "I know, but it's going to all work out and we're good with the rendezvous plans for this Friday."

Christy nodded her head.

Everyone had already packed their stuff in the disposable cars.

Roadhawg left in his Cadillac. Two minutes later, Jack and Ellen left.

Dan and Christy took a few minutes to go over the details of the house they were building on Vashon Island before they left. Their dream house had a sauna, steam room, a sewing suite for her and a 2000 sq. ft. shop for him. It overlooked the Sound, northeast of Gig Harbor.

"Tell George to continue on," Dan said to Christy. "He knows what to do. If he has any questions for me, tell him to do it like it was his. I'll call him from time to time." George, the contractor, was a God send.

"It's just that you've always been there helping, and..."

"Now I won't be for a while. I feel guilty because George is depending on getting the house done in the next two months," Jack said as they drove along the shore of Puget Sound.

"Honey, he'll be okay." Christy held Dan's forearm. "I'll be so glad when we get this all settled and behind us. I guess we'll have to let this attorney, Steve Mitchell, work out the details with the Feds."

"I wouldn't trust the Feds as far as I could throw them."

"I just worry with everything going crazy." Then she squeezed his arm.

"If the Feds want their money back, we'll be fine," Dan said.

"Everyone still has the money to give back?"

"Yes. I talked with the guys and we're all way ahead of what we deposited." Dan smiled

"I mean, do we have enough to finish the house?"

"Many times over, Christy. Don't you even begin to worry about that."

CHAPTER TEN

Dan told Christy he'd call Riley and Thomason, and leave word for them to contact Steve Mitchell because he would be representing Dan, knowing Roadhawg had left them the information in the briefcase. He dropped Christy off in downtown Seattle, a few blocks from Steve Mitchell's office. She walked the couple of blocks to the Law Offices of Hannah, Garrett and Taylor.

The receptionist asked her if she had an appointment. "Yes, I'm Christy Abbott to see Mr. Mitchell."

"Okay, he's expecting you. One moment." The receptionist pushed a button on her desk.

A man walked out from a door behind the reception desk. He was buttoning the third button on his tailored jacket. His wry smile, blue eyes, and brown hair made him appear mischievous. A little less than six feet, he looked quite dapper as he approached and took her hand.

"My, has anyone ever told you you'd pass for Natalie Wood?" He smiled.

"Everyone says that about mother and me."

"This way." He nodded to the secretary. "Janelle, hold all my calls, please." He guided Christy through the door he'd come from.

"First things first," Steve said after they entered his office.

Before he could finish, Christy handed him the

envelope.

"Yes." He took it and turned his head to the side as he raised his eyebrows, slipped the check out of the envelope, and placed it in his top desk drawer. He smiled. "Very well, have a seat."

"Thank you." Christy chose an overstuffed chair.

"Well, Mister Burton said you could fill me in on everything. Why don't you begin?" His eyes seemed to turn shifty as he leaned back in his chair.

Christy told him about the heisted military payroll from Okinawa the prior September. Then she told about her deceased ex and Dan's unfortunate involvement with them. All the while, he took pages of notes on a legal sized yellow pad.

"This ought to make a terrific novel." He stopped writing and cocked his head. "My, my, very interesting. Now, I understand the Feds' interest in all of this. Your fiancé should be a hero. You say all concerned, the other five, took the money from the thieves, waiting for a reward to be posted?"

Christy nodded.

"No reward was ever offered, and they felt stuck with it?"

She continued to nod, as he kept making notes.

"What a delightful problem. There might be some charges by the Feds but what I can't imagine. Other than possibly possession of…"

"What about it never happened in the United States?"

"Yes, that's very interesting." He pressed his fingertips together and put them to his lower lip. "And…and you said they're all willing to return it? How much reward do they want?"

"They said they'd let you negotiate that."

"That could be fun. Now, to this involvement with the illegal drugs and Mr. Anderson. I need to tell you his attorney, Bob Jones, is known in the legal community to be knee deep in defending drug money."

"Well, my ex was very involved, and it led to our separation and divorce. He was out of control. How do I say this…high, stoned twenty-four-seven."

"Well, I understand they've arrested Mr. Anderson…"

"Really?" she interrupted.

"He's out on bail, but the word is they have him for distribution. He's most likely going to plead that your ex was the culprit, and he knew nothing." Steve made quote marks with his hand.

The phone on his desk rang. Steve picked it up, shook his head, and clucked his tongue. "Please, I said no calls. Oh, okay. Put them through." He winked. "Yes, I'm Mr. Mitchell and you're Special Agent Thomason?" He smiled at Christy. "I understand. Mrs. Abbott will turn herself in. How about her house? Fine. I will accompany her there. Yes, say in an hour and a half? And I am looking forward to working with you, also. Is it Agent Thompson?" Steve appeared to have mispronounced it on purpose. "Yes, Thomason."

"Arrest?" Christy's heart skipped a beat.

"They're fishing. No arrest warrants. Seriously, at best you're a person of interest."

"Okay. Should I be worried?"

"Absolutely not. They're just scare tactics. We'll have some fun." He stood and motioned to the door. "I'll leave word with my secretary." Steve finished and they walked out of his office.

P.R. STEELE

CHAPTER ELEVEN

Steve and Christy arrived in separate cars and much to their surprise no federal agents were waiting. He had driven her to Bremerton so she could pick up Ellen's car from the evening before.

"Hey, Mom, I'm home," Christy announced as they walked in the door.

"I'm in the kitchen. Give me a minute. I'm taking cookies out of the oven."

Walking to the kitchen, Christy said, "Mom, this is Steve Mitchell. Steve, my mom. The FBI is on their way to ask some questions."

"My, my. Surely, your Christy's twin," Steve took her hand and held it.

"Stop it. You're teasing," Grace said, looking at him.

"Might I ask for a cookie?" Steve still held her hand.

"They're too warm." She pulled her hand away.

"Okay, but first a bit of business." Steve picked up a cookie and took a bite. "When the agents arrive, it's important that neither of you say a word. Not your name, nothing. Understand?" He glanced from Grace to Christy.

"Yes," they answered in unison.

Just then the doorbell rang.

"When I give the okay to answer their questions, try to make all your replies one word."

Christy nodded as the doorbell rang again.

"Let me get the door." Steve walked out of the kitchen.

Christy could hear Steve asking for their cards, and then to see the warrant.

Entering the kitchen Steve beamed with his hands in front of his coat, fingers pressed together, "They don't have a warrant, just yet." Then addressing Riley and Thomason, Steve began. "Let me say for the record, Mrs. Abbott wants to cooperate fully. You can ask her questions now that you've made it clear there's no warrant for her arrest."

"Mrs. Abbott, do you know the whereabouts of Mr. Daniel Burton?" Agent Riley spoke first.

Christy looked at Steve. He nodded. "No."

"Were you with him last night?"

Steve nodded yes.

"Yes."

"Okay. Where?"

Steve winked at her. As instructed, she gave them a slip of paper from her purse with the address in Poulsbo. Thomason took it and left the house for his car.

"Are they still there?" Riley said when Thomason returned.

Seeing Steve wink, Christy said, "They?"

"Yes," Riley snapped. "Higgins, Hegidio, and Mr. Burton."

"Agent Riley, please watch your tone." Steve cocked his head and smiled.

Riley exhaled through pursed lips. "Well?"

"I don't know, but I don't think so."

"Do you know where they are? Or where they're going?"

Steve blinked.

"No."

"Are you trying to tell me you spent the night and haven't a clue as to where they are?"

Steve took over. "Asked and answered, Agent Riley."

"We have warrants for their arrest. You know withholding evidence…"

"Pa-lezz…don't speak to my client with those threatening terms. If you must, direct the rhetoric to me, because this tactic won't get you anywhere." Steve turned toward Grace. "Are those cookies cool enough for a connoisseur, such as myself, to partake of another one, Grace?"

"Ah, yes. I think so." She lifted a warm cookie off the cookie sheet with a spatula.

Steve took a bite. "Most excellent. As scrumptious as the hot one right out of the oven." Then, he took her hand. "Oh, my God. You have won my heart."

"What the hell are you doing?" Riley interrupted.

Spinning on the balls of his feet, Steve glared at Riley. "Here, here. That kind of language is out of line. As for this ruse of withholding evidence, Agent Riley, you just ended your conversation with my client." Steve turned back toward Grace and again took her hand.

"Where was I? Oh, yes, most excellent cookies. Might I be so bold as to ask you out to dinner to repay you for this kindness?" He took another bite, closed his eyes, and swallowed.

"Excuse me, counselor." Riley interrupted, "Could we continue?"

Without taking his eyes off Grace, he said, "Only if the veiled threats cease. Excuse me, Grace." He pivoted to face Riley again. "You may continue."

Riley danced around his questions. Thomason joined him. The two could never get Christy to answer with more than a one-word reply. After about ten minutes, they left.

"You did fantastic, Christy," Steve said.

"No, you did." Christy hugged him.

"Grace, how about a hug?" Steve stood arms open, and then hugged her. She hugged him back. He held her longer than usual. Then stood back and said, "How about that dinner tonight? Say sevenish?"

Grace began to chuckle. "What? Are you serious?"

"I'm quite serious. Since I didn't hear a no, I take it you mean, yes." He winked at her.

"Ah, I'm old enough..."

Steve cut her off. "That's good to know. I don't want any statutory complications. Ladies, I must be off. Grace, thank you for the cookies, and I'm so looking forward to tonight."

After he left, Grace shook her head.

"Come on, Mom. I think he's serious."

"I don't know what to wear." A smile began to cross Grace's face.

"I've got a couple of numbers that'll do just fine."

Later that evening, at the prearranged time, Christy waited at the phone booth. She brought Dan up to date on everything.

"Honey, Steve is a kick-butt attorney. He's really good, but we've got a big problem with him."

Dan hesitated. "What?"

"He took Mom on a dinner date. I think he likes her."

CHAPTER TWELVE

Riley and Thomason had walked into the hideaway rental outside Poulsbo just before five that afternoon. The place left no clues except for Dan's handwritten note.

"So, what's it got to say?" Riley said.

"Says, he wants to clear the air, and the attorney has the authorization to broker a deal."

"That Mitchell is some piece of work." Riley shot back.

"A little too cute, but I'm afraid he's got some big ass balls." Thomason looked up from the letter in his hand.

"You know Washington isn't going to cut any deals. They want the money and some jail time. That's it."

"Letter says Burton, Hegidio, and Higgins didn't take it. They found it, and they know who took it."

"Bull shit. Lemme see that thing again." Riley reached for the letter.

"Let's get this back to the office. We'll call it in, in the morning," Thomason said.

The next morning, Dan meandered west on Highway 12 out of Olympia toward Aberdeen. Once there he took Highway 105 headed south westerly according to Dan's map. The community of Westport on the ocean included an airport he'd noticed several times flying for Ken. The lay of the land would offer several escape routes if he needed them.

This last weekend I was lucky. That won't happen again. I won't be caught wearing no disguises, anything recognizable. They're no doubt looking for this car. I'll get rid of it, but I've gotta start being more careful, or those morons will catch me.

Dan stood in front of an upscale mobile home park. He could throw a rock from there into Grays Harbor. He took notice of some of the "For Rent" signs. His stomach let him know it didn't appreciate skipping breakfast. At the only small diner in Westport, he enjoyed lunch while checking out the local weekly newspaper. His watch read a little after one.

Westport Realty was a few blocks from the diner. The streets were empty during the early afternoon. Besides that, the off season suited Dan just fine.

The reality office was small. Dan opened the door and a bell tinkled. A heavy set man in his forties jumped from his desk and extended his hand.

"I'm Bob Shepard," he said with a firm handshake.

"Ray Afton. I saw some of your ads for rent." Dan handed him the folded newspaper with the circled ads.

Dan and Ray Afton had grown up together, but Ray had died in Vietnam. When one has to change his name and lie about it, a good association helps the lying memory.

The realtor will remember me with my ponytail, and mustache. Dan smiled at his reflection in the real estate office's front window.

"Ahh, huh. Yes, we can go look at them right now," Shepard said.

Just as I suspected. Business must be slow.

On the way outside, Dan's antenna went up. But Shepard was asking qualifying questions, like about his car.

Dan said he left it at the diner.

"That's okay. We'll just take my truck."

Dan's story centered around his mother's failing health so he needed to be close by. The questions kept coming. To change the subject, Dan asked about the fishing.

They took a little over an hour, and looked at three mobile homes. Dan chose the one with a boat dock on the water. The small boat had a twenty-five horse outboard motor. Back at the office, Dan began filling out the rental agreement.

"Where's your mother live now? Is her situation serious?" Shepard was filling out background paperwork.

"Over in Olympia, but I'd rather not talk about it, if it's all the same."

Shepard finished the paper work. Dan left the deposit, and the realtor handed Ray Afton the keys.

The mobile home was newer, fully furnished with all the appliances, but most important, it offered seclusion with a good view of the access road. Grays Harbor was the entire rear view from the house. Standing on the back deck, Dan could see the small local airport runway less than a half-mile away, also on the water. The second bedroom closet backed up to a portion of the deck that extended to the water's edge. That was the clincher.

CHAPTER THIRTEEN

Dan walked to his four-door Ford at the diner and drove back to Tacoma. A used car lot advertised "We pay cash for cars." The transaction only took 10 minutes before he hailed a cab. He'd called the number in the newspaper advertising a '63 Buick for sale earlier, and got the address. He needed another car.

Dan loved the '63 Buick Electra. No ID was required to buy the disposable cars. He gave the seller cash and registered it in the same name, Ray Afton, but with a throw away address. He used a PO Box he rented in Olympia. After getting the car registered in his new name, he felt a little more secure.

His next two stops were a Tacoma hardware store that had everything he needed to modify the second bedroom closet, and then an automobile parts store for the Buick.

Dan drove the Buick to the Army base at Ft. Lewis. The auto hobby shop provided tools, space and equipment. There you could do anything to your car from painting to repairs. Before he got there he removed his disguises, the wig and facial hair. But he was cautious to use the Ray Afton name because he had to match his military ID card.

When the auto hobby shop manager didn't check his ID, Ray Afton's name appeared on the auto hobby shop's paperwork.

The shop manager had the tag but with a fake name, and he might remember me. But the state will never think to look up any vehicles registered to Ray Afton. Besides, it'll take a month to get it into the system. He breathed a little easier.

Dan changed the oil, spark plugs, rotor, distributer cap, and plug wires. The manager left the clip board on the counter. Dan smiled and changed the tag number and the vehicle description to a Pontiac. He felt better leaving because the now newly listed Pontiac started on the first try. It purred like a kitten the hour it took him to drive back to Westport.

Before Dan drove into the small town, he put on his disguise, again. Then he made a quick stop at the local hardware store. The check-out clerk at the hardware store in Tacoma didn't even bat an eye as he rang up the items, including a skill saw. The last thing I need is the local hardware store asking questions.

When he returned to his rental, he removed the wig, and headed into the second bedroom. He pulled the carpet up from the closet floor. In thirty minutes he finished cutting a square-hole in the old floor. He used 2 x 4's attached under the hole to leave a lip to support the piece of old floor. This would hold the new trapdoor. He squeezed Elmer's glue on the cut-out floor board. He took his time to place the cut piece of carpet back onto the trapdoor. It fit perfectly.

Okay, next.

The sign out front of the local filling station said Earl's. Dan parked at the side of the old building.

An older man walked toward him.

"How's business?" Dan said. "Are you Earl?"

"It don't matter much if it's off season or not. Business

is slow. And yes sir, I'm Earl, the owner of this here establishment."

"I have something that might be of interest to you, Earl."

"I'll listen, as long as it's legal."

Dan explained about his sick mother, her memory lapses, and his fear of what might happen if she tried to drive again.

Earl nodded as Dan continued about her getting lost or injuring someone. Earl's face lit up when Dan mentioned storing her car for a few weeks.

His smile grew even broader when Dan mentioned twenty dollars a month. Earl couldn't shake Dan's hand fast enough.

Dan parked the Buick and walked back to the mobile home. Maybe he was being too paranoid. He unlocked the front door walked to his bedroom to check out the emergency escape route. He pulled the carpet, and with a small tug, the trap door lifted up. He stepped down to the soft sand that surrounded the mobile home park, got on his knees, and pulled the trapdoor closed above him. The soft sand ran all the way to the water's edge.

Scrambling out from under the deck, he stood at the retaining wall by his dock. Inside the mobile home nobody would be able to tell he'd pulled the trap door closed from underneath.

The next morning, he caught the bus to Olympia where he bought a low-miles, four-door, 1958 Bel Air. He started out with five thousand in hundreds. With a little over three thousand left, he visited the bank in Olympia and made a withdrawal in twenties. Lot of places don't have change, and a hundred dollar bill could be a problem when someone's on the run.

Dan decided if he needed to leave in a hurry, he'd want extra cash. He divided five-hundred dollars into stacks of twenties and stuffed them into two airtight bags. He wanted to stash one in the Buick and the other one in the boat. If they came for him, he'd be ready.

After day break on Friday, Dan went to Earls and hid the five hundred dollars under the back seat of the Buick between the springs. He walked to the dock behind the house and taped the other bag under the seat at the boat's bow..

On Saturday morning, Dan waited for Christy at the mobile home.

At seven-forty-five in Christy's house, she took the wig off. Time to go. She got into her '66 Mustang convertible, and as the garage door closed behind her, she took a deep breath and put the top down. The ticket for her flight to Portland stuck out of the outside pocket of her purse on the front seat.

A government sedan fell in behind her, just as she expected. Her bright red scarf almost kept her hair in place, but she didn't care. At least her sun glasses made the morning drive tolerable. She smiled as she watched the sedan in her rearview mirror follow her off the I-5 exit for the airport. At the first gas station, she pulled in and hurried into the ladies room.

"So excited her weak bladder can't take it." Riley grinned at Thomason.

"Jeez, keep your eye on the Mustang. I can't believe she left it running."

"Nerves getting to her." Riley picked up the microphone. "Ah-h-h, unit two, do you still have us in sight?"

"Affirmative."

"Well, follow her when she comes out. She's obviously going to one of the terminal parking lots. We'll go to the Northwest gate. She's on the nine-fifty to Portland." Riley put the mic in its holder after the agent double clicked.

"There she is," Thomason said as she ran out of the

ladies room, putting on her glasses.

She got into the Mustang and peeled out from the station. The backup Feds followed her into the long term parking lot. On cue, they called Riley as they followed her into the terminal.

Riley and Thomason skipped the parking lot and went to her departure gate. They were there as she approached them.

"Mrs. Abbott, we need to speak with you." Riley said as he greeted her from inside the terminal. He pulled a folder from his briefcase.

"Excuse me," Christy's mom, Grace, said taking off her glasses and scarf. "But I think you have me confused with my daughter."

"What the hell?" Thomason's eyes bugged out.

"Maybe you should call Mr. Mitchell. Now excuse me. You've upset me, and I'm going to call my attorney." Grace walked away.

Christy drove north up I-5 toward Whidbey Island in the car her mom had parked behind the gas station near her home.

Dan surveyed the hot tub on the deck overlooking the Pacific. The weekend rental reeked of romance. He and Christy had spent several of his reserve weekends on Whidbey Island, but never at anything this cozy. Champagne sat in a bucket of ice. Glasses sparkled above the small ribbons tied around the stems. Christy's favorite shrimp cocktails awaited them in the fridge.

Dan heard the noise of a car being driven on the gravel driveway. He watched as Christy hurried to the cottage. He opened the front door, they embraced, and clothes began to fall on the floor piece-by-piece on their way to the hot tub. Dan popped the cork, and filled her glass. The covered patio kept the afternoon sun out of their eyes and the hot tub kept the Pacific chill away.

"Dan, this is fantastic. You did good." She placed a shrimp in his mouth followed by a kiss. She licked his fingers for the last bit of sauce as he returned the gesture. Dan pulled her over on top of him and fondled her butt.

"I've got something to ask you, Honey," Dan said.

CHAPTER FOURTEEN

"I'm worried about what the feds are up to." Dan inhaled the crisp afternoon air.

"What can they do?" Christy sat facing him on his lap. "Really. I mean, sooner or later they're going to get tired and hopefully come around and settle the whole mess."

"Baby, I'd like to think that, but so far they aren't. Maybe we need to be more careful."

"I'm on the pill." She grinned as she felt him responding.

"That's real funny. But, seriously, maybe we need to be in disguise every time we're out."

"Nawh. Oh my, little Dan isn't in disguise right now." She leaned over and kissed him.

"Oh Gawd. . .I know it. Lord have mercy, I've missed you."

"I can really tell. And I've missed you."

"That was the assistant to the director." Thomason said, hanging up the phone.

"So how much crap is coming down?" Riley glanced out the office window.

"When I read them Burton's letter, they all but laughed me off the phone."

The late afternoon shadows filled the room, but the silence reflected the dark atmosphere. The two agents had followed the trail to the hideaway, shared the contents of Dan's letter with the powers-to-be in D. C., and now waited for the decisions and directions to come down from on high.

"Well, Riles, they'll take the lead and send some hotshot to come ramrod the whole shebang." Thomason wadded up the telex he'd just read and threw it in the waste basket.

"So," Riley said as he slouched down on the couch. "J. Edgar wants to make an example, set precedence, and screw the possibility of getting the money back? Shit, the fact remains, and we both know it…those Marines aren't the ones who stole it to begin with."

"Well, that's what Burton says, and I believe him. Those guys are way ahead of us."

"No, shit. I think they're having fun screwing with us, but I'm with you. I believe 'em."

"Well, sir." Thomason paced the small office. "Remember, we were told not to contact that smart assed attorney Mitchell."

Pointing his finger like a gun, Riley broke out in a toothy grin. "But they didn't say if he contacted us we couldn't find out what he knows…unofficially, of course." He held up both hands giving the quote/unquote gesture.

Riley made a phone call to Steve Mitchell's office that led to Steve Mitchell calling them back. Steve must have caught the drift, for they set a meeting with him for five that evening.

McDonalds offered a neutral setting with semi-private booths. Steve Mitchell knew that because he checked out the place before the meeting. He smiled as he drove into the parking lot because none of them had home court advantage. He noticed the government-issued Ford parked there as he walked in. Riley and Thomason looked comfortable in a booth near the restrooms. Steve sauntered over.

Riley stood and gave his half of the booth to Steve. Riley grabbed a chair and sat at the end of the table. Restaurant chatter gave them extra privacy.

Thomason began. "Look counselor, we're here unofficially. So could we cut the crap?"

"Absolutely. Unofficially." Steve smirked.

"Your guy, Burton, said for us to deal with you." Riley leaned on the table.

"Okay. Let's say they could deliver most of those things you want back. What are you offering?"

Thomason's mouth twitched as he said, "Minimum time, and it'd be over."

Steve rolled his eyes. "They didn't take anything from the Federal Government. So first of all, no minimum time, and this is nonnegotiable…"

"They've got millions of the government's money. And it's stolen money. That's possession of." Riley poked his finger at Steve.

"They know who took it, and you're not pursuing that? My, my, very interesting."

"But they've got the money," Thomason shot back.

"Maybe they do. But let's get back on track. Here's an offer to consider. You get the missing property back, pursue the original thieves, give a reward for finding the missing property to the six Marines, and no more talk of time behind bars." Steve glared from Riley to Thomason.

"Offer a reward, and no jail time?" Thomason chuckled.

"D.C. will never accept that. Look, that money was stolen, and those guys have it. That's possession of stolen property. That equals time in jail. What are you missing?"

"They're far ahead of you. Keep that in mind and

remember this." Steve took his right hand and placed it above his heart and rippled his fingers. "They're prepared to vanish, go to the media, and tell their side of the whole mess. They have credibility, facts, and proof on their side."

"Credibility? Facts? Bull...shit." Riley shot back. "Fact...they have stolen money that equals zero credibility with J. Edgar Hoover."

"I want to thank you for this meeting." Steve eased out of the booth. Riley and Thomason both snapped their heads toward Steve. "Maybe, I should have had this meeting with J. Edgar."

"Wait. Hold on just a minute." Thomason stood. "This is going to spin out of our control and get very nasty."

"Thank you for that insight. I think that's exactly what my clients want. And they're looking forward to taking this to another level."

"What does that mean?" Riley knocked his chair backward as he stood, slamming it to the floor.

"I'm not at liberty to say." Steve rubbed his chin. "By the way, ever hear of Mike Wallace? Good day gentlemen," he said over his shoulder as he walked off.

"What'll we do now?" Riley said as he watched Steve leave.

"Officially, this little meeting never took place. And honestly, I think those guys are clean. Not squeaky clean, but I'm more on their side than D.C.'s." Thomason picked up Riley's chair and placed it back under the table.

Riley said, "Yeah, having some home office prick coming out here to take over the investigation is not a career enhancing feather in one's cap."

"Well, shit's about to hit the fan," Thomason said as they left McDonalds for their office.

CHAPTER FIFTEEN

Thomason paced behind his desk.

Riley fidgeted in the chair in front of it.

"Well, in some ways I'm glad," Thomason said.

"Tommy, I don't see the upside. D.C. sending her out here to take over sucks."

"Listen." Thomason still fretted. "Burton and those guys aren't stupid. This could work to our benefit. You know, let her be the lead dog on this...whole screwed-up investigation."

"Maybe. Maybe not. It's definitely not a step up for us. But, here's what else I don't like. One." Riley held up his index finger. "I truly believe we should be after the guys running the drugs, including that slime ball Anderson. Two." He raised two fingers. "We both agree they didn't originally take the money, and we should be after the ones who did."

Thomason still paced. He nodded his head in agreement as his intercom buzzed.

"Mr. Thomason," his secretary said, "Agent Clements is on her way in."

Before she finished, the office door burst open.

"Agent Thomason." She glared at him, "I'm Agent Roberta Clements. I've been assigned to take over the Burton investigation. I will be taking over your office until further notice."

"You what?" Thomason looked shocked.

"I'm sure you'd like to gather your personal effects. I'd like to get started immediately." She walked behind the desk, and faced Riley. "Agent Riley, I've read the file, and I, along with D.C., are concerned that two agents with your experience have let this investigation deteriorate."

"Well, well." Riley stood with hands on his hips, elbows extended, and his lips pursed. "I see you haven't changed since we went through the academy."

"Ah-h-h, but, things have changed. I'm two grades above you. Why don't we give agent Thomason a couple of minutes to gather up his effects and then you can bring me up to date." She placed a stack of folders on the desk stepping aside so Thomason could empty the drawers and remove pictures from the desk top and walked out.

In a few minutes Thomason re-entered the room.

"So, you two let this...Christy Abbott and Dan Burton affair embarrass you, this office and the entire FBI? They ran circles around you two clowns and all you can do is act like you're lost? Un-be-liev-able. Simply unbelievable."

"Well, let's see how good you can run the show," Riley said. "Is that all you can say? Well, two can play their game."

"And just how's that?" Thomason spoke in measured tones.

"The drug guys want this Burton character, right?" Clements broke out a snarly grin.

"And so?" Riley shot back.

"Contact the news media. Let it out that we want to question her as a person of interest." She made the quote sign with both hands. "We know the drug guys want Burton as bad as we do. Contact that attorney, ah-h-h,

Mitchell." She checked her paper work.

"And contact Mitchell for what?" Thomason raised his voice.

"You morons. Tell Mitchell that we have a warrant for her arrest, and if he has any contact with her he's to inform us."

"And when he asks for a copy of the warrant?"

"Yes?"

"We don't even have a warrant for Burton. Let alone one for Mrs. Abbott." Thomason pointed his finger at Clements.

"Get one. I don't care how, but get one. And contact the media. We're going to turn up the heat. They want to play games? Good, let the games begin."

"So, you're here to play games? I thought this was the investigative part of the Bureau." Riley was beginning to show his impatience.

"Riley, I'm here to clean up your mess. I get things done. So far, all you've done is waltz around whistling Dixie to your prostate. It's Friday. By Monday we'll make some progress. Now, you've both got calls to make. I want you back in here ASAP. That's all. I've got to check in with the director." She waved her hands to dismiss them.

Riley called his source at the newspapers, and Thomason his at the local television stations. They reported back to her. She told them to go pick up Ken Anderson. On their way to their car, Riley grumbled, "I don't like this at all. It's wrong giving out that information. We don't need Montoya's boys putting pressure on Mrs. Abbott. I worry that this is going to blow up on her."

"Me, too, Riles, me, too."

Saturday, at the secluded Sea Breeze Inn, Dan and Christy finished a hearty brunch. Dan began. "I know you think I'm nit-picking, but Monday you need to get to Ken."

"I don't think he'll admit anything." Christy shook her head.

"Tell him if he doesn't come clean, I'm coming for him. And it won't be for a walk in the park."

"He's not going to give us the drug guy." Christy said.

"Then, he'll be dealing with the guys and me. And when we get him, he'll talk." The dining table shook as Dan tapped his index finger on it.

Christy covered her face with her hands. "Baby, this is getting so screwed up."

"I know it. God, how I know it." He reached for her hands.

"Let's talk about something positive."

She appeared to relax.

"When you talk with George," Dan said, "tell him I like all the things he's changed in the master bath. And the breezeway between the house and the shop's a great idea."

"Do you think we should continue with the construction with everything else that's going on?"

"Yeah. This thing's gotta clear up. I mean, when they get their money back, it'll go away."

"But." She pointed with a circling motion. "All of this is not clearing up."

"I know, but George really has committed to finishing the house on time. I know he's passed up several jobs to finish ours."

"It's not as though you'd be letting George down. I think he'll understand if we put things on the back burner until this mess blows over."

"He's a Vietnam vet, and was really struggling when we first met. Ah-h-h," Dan inhaled. "Let's help him get our house finished at the same time."

"Okay. I'm cool with that." She squeezed his hand. "And we've got the money to finish the house?"

"Yes, there's more than enough money to finish it, but that reminds me to give you the check to deposit so you can pay him."

"Dan, they'll trace the check."

"Wait." He smirked as he got up from the table and opened his briefcase. He held up an envelope. "It's a cashier's check made out to you for five grand. Cash it and don't deposit the money. Pay George in cash. Cash doesn't leave a trail. "

"George'd love that, plus I don't have to explain a thing."

"Honey, let's take a ride around the island, and get away from all this talk." Dan helped her up from the table.

He put his arm around her waist, and gave her a hug as they walked to her car.

* * *

Janice Joplin was singing when Christy flipped on the radio. The windshield, wipers keeping a slight mist off the glass, seemed to be swishing in time with the song. All of a sudden, Christy began to sing along with the lyrics, making a new version.

Windshield wipers clapping time,
Bobby's hand in mine,
We sang every song that trucker knew,
Freedom's just another word for nothing left to lose...

Freedom was that weekend, but unlike the song, everyone had a hell of a lot to lose. For her it was all the planning and re-planning of their house, and their lives together. And it wasn't just Christy and Dan, but all the rest of the six guys.

Back at the rental, reality hit them like a rock. Watching the sunset over the water from the porch didn't help to keep Christy and Dan from planning next weekend's meeting.

"Baby, sooner or later the Feds are going to either follow me, arrest me or something. We can't keep this up forever. I mean, what's wrong with them?" Christy poured more merlot for both of them.

"Those idiots in D.C. are so screwed up. They're after us, not the drug guys. Plus, they're not even looking at Bedford, and he's the original thief." Dan sighed. "That's what's really wrong."

"I can tell you're thinking about something," Christy said.

"Yeah, let's go back over our plans for next week."

"Okay, but where are you and Jack meeting up?"

"It's not that I don't trust you, but if you don't know…"

Early Monday morning, the TV played in the background as they enjoyed their breakfast together. Dan happened to glance at the screen as he reached for the last blueberry muffin on the plate. He leaped from his chair. "Oh, my God," he yelled.

There on the screen were his and Christy faces.

"Look," he said as he pointed.

"And if anyone knows the whereabouts or has any information about these two suspects, call the FBI."

Dan grabbed Christy. "We've got to get out of here. I didn't wear a disguise when I checked in." He peeked out the window.

"I've got to get home and make sure the boys and Mom are okay," Christy said. "Oh, God. This can't be happening. I've got clients…and my neighbors and friends." She hurried to throw things in her suitcase.

"I think you'd better stop at Steve Mitchell's and see what's up." Dan closed his eyes.

"I was thinking the same thing." Christy bit her lower lip. "Shit, I feel like we're about to screw up." She had forgotten to give him his copy of the pay phone booths and the numbers there. It listed the first seven phone numbers that Dan would need to contact her for the coming week.

Christy rubbed her forehead. "But I think we're okay, if

you call the office and leave a message for me to call Mr. Bond at four." She nodded her head. "That means you'll call me back at location four. And if you like the second or third property, that means to add that many hours to four for the time you'll call."

Dan kissed her, holding her head with both hands, as they prepared to walk out of the cottage. "And, if I didn't like the second or third property, subtract that many hours."

"I think I've got it. Like add. Dislike subtract." She held him tight.

"I'll check at Steve's office in a couple of hours. You can have him update me. If you leave me a message with him, like 46, that means I'm to call at location six at four."

"Got it," she exhaled. "Okay, let's go. I'm afraid I might get stopped before I get there."

"If they do call Steve, don't say anything, okay?"

She nodded her head.

Dan carried her small suitcase as they hurried out to her rental car. "There's a whole lot going on this next week. I'll check with Steve's office. Sorry, I'm repeating myself."

"Love you, Baby." Tears began to run down her cheeks.

"You've got to go, Honey. I'm sorry," he said as she backed out of the drive.

From a gas station phone booth, Dan called Jack. When Jack answered, Dan closed the accordion door. He brought Jack up-to-date as dark clouds opened up letting rain pelt down on the phone booth.

P.R. STEELE

CHAPTER SIXTEEN

Christy sat in front of his desk. Steve Mitchell could tell she was frazzled. Her lack of makeup, and her overall demeanor spoke volumes. "Well, let me call the FBI agents and see exactly what they're up to. If in fact, they have a warrant, then we need to find out what law you've broken." Steve picked up the phone.

"As of last Friday, there was no warrant for Dan that I knew of," Christy said.

Steve held up his hand as the phone rang in his ear. "Agent Thomason or Riley, please." He furrowed his brow.

"May I ask who's calling?" A voice snapped at him.

"Yes, of course. I'm Steve Mitchell, representing Mrs. Christina Abbott."

"Are you returning a call?"

"No, no, I called you, and whom am I speaking with?

"This is Special Agent Clements."

"And who are you, agent Clements?" Steve made a face toward Christy.

"This call is being recorded." Clements ignored his question.

"Ah, for the record, why is this conversation being

87

recorded? And, is it Miss or Missus?" He slurred the word on purpose.

"For training purposes."

"Training purposes? Oh, please."

"Mr. Mitchell, I'm in charge of the investigation regarding your client, Mr. Burton."

"Ah, Miss Clements, then, I'm sure you've read the file."

"Mr. Mitchell, are you licensed in this state?"

"Yes, I am licensed in the State of Washington as an attorney. Thank you, it's so good of you to inquire. Now, exactly what charges do you purport to have against my client?"

After more banter, Steve said, "Well, that's good, Agent Clements. I'll gladly accompany Mrs. Abbott to your office. And for the record, what is your exact name and how do you spell it?"

"And, just why would you be asking?"

After another moment or two, "Why am I asking? I am filing charges of misconduct and flagrant abuse of authority against you in the Superior Court. I'll bring the paper work and serve you when we arrive at your office." Looking at his watch, Steve said, "It's around ten. Expect us after lunch. And for the record, we're fully cooperating."

"Well, we'll see you and your client then."

The phone went dead, "Well, I guess she didn't like that," Steve said to Christy.

Christy stood up and started pacing, "What are the charges?"

"Interfering with a federal investigation. Pure bullshit. Let me get my secretary started on the paper work."

Steve and Christy parked outside the bureau office in Tacoma. They entered Thomason's old office a little after one. Riley and Thomason stood. Clements, who sat behind the desk, then stood.

"Ms. Clements, so nice to meet you." Steve smiled as he

handed her some paperwork.

"What's this?"

"You've been served for filing false charges against my client." Steve cocked his head and smiled. "Now, I'd like to see the charges and warrant you purport to have had against my client. May we have a chair?" He pointed to one of the two chairs in front of her desk.

"Sure, have a seat. And here are the charges against Mrs. Abbott." Steve took the paperwork and began reading.

"Ah, ha. You filed charges against Mr. Burton last Friday, at three-seventeen p.m. Just how was my client supposed to know he was a person of interest that morning?" Steve cocked his head, and smiled. He couldn't miss Riley and Thomason elbowing each other as they stood beside Clements.

"I think you'd best have a better answer than silence when you go before the court this Wednesday. I see no charges against Christy Abbott. Now, we're here to cooperate with the Bureau. What would you like to know?"

When Clements started asking questions, Christy said nothing. Steve answered for her when Clements asked of her whereabouts during the past weekend.

"That would be the Sea Breeze Inn or Bed and Breakfast, located on Whidbey Island." Steve continued his unique hand and folding his arms antics.

After Clements asked several vague questions, Steve again took over. "You can rest assured they were not involved in any criminal activity."

Clements raised her voice. "I, by God, asked her the question."

"Well, now, did the kick starter break on the broom you flew in here on? Such temper. Very, very unprofessional." Thomason smirked. Riley choked.

"Thomason, Riley," Clements barked. "Check out that alibi. We're through here."

"Nice to see you two again," Steve said to Thomason

and Riley as they left the room. "And, once more, what charges are pending against Mrs. Abbott?

"We're still needing to question Mrs. Abbott, so don't be leaving the area." Clements said.

"No, not so fast, Agent Clements. We've answered all of your so-called questions. Mrs. Abbot has cooperated with the FBI one hundred percent. And, your leaking information to the press about her relationship with Mr. Burton was ill advised. We'll hold you and the Bureau accountable for any adverse effects that come to Mrs. Abbott or her family."

"First of all," Clements shouted. "No information came from here, Buster. Get your facts straight."

"Buster?" Steve looked around the office. "I don't know him. You must be addled. Would either of you be, Buster?" Steve spun around to Riley then Thomason as they re-entered the room.

They both shook their heads.

"We'll be leaving now, and here's my card." Steve reached in his vest pocket. "As you can see, it's Steve, not Buster. Only my family and friends call me Steve, but you can call me Mr. Mitchell." Again, he drew attention to his body language. When he made eye contact with Clements, he winked.

"Christy, come on. I'll drive you home." Steve took Christy by her arm.

At four o'clock, Dan called Christy at the predetermined pay phone. She covered the events of the day. Dan told her not to contact Ken, because Jack paid him a visit. Ken knew nothing and told Jack to contact his attorney, Bob Jones.

"Honey, I've put two and two together. Bob knows more than he's letting on. Remember that conversation I overheard between the two of them in Bob's office?"

"Yeah, kind of."

"Well he's going to be paid a visit, and that'll tell us what we need to know. It's closing in on four minutes. I've got to run. Be careful. I really feel kind of relieved that the Feds are parked outside your house."

"Me, too. Oh, yeah, Steve is having dinner at my place tonight with Mom."

"He's such a dog. I just love the guy, and he's got balls the size of Dallas." Dan laughed.

"I think something's going on with those two." Christy smiled as they both hung up.

Dan called Jack and Ellen in Portland, then headed to his mobile home in Grey's Harbor.

At 5:15, Thomason and Riley walked into Clements' new office. "He mailed us a new letter. It says the same thing. He's willing to make a deal, but only through Mitchell." Thomason handed her the letter.

"This is bullshit. What do they think they're doing? Do they think they're Faye Dunaway and Warren Beatty?" Clements snatched the letter and began reading.

"No, they're doing it a little bit better." Riley glared at her. "And boss lady, I'm not taking the fall if the media thing comes back to roost."

"This is utter bullshit. Who does this moron think he is? Wanting to deal? No deals." She ignored Riley's threat, and kept reading Dan's letter

"I'll tell you who he thinks he is? He's way better than Clyde Barrow. When they make this into a movie, you're going to look real good riding around on that broom with a broken kick starter." Thomason glared at her.

"Get out of here, and close the door."

Tuesday morning at 10:00, Bob Jones showed a prospective client into his office.

"What can I help you with, Mr. Bennett?" Bob asked.

"A friend of Ken Anderson's said to contact you if I

needed to get in touch with Carlos Montoya."

"I'm afraid you'd better leave. I don't know any Carlos Montoya." He stood to push his chair back.

"Sit down, Hot Rod. We can do this easy or...well, you can guess." Jack smiled.

Bob pressed his intercom button. "Alice, call security immediately and then the police."

"I'll be gone, but we aren't finished." Jack pointed to Bob as he hustled out of the office and toward the same stairway marked EXIT that Dan had used for his escape.

That evening Dan parked the `58 Bel Air and walked through the lobby of the Phoenix Inn in downtown Olympia. The hotel sat near the marina. The damp breeze reminded him he needed dinner. Dan rode the quaint but stylish elevator to the third floor where Jack and Ellen were staying. Jack let Dan in, and Jack told Dan about his visit with Bob Jones.

"He knows, and I think he's deeper in the deal than he's letting on," Dan said.

"Hell, yes, he is. If you could've seen the look on that maggot's face. He's guilty as sin. But what the hell? I'm starving. Have you had dinner?" Jack looked at Dan.

"Nawh. How about yawl?"

"Ellen said to wait on you. I scoped out a little barbeque joint a couple blocks over. The menu looks good and I'm buying."

Ellen grabbed her jacket. "Well, I'm ready. So, let's go. I'm starved."

After dinner, still seated at the table, Dan raved about the meal. "By God, that's some of the best ribs ever."

"I ate so much if they told me to haul ass right now, I'd have to make two trips," Jack said.

"You two stop it." Ellen clutched Jack's arm.

"Okay. Come on, it'll be safe to talk on the way back."

Dan left a healthy tip on the table since Jack had paid.

"Tomorrow, I need to get another car. If you don't mind, it'd be a big help if you could drive it back to Westport. It won't take long. I'll drive you back here and then we'll meet up the first of next week." Dan hunched his shoulders as they neared the hotel. When they approached Jack's car, Dan opened the passenger's front door and let Ellen in. They talked as they made their way to Grays Harbor.

"*Nada* big. I can do that. I'll call the Roadhawg and make sure he's cooling his jets. He's still pissed that he's not here with us."

"Yeah, but it's still dangerous for all of us to be together right now. We need to keep at least one of us separate from the other two. Anyway, tomorrow I'll show you all around the place. Although the real estate agent doesn't need to see you."

"That's cool. The place sounds really nice. Hey, man, new subject. I've been thinking."

"That always worries me."

"Seriously. I mean, you and Christy are building a house. She's sticking with you through all this. She knows about the money, and well, shit." Jack shrugged his shoulders and held his hands palms up.

"And what?"

"You dumb bastard. If you were married, they couldn't bug her about anything. You know the husband and wife thing?"

"I've talked with her, and what are you waiting on?" Ellen turned to face Dan.

"Yeah, I've been thinking the same thing, but with all this stuff, I mean, I almost asked her this weekend. I don't know. You know what I mean?"

"No, with your dumb butt, sometimes I don't know. Here's what I know. Ask her and if she says yes, get it done, like yesterday." Jack poked his thumb over his shoulder as he drove.

"I know, you're right, but I need to think about it."

"Dan, you're over-thinking it." Ellen sounded frustrated with him.

"Danny, just do it. She's stuck through all this shit and hasn't run."

Dan kept silent.

Jack pulled off the road, stopped the car and turned to face Dan.

"Jack, I'm afraid, man," Dan said.

"Afraid of what?"

"What if she say's no?"

Jack started laughing, "I don't need your money, or I'd give you ten to one odds on a grand that she'll say yes. You dumb bastard."

"I agree." Ellen winked at Dan as Jack parked in the hotel parking lot. Dan took a room for the night.

CHAPTER SEVENTEEN

The next morning, the section of the autos for sale in Olympia led Jack and Dan to a seller. They needed a couple of new cars. Jack sat in the car around the corner from the seller's house while Dan rang the doorbell.

"What are you planning on doing with the car?" the seller said.

Dan felt the skin on the back of his neck tingle. His paternal grandfather, a full-blooded Apache, warned him many times, when that happened be careful and beware.

Dan's appearance was well hidden in his disguise, but this guy was paying too much attention, and asking the wrong questions.

"Well, sir, I just need a reliable set of wheels."

"I just thought it mighty strange that a Mexican would want to buy my Galaxy. I thought you all liked Chevy's."

"Well, I'll think about it. Thanks, for letting me look at it." Dan turned and walked to the parked car.

"So, what was wrong with the car?" Jack said.

"He asked too many questions, and then made a Mexican remark. I got bad vibes and walked. He made a point out of my appearance, and that's dangerous. Besides we've got two more to check out."

"That's good with me. I trust your vibes. I know when I've got them in the past, I sure as hell paid attention." Jack started the car.

The next potential disposable car was about twenty minutes away. It had a huge dent in one of the front fenders. Anything out of the ordinary disqualified a car. The disposables had to be ordinary not sporty, flashy, or eye appealing.

The third time was a charm.

"Whew, now this is sweet. How much did you pay for it?" Jack admired the 1964 Ford pickup. It sported new tires, decent paint, and sounded a touch racy with the glass-pack mufflers.

"I had to pay six and a quarter, but the tires are brand spankin' new. Let's hit the trail." Dan checked his watch. "We're getting a little behind time."

They drove in tandem out of Olympia heading almost due west toward Aberdeen. Jack drove the Ford truck. Dan drove the car he told Earl was his mom's. The fifty miles clicked by, and then they skirted south around Grays Harbor to Westport. Dan signaled Jack to stop at the Seven Eleven to wait for him as planned. Dan parked his mom's car behind Earl's gas station, and left the keys.

Dan hustled back to the Seven Eleven and hopped into his newly acquired truck. Jack drove to the double covered carport at the mobile home. They got out and once inside, Jack took in Dan's location on the water.

"Danny, this is a great place and I really dig the vista. I wish Ellen was here."

That morning Ellen had stayed at the hotel with their '58 Chevy for the drive to Portland with Jack when the guys got back.

"And I wish Christy was here. It'd be nice to be normal," Dan said.

Dan showed Jack the trap door in the spare bedroom.

Dan told Jack to let him out under the deck as they walked to the sliding door out to the deck. Once on the redwood deck, Dan showed the unrestricted panorama of the small boat docks to their left. Jack followed and sat in one of the chairs by the outside table. Jack rubbed his hands, taking it all in.

"Like I said," Dan lowered his voice, "I've got great egress ability." He pointed under the deck and to the boat docks.

"Unless they had a boat, you'd be long gone." Jack nodded in approval.

"Plan B, is the filling station, just back there around the bend." He pointed to the heavily wooded area about seventy-five yards off to their right.

"Yeah, once you made the trees, you'd be outta sight in nothing flat," Jack said.

"And plan C is the small airport just past the trees. I'm going over there and rent a Cessna. While I've got the keys, I'll have a spare key made and use it if push comes to shove."

"Man, this is way better than our place in Tahoe." Jack continued to look over the water.

"What's your getaway plan in Tahoe?"

"Dirt bikes in the woods, and snowmobiles when it snows. But we both know if they're coming, the bastards will surround the place first. In that case, you boys are the backup plan."

"I know. Hey, man, I hate parting with such dandy company, but I know you've got to be missing El. Let's get moving." Dan jingled the keys. "You want to drive the truck?"

"Why not?"

"How's it doin'?" Dan said.

"I really like it. The thing can actually get a little scratch in second gear." Jack raised his eyebrows.

Dan chuckled. He knew the drive to the hotel in

Portland would put Jack back with Ellen a little after dark.

"I know you're dying to get on the road, but I'll buy you and Ellen some dinner if you want." Dan said once they arrived in Olympia.

"Thanks, brother, but we'll grab a quick bite to go and eat on the run. That way we'll be there that much sooner."

"The proverbial Oklahoma Sooner." Dan nodded as Jack started the car. "Hey Jack, thanks for everything."

"Would you shut up? Shit, next thing you'll probably want to hug me. Good bye." They both laughed. "And Danny, ask her."

Dan smiled and nodded as Jack walked into the hotel.

Dan stopped at a local Safeway in Olympia and bought kitchen stuff and groceries. The hour-plus drive back to the rental wasn't wasted. He planned his early warning devices while enjoying the ride in the new truck.

He stopped at Earl's filling station near the mobile home park, and began filling it up.

"Nice truck," Earl said.

"Thanks, she gets me around."

"How long have you had her?" Earl said.

Dan's alarm sounded. Be cool. He's just being friendly. "Oh, a while."

"Well I gotta tell you, she looks almost new."

Dan paid Earl for the gas.

"Well, I've gotta get. See ya, Earl," Dan walked to the truck. The gray overcast had never burned off making the onshore breeze have a bit of a bite. Dan felt the chill as he put on his dark sock hat.

Once he got home, he began to set up the kitchen. He turned on the heat, and then checked out the TV. Couldn't be any better. That antenna picks up all three Seattle stations. He turned his thoughts to getting his early warning devices set up. The place was turning out to be okay.

That evening, Steve talked with Christy and her mother in Christy's kitchen. "I don't see any reason not to see Dan. He's only a person of interest. And they're still, in my opinion, harassing you with all this surveillance crap."

"Well, then we'll see what happens tomorrow." Christy looked at her mother.

"So, I guess Grace will be with the boys this weekend?" Steve said. "Would it be okay with you, if we took them out with us sailing on the Sound?"

"Sure, after what Mom told me about it, I think they'd have a ball. But make sure they wear a life vest all the time." Christy looked toward her mom who nodded in agreement.

"Christy, you know me. The boy's will be safe as can be," Steve said.

Grace said, "That goes without saying. And Christy, make sure you're careful this weekend."

Steve reached over and took Grace's hand. Christy noticed Grace squeeze his. She also, when the couple left for dinner, saw Steve put his arm around Grace's waist.

They're so lucky. Christy watched them walk to Steve's car and Steve open the car door for Grace.

The next morning, Christy drove to the SeaTac airport. She smiled as she parked her car in the covered lot there. Out of the corner of her eye, she noticed two agents parked nearby reading newspapers.

She walked into the terminal and approached the ticket counter. "Round trip to Portland."

"That'll be fifty-two dollars," the PSA agent said, taking the money and handing Christy a boarding passes.

Christy took the tickets, all the while noticing a woman she assumed was agent Clements with the two agents Christy had noticed from the parking lot. Christy turned and walked out to the hotel courtesy vans. The Holiday Inn's shuttle driver opened the door. Christy boarded. She smiled as she sat by the driver and the door closed. She couldn't miss the agents with walkie-talkies to their ears as they scrambled to catch the van. After the shuttle turned the corner and drove past the covered parking, she said to the driver, "Oh, darn it. Please stop. I need to get out. I left my sun glasses in the terminal."

"Sure thing. I'll pick you back up when I return," the driver said as Christy hurried off the shuttle.

She rushed into the open parking garage and watched as the shuttle drove away with the agency car in pursuit.

Out of sight in the garage, she opened her small suitcase, took off her blue sweater and slipped the pink one on along with a wig. She stayed out of sight until the Best Western shuttle approached the drop off area. She walked to the van and made sure no one boarded after her.

When the shuttle arrived at the motel, she walked into the reception area and out the back entrance to the parking lot. She took her time making sure no agency guys had followed her.

She and her mother had left her getaway car there. She was on her way.

CHAPTER EIGHTEEN

Christy noticed a strip mall ahead on the other side of the street. She made a sudden turn into a parking lot, then sighed as the Ford drove on. But, she waited to see if a second agency car might appear. After a couple of minutes, she began her journey south on Interstate 5. Before passing Tacoma, she exited and made several more turns, until she was sure she wasn't followed.

Entering the pre-planned drop at one of Olympia's long term parking lots down the street from the Sears Department Store, Christy began to feel a little bit safer. She walked to the Sears store, checking the windows for someone following her. In the women's restroom, she changed clothes, and her wig. Now she wore blue jeans and a sweatshirt. When she walked out of the store, she saw in the reflection of the window a man approach from behind. The dark suit, thin tie, and government issued sunglasses screamed FBI. She panicked.

"Ma'am I'd like you to come with me," he said as he took her arm.

"Damn it, Dan, you scared the crap out of me."

"Really? I thought I looked quite professional." He

turned the corner and walked her to the truck.

"Did Thompson and Riley do your haberdashery?" she said.

"Ma'am, let me get the door for you." He opened it. "And, no, I picked out the threads from the local Society of Purple Hearts, thank you."

On their drive to Westport, they got caught up on the past week. Dan stopped, changed clothes, and then they strolled into a deli for lunch.

"There's something I've been wanting to ask you." Dan stammered while playing with the water glass.

"Okay." She looked at him but he avoided eye contact.

"I know there's a whole bunch of stuff going on and…" he hesitated.

"And what?"

"Ah, how's your mother and Steve doing?"

She giggled and took his hand. "Seriously? I think they're doing it."

On the east side, just outside the back gate of McChord Air Force Base, sprawls the town of Spanaway. Near the southeast side in the commercial area was the headquarters for Carlos Montoyo.

The storage facility accommodated a lot of the military families from Fort Lewis and McChord Air Force Base. Trucks coming and going attracted little attention, and the high electric fence and guards Montoyo had posted caused no concerns. Late at night, drugs moved to and from an elaborate underground facility, but during the day the upstairs passed for a furniture storage building.

Carlos Montoyo was first generation from Jalisco, Mexico. His hair glistened in a tight ponytail. His eyes matched his dark hair. He was tall and well-manicured. He wreaked drug-lord.

Inside the elaborate offices, Carlos demanded payback for the death of his brother from the disastrous shootout at

Ken's helo landing site in Tacoma.

"I don't give two rat shits," Carlos shouted at his hit man. "The son of a bitch, Burton's fiancé, is the ex of that bastard you just took care of." He glared at the man who had shot and killed John Abbott. "His address and hers is in the phone book. How hard can it be? I want it done yesterday."

The hit man shifted his eyes from the floor to Carlos.

"Alright, it'll be done tonight, but it's risky. The Feds have a car out front, and..."

Carlos jumped up to his full six feet, and rolled his head. "And I don't care. Raphael was our brother. Take the Feds out first, and then the bitch. That Burton will pay. Blood for blood. See how he likes it. And to hell with the Feds. Piss on all of 'em," He shook his finger at the hit man.

"But, Brother." Carlos's new second in command was his younger brother, Juan. Juan pleaded, "We don't need the heat right now."

"Juan, Raphael was our brother, and you say..." Carlos shook his head.

"Okay, okay, but it could wait. That's all," Juan said.

The hit man put out his cigarette. "As you wish, Carlos. It will be done before tomorrow night, but taking out the Feds will cost more."

"I said, do it," Carlos yelled.

Saturday, late afternoon, their day out on the Sound having ended, Grace drove into the garage with the two boys in the backseat. "Are you guys about ready for some dinner?" she said.

"I'm ready, and Grandma, I really like Steve's sail-boat." Allen and his brother scrambled out of the car.

"How about chili dogs, and Grandma, I really like Steve, too. He's funny." Josh picked up a bag of groceries to help his grandma unload the car.

"I like him, too. Now, get in the house, and you boys

need to get your homework finished after you get your chores done. I'm going to get the mail, and start dinner." Grace moved along the side the car.

"Grandma, please can we have chili dogs?" Allen asked again.

"Oh, okay, I guess so, but you two get a move on. And Allen go in the house and let the dog out. Make sure he's got some water in his bowl in the back yard."

"Is Dan coming home today?" Josh said.

"I don't think so. Now, Josh, hurry up and get the hot dogs out of the refrigerator freezer." Grace walked out the double garage door and closed it. Both boys entered the kitchen through the garage door in front of the car.

Down the street, a van appeared, but it was the explosion that got Grace's attention. She couldn't miss the fire ball and the white smoke trail. The explosion startled her. She ran to the front door, unlocked it, and slammed the door shut. She grabbed Josh as he ran to her in the kitchen doorway when a second explosion hit the front door.

The van disappeared from sight leaving the blazing agency car and the house smoldering.

The news media from both the TV and radio stations converged on the burned house as the fire men mopped up the blaze. The reporters interviewed the ER physicians at the hospital. The fire devastated Christy's home, but the scene at the hospital took on a complete sense of finality with the media pressing for any word on the two FBI agents and the three other victims.

CHAPTER NINETEEN

Christy and Dan finished their outdoor barbeque in Westport. They'd worked out the details that afternoon for Dan to turn himself in.

"I don't know, Dan. I just don't trust those guys," Christy said as they cleaned up.

"Well, it's gone on too long, and I don't think they'll work a deal until I get to talk with them. And, if they screw us, Jack and Roadhawg are ready. But, are you sure you'd really vanish in a year or so, if we have to? I mean the boys, and your mom, our house? It just seems like a lot to ask."

"It'll be a while before we'd know what they're going to do. And I don't think they'll put anyone in jail once they have all the facts."

"We hope so," Dan said.

"If I had to, I think I could go on the run, and it'd be okay, because I think the boys would be older. Plus, they'd be with Mom."

"Yeah, but in the meantime, it's a long time to wait and see what the Feds have up their sleeves."

"Well, count me in." She turned and wrapped her arms around him.

"Something's come up."

"What?"

"Wanna fool around?" He hugged her. "But," he reached in his pocket and handed her the box with the ring. "But first, would you marry me?"

"Are you serious?" She hugged him. "Yes, yes, yes." Tears filled her eyes.

"I have the paper work, and the Justice of the Peace said come by early. And..."

"What'll I wear?" She reached for a tissue to dry her tears, and kissed him.

"Wearing nothing would be cute. But you look mighty fine to me just the way you are. Let's go."

The ceremony included the J.P.'s wife as a witness. The newlyweds hurried back to the trailer park and their honeymoon suite.

Later that evening, recovering with a bottle of wine, they decided to watch TV as Dan started the barbeque. Their happiness evaporated when the station cut to the late breaking news.

Christy fell on to the couch, and held her mouth. Dan ran to the TV and turned up the sound. The newlyweds sat in silence. Dan put his arm around Christy. She held his hand. The news was still jumping from the destroyed house to the hospital.

"I've gotta go," Christy cried.

"Let's go make some phone calls," Dan said. "I've got Steve's home phone for emergencies, but I doubt he's there. Let's call the hospital, and I'll have him paged."

They hurried to the pay phone booth at Earl's. Christy called one of her best friends and got some information. Then Dan called the hospital and after a few minutes, Steve picked up the phone. He relayed most all of the information to Christy. They decided to have Christy go back to the mobile home and close everything. Dan stayed at the phone booth.

"I'll call Jack and Roadhawg." He began to get the paper with their phone numbers.

From the payphone Dan called Roadhawg first. He brought Roadhawg up to date on all the happenings.

"Okay, that all sounds unbelievable. I'll catch the nine-ten flight out of Sacramento, grab a rental and meet you there," Roadhawg said.

"I'll meet you at the airport so you don't need to rent a car. I'll pick you up outside the terminal, and thanks, man. I'm at a loss for words." Dan felt like he was rambling.

"Danny boy, keep focused on the important shit. Tell Christy that everything will be okay. And we all need to pray."

"Amen to that. I'll be out front at ten fifty-five," Dan said.

Back at the mobile home, Dan watched the TV as Christy got her things together to leave. "I can't believe it," Dan said to Christy, "Honey, come here. There's a news update about your mom."

"Ssh-h." Christy sat down and put her hand across his mouth.

"...from the burned house. The two deceased FBI Agent's names are being withheld until notification of the next of kin."

"Oh, my God," Christy said. She covered her mouth again.

"...a woman believed to be the grandmother, is in intensive care. One of her grandsons is being held for observation."

The reporter continued. "It looks like the grandmother may have picked up the boy just as the blast occurred. I've been told by a hospital spokesperson, her body appeared to have shielded him. He apparently has a broken arm and lacerations. The spokesperson also said, the other grandson was in the back yard at the time, and was okay. Both of the boys are expected to make full recoveries. As of this report, the grandmother's condition is unknown. This is Brian Holter reporting for KOMO News, Channel four Tacoma."

In tears, Christy leaned into Dan's open arms. Outside the evening shadows matched their mood.

"I'm so sorry, Christy. This is all my fault."

"I've got to get to the hospital."

"Christy, if you'd never met me, none of this would've happened."

"Not another word."

The curves in the road flew by on the way to her rental car in Olympia. When they arrived, she left for the hospital.

CHAPTER TWENTY

In Spanaway, a little after eight, a meeting was underway.

Carlos Montoyo lit a Cuban cigar and pointed at his younger brother. "Well, I'm pissed. But, that's how we take care of our own. That Burton will still get his."

"Carlos," Juan said, "I hope this doesn't backfire. The FBI isn't going to let this just disappear. We need to be extra cautious."

At the FBI offices in Tacoma, Riley and Thomason had just caught the Channel 4 update. "Miz-turn-up-the-heat just screwed up big time," Thomason mumbled.

"Knowing her, she'll try to blame everything on us. I can't believe we lost those two guys." Riley walked to his desk and held up a small recorder. "But, this is our insurance. This whole thing's terrible."

"I knew one of those guys for several years."

"Yeah, me, too. They both had families."

Riley still held up the small recorder.

"Is that what I think it is? Riley, you didn't, did you? Did you get it all?"

"Every last word clear as a bell. And, if Clements tries to screw us, we'll let her lie about it back in D. C. first. Then, we'll play it. I don't want her to know doodley shit. If, she comes clean, good. If not..." Riley waved the recorder in the air.

Later that night, Dan picked up Roadhawg at SeaTac. They rode in silence in Dan's truck. After a bit, Dan told him Christy was at the hospital.

"How's Christy's mom and boys?" Roadhawg said.

"Grace is holding on and doing good. The boys are resting. Allen had gone out to the back yard, and Grace had evidently seen the shit coming, because she picked up Josh, and had just turned into the kitchen when the thing hit the house."

"Shit, this whole thing is unbelievable."

"Good thing is, Steve Mitchell is there with Christy since I can't." Dan pounded the steering wheel.

"Jack thought it a good idea for Ellen to stay with Christy at the hospital when they get up here."

"Yeah, that'd be good, but I gotta tell you, that drug guy just signed his death warrant."

"Danny, I'm with you a hundred percent," Roadhawg said. "We'll work it all out. I understand the news media broadcasted the info about ya'll being engaged."

"Yeah, but all of this is over stupid shit. Ken running drugs, and me shooting the shit out of the drug guys. Why didn't I let them waste Ken's worthless ass? And another thing, Ken knows more than he's letting on. As soon as Jack gets here, Ken's going to disappear and sing like a canary. When we find out who did this, I swear, they're going to pay."

CHAPTER TWENTY-ONE

A little before ten the next morning, Dan and Roadhawg sat glued to the TV. They both turned when they heard a car enter the carport. Dan peeked through the blinds just as Jack and Ellen stepped out of their '58 Bel Air.

Once inside, Dan brought them up-to-date. "The latest news is that Grace is still critical, but the boys are okay and with Christy now."

"I'd like to hurry on over there and be with Christy. I just can't begin to imagine..." Ellen looked at Dan.

"Let's head out, then," Dan said. "You can follow me and Roadhawg in my truck, and when we get close to the hospital, Jack, I'll pull over and you can get in with Roadhawg and me. And Ellen you can drive on to the hospital. I don't think they'll make the truck. Let me lock up and if everybody's ready, let's go."

Dan checked the back door as the others left. He locked the front door on his way out. They sped to Tacoma. Jack stopped near the hospital at a filling station with a phone booth. Dan wrote down the pay phone's number. He walked over to the Bel Air and gave the phone number to Ellen. When they were about a block away from the hospital, Ellen pulled over. Jack got out and climbed in the cab of the truck with Dan and Roadhawg.

"Ellen will call us in thirty minutes to the phone booth we stopped at back there," Jack said. "Ellen wants to talk a bit with Christy and will call the number you gave her."

It was almost thirty minutes on the nose when the phone rang at the phone booth they'd stopped at earlier. Ellen told Dan about Grace's condition and that the boys were fine. Christy, the boys, and Ellen were leaving for Christy's sister's house in Gig Harbor.

Dan thanked Ellen and gave her phone numbers from a copy of Christy's info sheet. He left a time and location saying he'd call her if she could get away later.

Dan, Roadhawg and Jack left for the mobile home. "Okay, here's the long and tall of it," Dan said.

He told the guys about Christy's mom and the boys.

"Is there anything else we can be doing?" Jack said.

"I'm going to need both of you guy's help." Dan asked more than stated.

"Come on, man. You don't even have to ask," Jack said.

"What's the plan?" Roadhawg tapped his finger on the dashboard.

"First, we're going to need a couple more sets of wheels for each of you. Tomorrow, first thing, we'll get on it. And then that son of a bitch Bob Jones is going to tell us everything we want to know."

CHAPTER TWENTY-TWO

From a phone booth in Westport, Roadhawg got the update from Christy and Ellen. Then Steve Mitchell gave him more information after he'd talked with Christy. He hustled back to the mobile home and relate the news to Dan. The most important terms of the negotiation gave them both hope. Steve Mitchell, in no uncertain words, told Roadhawg Bob Jones knew a bunch.

Roadhawg and Dan left for Ken's house in Tacoma. Dan parked a half a block away. Their stakeout began a little after nine that evening.

"You've got a good plan. But can you really go through with it?" Roadhawg checked his pistol for the hundredth time.

Dan raised his voice. "Not only yes, but hell yes. When we nab this douche bag, I'm going to love making him talk. I mean it."

"Dan, I'm with you one-hundred percent, but this could get nasty. I mean kidnapping is jail time."

"Yes. What time is it?"

"A little after ten. We've been here for about an hour, and I don't think he's in there." Roadhawg motioned toward Ken's house.

"Jack's still back at Westport. Let's knock it off here and head out."

"I'm sure Jack'll have some information on what's going on."

Their drive to Westport sped by in silence as both veterans prepared for battle. Jack's car sat outside the well-lit mobile home. The abundance of lights worried Dan.

He parked at the gas station, then snuck around behind a vacant mobile home as Roadhawg entered his rental. The porch light flashed once, giving Dan the all clear signal.

Dan went inside and found Jack on the phone with Steve Mitchell.

"Yes, sir. I understand and we'll contact your office tomorrow. Okay, and I'll be Chris Montano. Yes, sir. Will do." Jack held several pages of notes. Without looking up from his papers he said, "Your attorney Steve is stoked. I mean pissed. He's really upset by what happened to Grace and the boys."

"He's not the only one. I'm ready to get some answers and find that drug dealing dirt-bag." Dan kept pointing his finger like a gun.

"Well, here's that moron Jones's home address." A Steve McQueen smile broke out on his face.

"Okay, let's go."

"Hold on cowboy. There's more. Steve says every attorney in town knows Jones is dirty right along with all his slime ball clients. He also said Jones's flashing too much money around to be coming from his practice."

Dan told his plan to Jack as Roadhawg chimed in with some of the details.

"I rented a quiet warehouse down by the loading docks in Tacoma by the water," Dan said. "I thought it'd be a good place to store a car or two. It's perfect for what we've got planned."

"Man, it's going to get dicey. Are you sure you want to go through with it?" Jack said.

"With a grin on my face."

"Danny boy, you're beginning to scare me," Jack said.

"After what they've done? He's convinced me, and I'm in," Roadhawg said. "The law won't take care of it, so we will." He didn't break eye contact with Jack. "So Whadda ya say, Jackson?"

"I'm in, but I don't know that I could do the meat clever deal to make him talk." Jack glanced from Dan to Roadhawg. "I mean, we'll all be guilty of jail-time crimes."

"Don't sweat it," Dan said.

Jack nodded his head. "Alright, Dan, I'm with you a hundred percent."

"Okay, then at first light, we need to get one of those vans the hippies hang out in. Set up the warehouse, and get a cigar lighter, battery, and charger from the auto parts store." Dan closed his eyes in thought.

"And then start picking up those bastards." Roadhawg's grin broke into a chuckle.

Dan tossed and turned most of the night, unable to fully come to grips with the anger that possessed his every thought. They're going to pay ran across his mind like an Oklahoma tornado through a trailer park.

The next morning, Dan entered the Tacoma Chevrolet Dealership because used vans were non-existent. He approached the salesman. "I saw the $1500 van for sale on the used car lot."

"The light blue one?" the man said.

Dan nodded his head.

"Well, she's practically new. Still under warranty. I can make you a sweet deal."

"Can you take me for a drive?"

"Let me get the keys. Wait here. I'll be right back."

The test drive sealed the deal. Dan said, "What's your bottom dollar?"

"Are you going to finance it?"

Dan shook his head no.

"They're asking thirty-one hundred." The salesman rubbed his hands together.

"I'll give you twenty-six cash."

"Cash helps but they won't go below twenty-nine."

"I just walked out on the Ford dealership. It's twenty-seven or I'll go to the Chrysler dealership."

"All cash?"

He's going to do it. Dan continued to stare at the salesman as he nodded his head and patted his jacket pocket.

Dan walked out toward Jack and Roadhawg with the keys dangling from his finger.

"Wow. You got it. Sweet." Roadhawg jumped into the passenger's seat.

"The cargo door will make it easy to stuff them into the back." Dan made sure Jack was following as he drove out of the used car lot. Okay, Ken, here we come.

Roadhawg and Dan finished up their last bit of shopping. Jack checked in with Ellen. Grace's condition improved to guarded from critical. The boys had spent the night with Christy at an undisclosed location.

Once inside the warehouse, the three set up their equipment.

"Well, boys, let's go get some information from Ken." Dan cracked his knuckles.

Thomason and Riley sat in Clements appropriated office. Thomason glared at her, but Riley just blinked his eyes as she spoke. "This has all the makings of a disaster. We have two dead agents and Mrs. Abbott's mother and sons are recovering. D.C. is going ballistic. We need to play this close to the cuff. Do I make myself clear?"

After a few seconds, Thomason frowned. "You said, we?"

"You might have a huge problem." Riley pointed at her.

"We have several teams working on the two agent's deaths. I mean someone's going to fry over this." Clements paused, "And just so you two are on the same page, we're in this together. So let's get the story straight. Got it?"

Riley glared at her. Then he chuckled. What a pompous ass.

"What's so funny, Riley? We lost two damned good agents and you think it's funny?"

He stood. "No, it makes me sick. Two agents who were very good friends died because you wanted to turn up the heat. Oh, yeah, if they want to play games, let's show them how. That's what you said." You back-stabbing, lying two-grades-above-me bitch.

"I don't know what you're talking about," she shot back, straightened her back, and stuck her chin in their direction.

Thomason snarled. "If you say so."

Clements cleared her throat and continued. "Well, we have leads to follow up. Those RPG's were stolen from the Army reserve unit in Pleasanton, California. So, we need to round up all the usual suspects, starting with the drug shoot-out survivors."

Riley remained seated. "So you want us to leak the info to the local news outlets, again?" Riley baited her.

"Get your ass up and out of here," she shouted.

"Yes, sir. I mean ma'am." Riley wagged his head as he sauntered out.

P.R. STEELE

CHAPTER TWENTY-THREE

Jack, Dan, and Roadhawg, kept watch from dawn until 8:50 that morning. Then Ken shuffled out. The snatch took place as smooth as clock work. Ken found himself gagged and hog tied in less than fifteen seconds.

Dan drove the van to the storage unit near the waterfront in Tacoma. Roadhawg opened the pull-up-door at the warehouse, and closed it after Jack drove in.

Ken fought as they removed him from the van and taped him into a metal armchair in the warehouse. The shop light glared in his face. Dan removed the gag. "Ken, Ken, Ken. You're in deep do-do, buddy. Here's the deal. You start yelling. And the gag goes back on. So don't. Understand?"

Ken's Adams apple bobbed as he tried to swallow. "What do you want?"

"I want the drug guy's name, address, and who's really in charge." Dan sat in front of him with the light behind so Ken couldn't see Dan's facial expressions.

"I can't. They'll kill me." He began to squirm.

Jack strapped gray duct tape back around Ken's head covering Ken's mouth. Then Roadhawg cut the tape from Ken's left hand and arm so they could tie it to a plywood table that sat beside Ken. Jack fit Ken's hand on top of an outline of a hand with six holes...one beside each finger. Jack began lacing Ken's fingers to the table with clothesline rope. Roadhawg bound Ken's wrist to the table through two more holes that they'd predrilled.

The three of them stood back to observe their work. Ken's splayed hand and bound wrist were secure.

"Now Ken, you know who blew up Christy's house. And injured her boys and her mom. I'm not going to ask you who it was but once.

Roadhawg opened a package of hot dogs and placed one by Ken's hand. Jack handed Dan the meat cleaver. Dan slammed it on the hot dog, severing it in half.

Ken struggled to get away.

Dan registered Ken's fear. "Now Ken, I'm going to start with the first joint of your pinky finger. Then we'll cauterize it with a cigar lighter."

Jack placed the battery they'd bought next to the table with the cables attached to the cigar lighter and Dan pushed the it in. A few seconds later it glowed bright orange. He placed it next to the pinky in question.

"So, Ken, without further interruptions, I'm going to start, joint by joint. When I've taken each joint from each finger on both hands, then it's going to get interesting. Wanna know what's next?"

Ken shook his head.

"Well, old buddy, you're going to be...well let's say you'll have to squat to piss the rest of your life."

Ken shook his head from side to side.

"Alright then, I'm going to get started." Dan placed the cleaver on the first joint of a little finger, lifted a four-pound, small sledge hammer and placed it on the cutting instrument. A thin line of blood began to run. "Let me know if you're ready to talk."

Ken tried to scream through the gag, as he nodded his head to indicate yes.

CHAPTER TWENTY-FOUR

"Ken sure gave up Jones in nothing flat," Roadhawg said as he drove Dan and Jack toward Seattle.

"I believed Ken when he said he didn't know where Montoyo is," Jack said.

Dan began to grin. "And the bastard doesn't even know we're coming."

"I'm actually beginning to look forward to this," Jack said. "Let's see how much Jones gives us before we get that info out."

Dan just nodded his head. Sure hope he plays hard to get, because, I won't hesitate.

"Hey, ah, Danny," Roadhawg said. "Would you've really chopped off fingers if Ken hadn't talked?" Jack drove as Roadhawg and Dan sat in the empty van's cavernous cargo area.

Dan nodded his head. "And what's scary...I'd feel good about it. Like, I was finally doing something to protect my family. Not like that shit in Vietnam, where we were doing nothing, just kept doing what we knew wasn't right."

"Danny boy, you're almost scaring me," Roadhawg mumbled.

"That's good." Dan said.

Jack drove through the morning commute traffic in the slow lane. They found out Jones had parked in the downstairs lot under his building. The parking area appeared unattended.

"Okay, there's Jones's spot and he's already here. So let's head back to the warehouse and wait until quittin' time," Roadhawg said as he drove toward the exit.

"Here's how I see it." Dan didn't finish.

"Well, come on, how do you see it? Here's how I see it." Jack pointed to Jones's parking spot. "I think it'd be easiest if we could back in next to his driver's door. That would put our slider next to his car on the driver's side."

"What if the parking space isn't open?" Roadhawg said.

"Well here's my plan," Dan began. "We pull in behind his car, blocking him in, and open the slider. We need to jack up the van like we've got a flat."

"I like that," Jack said

"We'll be dressed like a bunch of hippies with long hair, bell bottoms, the whole nine yards."

Roadhawg butted in. "That sounds solid. Then when he walks up we nab him."

"If anyone sees anything…we'll just be a bunch of hippies with a flat tire." Dan finished Roadhawg's thought. "We've still got the paper license plates on the van. That'll make it hard to trace us, if they can't get a tag number. "

"Well, okay girls." Jack rubbed his hands together. "We've got about an hour before I need to check in with Ellen. Let's go baby sit Ken boy and make sure he's not done anything stupid."

When they opened the door to the warehouse, Ken appeared comatose, lying on the cot they'd tied him to. Dan stretched out on one of the other cots in the chain link cage they'd built. Thirty minutes later Jack slipped out of the warehouse to go make the call to Ellen.

Ken began to stir, then tried to sit up. Dan walked over

to where he was strapped to the cot. "Hey, Ken, you'd better hope nothing, and I mean nothing goes wrong with my mother-in-law."

Ken tried to mumble something.

"If you yell," Dan held up the razor sharp meat clever, then he yanked the tape off Ken's mouth.

"Oh-h-h, man," Ken struggled to speak. "Dan, you've gotta believe me. I didn't know shit about what Montoyo had planned. I swear. I'd never do anything to harm the boys or Christy's mom. Think about it. The son of a bitch tried to kill both of us."

Dan digested what Ken had. "Okay, okay. But answer me this. When I was in Jones's office, I heard him say, 'I told you to take care of him,' and then he said, 'so, I had to do it.' What was that all about?"

Ken swallowed and seemed to struggle for words.

"Roadhawg, get the chair and hand holder ready. Ken's forgot how to talk."

"No, I'm talking." Ken rubbed his jaw. "Jones told me to waste John Abbott."

"I thought so," Dan said.

"Man, I couldn't do it, so he let me know I was on his shit list. Like I'd be next."

"So, he had John killed."

"Yes, I think so, Dan. I don't know for sure, but I'd bet big time on it."

"Just as I thought." Dan closed his eyes." Let's just see if Jones will confirm it before I have to start on his ass.

Jack rolled in about twenty-five minutes later. The latest update was all good. Grace was recovering, and the boys went home with Christy and Ellen. "Ellen reminded me that we have to make the call to Steve in about fifteen minutes."

"Oh, damn it," Dan said. "I'd forgotten all about that." I can't be screwing up right now.

Fifteen minutes later, Dan and Roadhawg left the

warehouse. Dan made the call from a phone booth. Roadhawg stood by to keep an eye out.

Dan identified himself as Bob Jones, then Steve came on the line.

"Ah Robert, old buddy, don't say anything, let me talk. Is that okay with you?"

"Absolutely," Dan whispered trying to disguise his voice.

"Okay, first things first. Everything on the home front is well. The condition is improving. The complainant with the FBI is still out to lunch. I've been told you might be considering a face-to-face and see if we could straighten the whole mess out."

"That's correct." Dan covered the mouthpiece.

"But for now, they're being too unreasonable, so I say we do nothing but what you're doing. Be careful with the medicine man."

"I understand." They might not need Jones's information just yet.

"Let's play it by ear. Contact me tomorrow. Is this a good time? I'm available if it is."

"This is good," Dan said.

"If something changes, I'll contact your answering service, and you can do the same. So, in the meantime, let's see what I can get done to get a settlement."

"Sounds good."

Dan relayed the information to Roadhawg.

Before they left, Dan picked up the phone and called Bob Jones's office.

"Good morning, this is Ken Anderson. Bob was going to meet me this afternoon."

"Yes," Brenda said.

"He said for me to check in with you, to get a ball park on when his last appointment is today."

"Let me see, Mr. Anderson. Okay, his last appointment is at three and he should be out of here by four."

"Okay, good. So, he'll be done by four. That'll work. Thanks, Brenda." Dan hung up and nodded toward Roadhawg.

"We'll have 'er on the jack by fifteen 'til four," Roadhawg said. "He's going to love our little date."

At 3:30, they pulled the light blue van into the underground parking lot. Jones's Deville sat waiting. Roadhawg parked behind the Caddy. Acting casual, Dan and Jack got out. All three wore long hair wigs, bell bottoms, t-shirts, and construction boots.

"Okay, Roadhawg and I'll sit here at the open slider, and Jack you get the van up on the jack. As soon as he comes out, we'll stuff him in the van, and close the door. Jack, you let the thing down and Roadhawg, you drive us the hell out of here."

"We're all good, but you aren't using the gun are you?" Jack held his palms up.

"Only as show." Dan's expression never changed. "But, I will if I have to."

At 4:00, no Jones. Dan stayed seated in the door opening. Perspiration from the wig ran down his face. He looked at Roadhawg. "Are you sleeping or praying?"

"In Jesus name we pray." Roadhawg grinned as he toyed with Dan.

"That's a good one. I gotta remember that."

At three after four, Dan double checked his watch. Then he heard the elevator bell ring as it announced an arrival.

Jones and another attorney-type walked toward them. "Aw shit, who's with him?" Jack whispered.

"What the hell do you think you're doing blocking my car?" Jones yelled.

"We're about finished." Roadhawg pretended to fiddle with the lug nuts.

"Hey, Jones, I'll meet you there." The other man got into his car parked next to Jones.

"Hurry up, and move it. you deadbeats."

"Give it thirty seconds and we'll be outta here." Jones approached the slider. The other man backed out his car. When he was no longer in sight, Roadhawg said, "Sir?"

"What is it, now?"

"Someone broke your tail light lens, and I wanted you to know it wasn't us." Roadhawg hemmed and hawed, as Jones bent over to look at the broken lens. Dan grabbed him and Jack wrapped duct tape around Jones twice before Jones realized what was happening.

"What the?"

Roadhawg stuffed a rag in Jones's mouth and taped it closed.

Jack secured Jones's ankles with tape.

Dan and Roadhawg picked him up, threw him in the back of the van, and slammed the slider shut.

Jack lowered the van off the jack in less than five seconds.

Roadhawg started the van. Jack and Dan climbed in the back beside Jones.

Dan removed his wig and glasses. "Hey, there, Robert. Your worst nightmare just arrived. Sit back, and enjoy the ride. Ken will be glad to see you."

Roadhawg took the exit a little too fast. All three riders bounced around in the back. Jones kicked the side of the van.

"Jones, if you don't settle down, I'm going to beat you like a drum, with a smile on my face. Now, you don't want to get me started, because when I think of those two boys and their grandma. Well, I've got some anger issues. And, I'm dying to show you how much anger that is."

CHAPTER TWENTY-FIVE

Jones squirmed, tried to yell, and generally made a nuisance of himself.

Roadhawg spoke from the front seat. "What the hell is all that commotion back there. I'm trying to drive and it's gettin' on my nerves. Danny, can't you do somethin'?"

"Jones, I warned you. Last chance." Dan shook his finger in front of Jones's face.

Jones squirmed and kicked the walls of the van with both feet.

"Danny, come on. This is annoyin' the piss outta me. I've gotta concentrate on drivin'."

"Okay, counselor, I want you to realize I mean what I say."

Dan picked up a length of garden hose and dangled it in front of Jones's head so he could see it. Jones continued to bang on the side of the van.

"Once you come to grips with what I'm telling you, well, you're going to be so much better off. You can't tell yet, but this hose is filled with sand." Dan raised it to the roof of the van and swung it hitting Jones on his buttocks. The scream that followed didn't raise many decibels through the gag and tape.

"Danny, that didn't seemed to make him scream very loud," Jack said.

"Well, watch this." Dan swung the hose at him again. "Bobby, Bobby, Bobby, shut up…or I'll make mincemeat of that pretty face of yours."

Tears streaked down Jones's cheeks as he lay motionless.

"That's so much better."

Jones turned his head away.

"Damn it, Jones." Dan hit him again with an open hand on his face.

"Danny, I think he's got a lot of learning to do." Jack shouted out as Jones nodded his head.

"There, now. That wasn't so hard was it, Jones?"

Jones shook his head to answer.

Roadhawg yelled from the front seat. "Well, hell, it's about time the racket back there came to a halt."

In thirty minutes, the van approached the storage unit. Roadhawg looked around and gave a thumbs up for all clear. Jack opened the slider, pushed up the roll-up door to the unit. Roadhawg drove in.

They made sure Ken was okay, then once again they set up the table with the pre-drilled holes, and hooked up the battery cables to the cigar lighter. They drug Jones out of the van and that's when a scuffle began. Jack and Roadhawg tried to manhandle Jones, but he struggled and fell down. Then, he kicked Roadhawg in the shin.

"Damn it, that hurt, you idiot." Roadhawg hissed as he limped toward Jones.

Dan handed Roadhawg the hose, and he administered three good strokes on Jones with the sand filled hose.

Jones froze, but his muffled screams sounded serious.

"I hate it when he makes me do that," Roadhawg said to Dan.

"Now, see if that makes him behave himself. And Jones,

please act up again. I think you've improved my golf swing." Dan demonstrated a perfect Arnold Palmer swing.

They pulled out a wooden chair and taped Jones in it. They fastened each of his legs to a chair leg, and one of his arms taped to his side.

Jones offered no resistance.

Next, they strapped his other hand to the table, this time with leather shoe laces. The predrilled holes allowed his hand to be spread-eagled yet bound just like Ken's had been tied to the table. Jones could sit, but he had no wiggle room.

Dan whispered to Jones that all he wanted was some information.

Jones glared in return.

"I like that look. Defiant and ignorant. Okay, I'm going to let Jack begin, and then Roadhawg. I'm batting cleanup."

"Jones, my name is John Charles Higgins, but my friends call me Jack. Ahh, you're getting it. That's right. I don't give one iota that you know who we are. Besides me there's one Joseph Hegidio, and he wants you to know the same thing."

Roadhawg took over and explained that, if anything happened to any of them, there would be payback. Not only would Jones be dealt with, but so would his family. He reminded Jones that they had many Marine Corps friends who would do the job if something ever happened to any of them.

Jack made sure Jones knew they were damn dead serious, then Jack pointed to Dan.

"Alright, as to why we're here," Dan said, "we want to know who put the rocket-propelled grenade in my wife's house? Well, specifically who ordered it? Now, listen up. I'm going to untape your mouth. And then you're going to tell me. Got it?"

Jones stared straight ahead.

"Well, Jones, here's where it's going to get interesting."

Dan nodded his head toward Jack.

Jack approached with the meat cleaver, hammer, and a knife sharpener. He shook his head in mock disbelief, rolled his eyes, and exhaled. "Danny, he's not looking like he wants to cooperate." Jack placed everything on the table.

"Well, since you ignored my last statement, let me explain what's about to happen." Dan sharpened the cleaver. He smiled as Jones's eyes bugged out. "Yes, the cleaver is for chopping. Have you noticed your splayed fingers?"

Jones nodded.

"I think the light went on for Jones." Roadhawg laughed.

Jones closed his eyes.

"Are you following me, Bobby? Let's do the math. Including your thumbs you have ten digits, multiply that by three knuckles. Bobby, pay attention. Did you do the math?"

When Jones nodded his head, he almost turned the chair over.

"Well, good," Dan said. "Now, who ordered the hit on my wife's house. Take the tape off, Roadhawg. If you yell, Robert, Jack will tape your mouth again."

Dan explained he wanted the guy's address and all of Jones's files on the guy. Jones, of course, screamed client/attorney privilege and that made the boys laugh. Dan pushed the cigar lighter in for effect. "Are you ready?

"Yes."

"Well, good. Now who ordered the hit on my wife's house?"

"I don't know for sure who did it. They'll kill me," he cried.

"Uh, oh, wrong answer, Robert. Tape his mouth, Roadhawg," Dan said.

"Listen, I'll tell you, but this is crazy."

"No, it's justice, and I'm going to see that it happens."

"Justice? This is kidnapping, torture and…"

"Shut the hell up," Dan shouted.

"You don't have the balls to do it." Jones's bravado began to show.

Dan picked up the cleaver.

"Beating me is one thing. But, you don't have the balls to do that." Jones wiggled, trying to keep the gag from being taped to his mouth.

"You might be right, but we're going to find out. Just as soon as we get the cigar lighter glowing."

Jack got the gag in place and wrapped an extra layer of tape around Jones's head.

Dan took the cleaver and slid it on top of the little finger knuckle next to the nail. He drew blood.

"You see, Jones, we already know who did it. We were giving you a chance to come clean. But…you seem to have your head so far up your ass you wouldn't recognize a breath of fresh air if it hit you in the face. Just for the record, counselor, I've got the balls to do it. And with a grin on my face, you dumb bastard."

"Dan, I need to see you for a second while the lighter is getting ready," Jack said.

Dan got up and followed Jack to the far side of the van. "Man, are you really going to do this?" Jack whispered.

"Yes."

"I'm with you a hundred percent, but…"

Dan cut him off. "Jack, if it were Ellen?"

"Okay, okay. I just wanted to make sure."

Dan growled. "Hey, they started it."

"But we're talking kidnapping, murder and…"

"I know, but they crossed the line and went after family. I'm tired of the system screwing around. Screwing us."

"Okay, you're right Danny. Want me to do it for you?"

Dan shook his head. "Thanks, man. But, I can do it."

They returned to where Jones sat.

Dan sat back down. The cigar lighter glowed bright

orange. "Jones, I want the thing hot enough to cut down the bleeding. I just hate messes. Now, last chance. Want to tell me where to find Juan Montoyo?"

Jones sat motionless.

Dan frowned. Then he pursed his lips, placed the meat cleaver on the knuckle of Jones's little finger and raised the hammer.

CHAPTER TWENTY-SIX

The hammer struck the flat surface of the cleaver with a definite bang. Dan pried the cleaver from the plywood table, picked up the glowing cigar lighter and seared the finger.

Jones jerked in the chair, his screams muted by the gag. Roadhawg stood behind the chair to insure Jones didn't fall backwards. This time Roadhawg held the back of the chair, because Jones became more violent. The smoky stench almost gagged Dan, but he gathered himself together.

Dan wiped the cleaver with a damp cloth in front of Jones for effect. "Are you ready to talk now?

Jones's whole body nodded with his head. Roadhawg removed the tape from the gag. Jones appeared to about pass out a couple of times as he stared at the missing tip of his pinky finger. After about fifteen minutes answering their questions he settled down and cooperated.

"Jones, this has been very good, but in the morning, I'll call your office. You'll tell them Roadhawg will stop by to pick up the Montoyo files. If you even begin to screw up..." Dan waved the cleaver and hammer.

The next morning, Dan called the office. He held the

phone next to Jones's ear. Jones, gave the secretary instructions to gather all of the Montoyo files. Then Roadhawg left for Jones's office. After about an hour and a half, Roadhawg returned with several boxes of legal paperwork.

"Jones, this is going a whole lot better, now, don't you think?" Dan leafed through Montoyo's files.

"Yes." Jones exhaled.

Dan, Jack, and Roadhawg pored over the files with Jones, and got everything they needed. Roadhawg left for the airport to catch the next available flight to the East Coast. Jack and Dan finalized their plans for each of them to spend some time with their wives.

In private, Jack said to Dan. "Hey, it's almost time to call Steve Mitchell."

Jack left to make the call. When he returned, he spoke to Dan away from the cage that held Ken and Jones. "So, Steve said, they're considering some sort of deal."

"Huh? I don't trust them." Dan closed his eyes.

"Well, Ellen said they're ready for Christy to make her getaway. The boys are fine and staying with her sister. She said Steve has been at the hospital almost all night...every night."

"I like him a whole lot and I don't like many attorneys. I'm really glad Grace is getting better. Okay, let's change the subject. After Ellen and I meet, we'll plan our next move on Juan Montoyo. Roadhawg should be back by Friday."

"Hey, Danny, you seem, I dunno, ah, scattered. Are you sure you're okay?" Jack searched Dan's face.

"Hell, yeah. I just hate turning myself in. I don't trust the bastards."

"But Steve said they were willing to talk no jail time if they got the money back."

"I still don't trust them. You know that sick-to-your-gut feeling? Even if Roadhawg finds something, we'll still have no solid proof."

"Yeah. I know what you mean. But back to you taking off."

"Today's Sunday," Dan said. "I'll roll out of here in the morning, and be back Wednesday afternoon. Then you and Ellen can get together after you pick up Roadhawg on Friday."

"Babysitting these two is beginning to be a pain in the ass." Jack motioned with his chin toward Ken and Jones. "We outta be fine with just one of us watching these jokers. That make-shift jail cell is doing the job, but I still worry about only one of us being here."

"Yeah, we gotta sleep some time. But, I warned them, if they try something they're in big shit trouble."

They secured Ken and Jones to the concrete wall by a length of chain. The two had access to the toilet and the igloo water cooler inside the cage. They both rested on their army cots. The meals created a problem. One of the three would have to go out and buy take-out, but being solo created a problem.

"If they try something," Jack narrowed his eyes, "it'd be two against one. But I don't think they can get out of their handcuffs. And with their feet cuffed with those stupid cow bells, it'd be hard for them to do doodlely shit."

"We just need to be super careful. But, I really worry how all of this is affecting Christy. I mean it's a lot to come to grips with. She might want to just call the whole thing off."

Jack shook his head. "That's not what El said. Christy misses and needs you a bunch. I think you're solid. So get your stuff and get a move on."

"I hope Roadhawg gets the information and gets back here okay. It'd make things a little easier having a couple of us here."

"If they bust you." Jack pointed toward Dan. "In the meantime, Roadhawg and I'll carry out the rest of the plan. If things get screwed up, we've got the contingencies all figured out. We'll be okay here."

"I just worry, that's all."

"Quit worrying, would you? Get your butt out of here. Oh, yeah, enjoy the honeymoon."

"Yeah, right." Dan sighed.

"And, you've got the times to call the phone booth to check in, don't you?"

"Right here." Dan held up the paper and walked out.

The drive to Olympia took less than forty-five minutes. Christy arrived at the rendezvous a few minutes after Dan. He checked for possible tails. When he felt sure she wasn't followed, he approached her.

The hour to Westport gave both of them time to catch up. She kept talking about the house being destroyed, and the boys and her mom's recovery.

"Steve has really been a God send," she said. "How old do you think he is?"

"I don't know." Dan frowned. "Early to mid-thirties?"

"Nope." A slight grin broke out on her face. "He's only three years younger than Mom. He's forty-one."

"I knew your mom looked young, but I didn't know she was that young."

"She had me when she was seventeen. Dad was five years older than Mom. They got married in forty-four and Dad was shipped out soon thereafter. Anyway, Steve thinks the Feds are ready to maybe listen."

"Talk's cheap. I don't trust them as far as I could throw them." Dan squinted as he checked the rearview when they pulled into Westport.

"What's the matter?" Christy said.

"Just checking. We're okay." He continued with caution toward the mobile home park.

Dan eased into the covered parking stall behind the singlewide. They took their time as they entered through the back door. Once inside, Dan checked all his markers to see if any unwanted visitors had stopped by. He felt better after he checked the last device.

"Well, we appear to be undiscovered." He relaxed.

Christy stretched out on the couch with her head fully resting on the back cushion. She appeared to be staring at the ceiling. "I'm still worried about you turning yourself in."

They talked late into the afternoon, discussing the repercussions, both good and bad. Two bottles of wine and the flickering light from the gas fireplace made for a relaxed conversation.

"Let's go over it one more time to be sure I've got it." Christy said.

"I have Steve set up to do the surrender." Dan rubbed his temples.

"That's after we get assurances they'll take the money and no jail time."

"That's right. And all of us have more than enough to give them back what we took from Bedford."

Christy closed her eyes and nodded. Dan was glad she knew about their finances.

"And, if they screw me, the boys will spring me." Dan refilled their wine glasses.

"It all seems very risky, Honey," Christy paused. "How do you feel about all this?"

"Like the country dog that went to the city. I feel like I'm going to get screwed if I move, and screwed if I sit still. But I can't allow the crap to continue that's resulted from all of this."

"I agree, but I still worry…"

"Let's take a break." He winked at her.

They decided to have dinner before the local fish diner closed. When they returned, their conversation revolved around the plan for Carlos Montoyo. Carlos and his operation's next drug shipment was going to be leaked to the Feds by Dan through Steve Mitchell. With any luck, Carlos would be in jail.

Christy worried that information wouldn't buy them any credibility with the Feds. Dan told her it couldn't hurt. The conversation continued with both of them warming up to Ken and Jones's role of assisting Christy in the new venture. Dan assured her that Jones and Ken had too much to lose if they screwed up. He felt they'd do well. Dan added the big motivational factor they held over Ken and Jones. Christy worried if having Ken and Jones didn't work out.

But, Dan's thoughts returned to Roadhawg's trip back East. He knew if it turned out well, they'd finally have some leverage.

CHAPTER TWENTY-SEVEN

Tuesday flew by. Christy more than once tried to convince Dan that the whole mess didn't fall on his shoulders. Yet he knew that flying for Ken brought all the bad attention on the other Marines. He felt responsible for the tragedy to Grace and the boys. The information Bob Jones delivered meant Montoyo was on borrowed time. Dan wished he could be there when the Feds made the bust. He called Jack at the appointed time and Jack reported Roadhawg needed to be picked up the next morning. The news put a smile on Dan's face because he and Jack needed more help watching Ken and Jones.

Wednesday morning, Dan cleaned out the cash stashed in both the boat and the '63 Buick parked at Earl's gas station. Christy drove the Buick back to long term parking in Olympia, and Dan followed in the truck. They needed the extra set of wheels. Dan had rented a motel room on the second floor overlooking the lot where Christy had parked her car. The parking lot was unattended.

Christy and Dan went to the motel room. From the balcony, he couldn't see any visible tails. They kissed and she left the room to go to her car. Dan wiped the sweat from his forehead as Christy drove away.

"Okay, let the games begin," he said out loud. He adjusted his wig and left the balcony vantage point.

Dan circled the departure lanes at SeaTac. He almost bumped the car in front of him. He couldn't believe his eyes. Their crew chief, Charles Pogany, from Vietnam and Okinawa, waltzed out of the terminal with Roadhawg. In the fall of 1971, Dan, Jack, Roadhawg, the crew chief, Charles Pogany, and the two other original 1968 Vietnam Veterans, liberated the stolen military payroll from the original thieves, Lt. Col. Fred Bedford and his cohorts.

Dan, and the other five took it from Bedford. They waited for a reward. None was posted. So they deposited close to 3 million each into a Swiss bank. The accounts drew close to 8% interest on 90% of their original deposit. The bank invested 10% of it in oil futures.

Oil exploded on the upside that spring. The 10% increased close to thirty fold before the Swiss bank funds manager took them out of the oil futures. Each one sat on a little over 6.5 million. Now, all six of them agreed on giving back their original 3 million, because it had doubled in value.

"Well, if this ain't the cat's ass," Pogy said, sliding in next to Dan. He and Roadhawg filled the cab of the truck.

"You gotta be kidding me. What are you doing here?" Dan said. Pogy put his arm around Dan and kept hugging him.

"After you called Ludwig, we decided I should disappear. Saint Thomas is too small and we felt there were going to be eyes looking. So, when Roadhawg called Luds to check in, we made arrangements for me to meet him in D.C."

Roadhawg leaned forward nodding his head. He closed one eye to exaggerate the wink, and pointed a gun-like finger at Dan.

"Well, I gotta tell you we can sure as hell use your help," Dan said to Pog. "Now, quit hugging me." Pogy kissed him on the cheek.

"Quit being such a homo," Pogy said. "I can't believe the crap that's going on. Two dead FBI types, your wife's family... And, now, you clowns are guilty of kidnapping?

"So, Dr. Frankenstein, tell us what's going on." Roadhawg referred to Jones's pinky stub.

Dan brought them up to date on all they'd learned from Jones and the files they'd picked up. Dan went into detail on the plan for the Montoyo drug gang, and the future for Jones and Ken. Dan asked if Pogy would like to join in.

"Hell, yes. I'll contribute a couple hundred grand," Pogy blurted out.

Roadhawg said, "I like the whole deal. I'm in, plus I'd like to stick around and help out."

"Okay, that's way cool, but here's what we've got in store for me turning myself in after we hand Thomason and Riley, the Montoyo boys on a silver platter." Dan merged on to I-5 south to pick up the '63 Buick Christy had driven from Westport and dropped off at the motel parking lot. Dan told them about the plans for his surrender. They all added more ideas, and contingencies.

A couple hours later, they drove to the warehouse down by the docks in Tacoma. As they got out, Roadhawg inhaled and said, "I love the aroma of dock-side stagnate polluted water. It gives me a rustle in my loins."

"Don't let me get too near him," Pogy hurried to get in front of Roadhawg.

"Hey, Jackson," Danny announced after they stepped into the warehouse area and closed the entrance door. "Looky here what the cat drug in." He cocked his head toward Pog.

"Hey, I'll be damned. Lord, have mercy, Buddy, it's good to see your worthless ass." Jack slapped Pog on his back.

After they got caught up on what had been going on, Jack said, "So, Ludwig thinks the climate on Saint Thomas might get a little sticky?"

"Yeah. Just gives them more questions to ask. Although, I gotta tell ya, he's making good money turning those sailboats down there. And I just finished my first run back on a thirty-six footer."

"No, kidding. I didn't think you enlisted pukes would be smart enough to learn how to sail," Roadhawg teased.

Pog chuckled while he gave Roadhawg the finger.

"Okay, I'd love to carry on all day," Jack said, "but El is waiting and I feel the need to breed. So, lemme turn these two reformers over to you." He headed to the enclosed back room with Jones and Trevor.

"So, does this make me an accessory?" Pog chuckled.

"Not only yes, but hell, yes," Roadhawg shot back as he slugged Pogy in the bicep.

Ken and Jones sat silent as the guys approached their cell. Jack explained how he'd gone over their options for Ken and Jones's release.

"So, you've agreed to join in our little operation and turn over a new leaf?" Dan said to Jones and Ken.

They both shook their heads. Jones spoke first. "If your plan to eradicate Montoyo doesn't work…we're all dead men."

"Notta prob, Jones. I'll personally do it if the Feds don't.

"As much as I'd love to stay and kibitz, Ellen is waiting, and I'm gonna make like horse poop and hitting the trail." Jack headed toward the front door.

"Check-in times remain the same," Dan hollered.

Jack nodded his head and held a thumbs up for them to see as he walked outside.

Dan, Pog, and Roadhawg sat down in front of Ken and Jones. Well, let's see if they're really on board Dan asked himself.

"Let's begin with the Montoyo operation. Jones, why don't you go over it in detail and I'll take notes."

"If they ever find out I talked, I'm dead."

"Yes, that's true, but…" Dan circled his index finger motioning to himself and Roadhawg and Pog. "You've got us covering your back. And you know what we're capable of." Dan looked at Jones's shortened pinky.

"Yes, I know. Anyway, since the offshore helo runs are over, they've had to resort to bringing in the dope in furniture from Canada. The next delivery will be this Saturday around two in the morning. And it's a big one."

Dan nodded his head, "And, one truck will be coming to their storage facility in Spanaway."

"That's right, and only with the regular night guards outside. Carlos will personally be there with his bevy of buddies. I gotta tell you, they will fight to the end."

"I only wish I could be there to help finish them off." Dan blurted out in anger.

Roadhawg put his arm around him. "Danny, don't let it get personal. We're counting on you."

"You're right, and I'll be okay, But I'd still like to hit Montoyo with a baseball bat."

In a drugstore down the street from the FBI building, Dan, in disguise, picked up the phone in a phone booth, deposited the money, and listened to it ring.

He asked for Agent Thomason or Riley. The operator asked who was calling.

"Tell them it's Dan Burton, and I won't wait over ten seconds. You can put the tracer on the phone once they're on the line."

Dan listened and in less than ten seconds, the phone came alive. Agent Riley answered and told Dan agent Thomason was listening on another phone.

"Agent Riley…this is Dan Burton. I want you to know

Carlos Montoyo will be personally taking delivery of over two million dollars of drugs in street value."

"Who is this?"

Dan knew Riley was attempting to stall. "Come on, Agent Riley. We know they're hurrying to put a trace on this call. So, here's the deal. I've given all the information as to times and places to my attorney, Steve Mitchell. I hope you finally realize I'm on your side."

"Where the hell are you?" Riley snapped, still stalling.

"All we ask is that Ken Anderson be given immunity for supplying me this information. Now, you've got less than fifteen seconds according to my watch. Any more questions?"

"Don't hang up. I need to get the time and address…" Riley listened to the dial tone. "Did you get an address?" he shouted into the phone to Thomason.

Thomason said, "They've got his location narrowed down to a couple of blocks from here. He's still staying way ahead of us. Damn it, he's calling from right under our nose and enjoying it."

"I suppose we have to call that smart assed attorney of his," Riley said as his phone rang. He snatched it up, "Yes?"

"Agent Riley, there's a Steve Mitchell on your line one."

Dan left the drug store by all appearances an old man using a cane with a noticeable walking disability. He struggled into his truck and drove away. Twenty minutes later, he called Steve's office as planned. After Steve gave him Grace's progress report, they got down to business.

"The Feds have all the information," Steve said. "And you better be sure Ken is on board, because they agreed to give him immunity on the drug charges."

"We'll know soon enough if both of them are on board. And if they aren't…"

"Dan, new topic. I've thought it over, and I'd like to buy

into you guy's Veteran's real estate deal that Christy's starting, if that's okay."

"It'd mean a lot to all of us. Thanks, Steve."

"Dan you mentioned you guys were putting in two hundred thousand a peace. So, count me in for the same amount as you guys. I think it's a great idea. But more important, I think it'll make a lot of money. Okay, I've got to take this other call. They say it's Grace. I'll talk to you later."

Dan smiled as he ended the phone call.

CHAPTER TWENTY-EIGHT

"Okay, you two," Dan spoke to Ken and Jones. "Here's the deal. Ken, they're going to deliver your immunity to our attorney. And after the bust on Saturday night, or Sunday morning, it outta be safe to let you two loose."

"How will we know if they have Montoyo's bunch all in custody or the morgue?" Jones said.

"Steve'll call Christy. She'll pass it on to Ellen and Dan." Roadhawg took center stage. "Let's go over the financials and your involvement Jones."

"I know," Jones began. "I leave my law firm. And incorporate our new business. I'll contribute three-hundred and fifty thousand, and Ken there ..." he rolled his eyes toward Ken, "is putting up the other fifty."

Dan pointed at Jones and Ken, and then at Roadhawg. "Just so we're clear here. Roadhawg's going to honcho the deal, and Steve Mitchell will be on board so there'll be plenty of eyes on your performance."

"So, I leave my practice, and run the operation along with Ken. And it's costing me every cent I've got." Jones stated more than asked.

"Jones, that sounded a bit testy." Pog stepped up.

"No, it's just hard for me to walk away,"

Dan interrupted. "We're handing you a gift."

"I'm sorry. It's still setting in. That's all. It's all so new."

"I'll go over the financials." Roadhawg joined in. "You and Ken, here, are contributing four, Steve Mitchell two, and then one point two from the Marine Corps contingency."

"That's a lot," Ken said.

"No, that's only one point eight million. We expect it to grow significantly from our endeavors," Roadhawg said.

"So, we're going to hire Vietnam vets, put them to work remodeling, building houses, and developing real estate?" Pog said.

Dan nodded in agreement, "Along with several other businesses, like buying our own hardware and lumber yards, and opening a garage to buy and maintain the corporation's automobiles to give or make available to the vets that need transportation."

"Your wife, Christy, will she broker all the real estate transactions?" Ken said.

"She'll open her own office, but Ken, she'll work for a salary, just like you. She'll donate all her commissions to the corporation. And just like you and Jones, along with the other investors, there'll be an equal split of profits at year-end."

"Let me make sure of this one," Pog asserted. "Fifty percent of the profits go to the retirement fund, the deferred compensation plan that all of us and every employee are in. The other fifty percent is a bonus for the original investors."

"So, we get a salary, and year-end bonus as original investors, plus the retirement contribution from the operations?" At last Ken seemed to grasp the financial agreement.

"That's right, Ken." Dan nodded.

"I was making a hell of a lot more," Jones said with his

head down.

"Yeah, but in three years, you can opt out. We'll buy anyone out in three years. If it makes as much as we think, you'll be a millionaire. But let me be crystal clear on this one. You're through fronting a drugs business and lawyering for the crooks." Roadhawg pointed his finger at Jones.

Jones inhaled, then said, "I know, I know. And I'm on board."

"You have a lot to gain, and we'll keep our word if you screw up," Dan said.

"I'm on board, but I don't think it's fair for me to front the hundred and fifty for Ken's share. I mean ..."

"You crawled into bed with him. Now, get over it or..." Dan's ire rose.

"You're right. You're right. I'm good with it. Really, I am." Jones sighed.

"Nice to have you on board. Now let's get Sunday and Monday ironed out," Dan said.

The Senior Agent in charge, Clements, led the flurry of activity at the FBI office. She strutted around dictating the order of events for the Sunday morning drug raid at Montoyo's facility. When Riley and Thomason presented her the details from Steve Mitchell, she contacted D.C., taking all the credit for the lead and information. Now, she exerted her expertise on the two agents. Riley slouched, looking bored.

"What?" Clements yelled at Riley.

"Your plan of knocking on the door with a search warrant at two in the morning sucks. I'll let you do that. What do you want on your tombstone? Or are you going to sacrifice some poor sons of bitches? Again."

"Just what does that mean, Riley?" She glared at him.

"It means, they've got fire power out the ass. They've already shown their willingness to blow away two agents on stakeout, and you want to present them with a search warrant? I'll watch you take the lead. That's the stupidest plan of attack I've ever heard."

"Oh, you've got something better?"

"What we're saying is simply this, Agent Clements," Thomason interrupted. "With their past actions, we could get the authority, and have it well documented. The shootout at the helicopter pad, losing two agents, and the attack on Ms. Burton's residence is more than enough proof to go in loaded for bear. I say you go in with military armed-personnel vehicles."

"APV's?"

"APV's locked and loaded. Not one, but as many as we can get. Along with tanks, if we could get them. We've got probable cause." Thomason stood, raising his index finger. "Their past record for violence." He raised two fingers. "And good proof of moving major drugs." He held up three fingers.

"And, what if it's a bust? We've got nothing accomplished."

"You moron." Riley stood up.

"What'd you call me?"

"You heard me. You've got intel that they've killed two agents, and that's all you need. Even if the drugs aren't there, arrest them with a warrant." Riley shouted.

Clements glared at Riley. "You don't talk to me that way. Do you understand me?"

"Oh, yeah. Want us to contact the media, again? Huh?"

"Just what does that mean?"

"Do your job. You're not the only one with contacts in D.C." Thomason joined in the fray.

"Don't either one of you ever threaten me, or your career is over." She poked a finger at him.

"Do your job, Clements, and don't ever threaten us." Riley broke out in a grin.

"Get out of here. Both of you. Now," She shouted.

"If, you try going in with anything less than APV's ...you're history." Riley said as he left.

"History my ass. You're through. Do you hear me? You're through. Get out of here." She picked up a stapler and threw it at the door as they left.

In the quiet of Christy's office, she and Ellen finalized her escape plan to meet Dan on Monday morning.

"I think it covers most every contingency," Ellen spoke a few decibels above a whisper.

"Yes, and if it gets messed up, I've got several ways to drop it." After a few moments, Christy said. "But I'm looking forward to a couple of days alone with Dan." She tried to smile as a tear trickled down her cheek.

"It all seems so scary."

"I don't look forward to Dan turning himself in. You know they're going to lock him up, at least for a while." She started to cry.

Ellen walked over to Christy's chair, knelt down and hugged her. "I know. I know. I just wish it were all over and done with."

"What I feel the worst about is seeing him in jail. But, really, after what's happened to the boys and Mom, I couldn't leave them. I'm so screwed up."

"I know. I couldn't imagine if Jack were in jail. But I don't have a family to leave, if we have to go on the run."

"Let's change the subject." Christy wiped her eyes, picking up the plot maps. "Look at the real estate plans I've got finalized. Here's the quarter section, all one-hundred and sixty acres, with the lake and views of the Sound."

Ellen took the large scrolled paper and said, "I'll help you get them working on it. Also, I agree with you. We ought to net at least eighty-plus home sites."

"And the seller is down to two-twenty, and subtracting the commission. We can get it for under two." Christy's demeanor began to brighten. "It's so exciting. I mean it's really coming together. And, tell the guys George is on board with contracting, construction, and joining the corporation."

George's plan consisted of a working crew per project. A well-experienced carpenter and a crew/team of four or five veterans. The on-the-job experience and learning as they formed a cohesive working unit made sense to everyone.

The concept the guys came up with would be a crew to rough in the framing, with a plumbing team, an electrical team, a drywall team, and a painting and finishing team. They'd also need a landscaping team.

The home owner's bylaws were simple and few. Everyone must keep the landscaping natural, along with up-keep. Each home site offered seclusion or views. The association would have an enclosed RV storage area, a community center with an indoor pool, sauna and steam rooms, plus a big recreation area and a meeting room with a full kitchen.

From start to finish, the hiring of workers would give preference to veterans. If they lacked particular skills, the head of the crews would provide the experience and know how to teach the crew/team. The concept would be much like the military—show them, and then have them apply their learned skills. Everyone would have full benefits and share in the profits for their retirement accounts.

Holding the plot diagrams and details, Ellen said her goodbye to Christy as she started to leave.

"Christy, I'll be here Tuesday when you get back."

"There's too much going on right now. I'll be so relieved when Montoyo is either gone or in jail. I know it's wrong, but I want him dead." Christy's voice quivered. "I haven't begun to think of Dan being in jail."

CHAPTER TWENTY-NINE

Christy parked in short term parking at SeaTac and made no attempt to disguise her movements. She'd already bought a prepaid ticket on PSA to Portland, yet she walked in plain sight to the ticket counter and purchased a ticket to San Francisco. The two flights were only ten minutes apart on departure. She'd picked up on the agents following her on her way into the terminal.

After she'd boarded the San Francisco flight, along with the two agents, she deplaned at the last moment and hurried to the Portland flight at the adjoining gate. Seated, she made sure no other passengers boarded as the stewardesses closed the door. After landing a little past noon, she did a switch with the shuttles and arrived at the predetermined hotel. With no agents in sight, she walked past the front desk area, then out the back door. An old Ford drove up beside her. She shot into the back seat while it still moved. The driver, disguised for all those who might be watching, appeared to be an older gentleman. He'd left the motel for all intents and purpose, alone.

On the drive to Westport, she and Dan went over the plans for the evening and the weekend. They were to call

Jack and Ellen at their undisclosed residence, arranged in advance by both Christy and Ellen.

Dan got out before they got close to the mobile home, and began his walk along the shore as Christy drove. In the safety of the trees, he watched her take her suitcase in. After a short wait he approached the back door, assured everything appeared okay.

Once inside the Westport mobile home and after Dan poured two glasses of wine, Christy began. "Steve is comfortable with the tentative plan, but would like more assurance the monies will be ready to be returned." She twirled the chardonnay in her stem glass, not looking at Dan.

"Here's the deal. Most of the guys have talked about what their shares are invested in. But, now we've all agreed to give it back."

Dan explained again how the money had more than doubled and how everyone could well afford to give the original money back. Dan and Christy went into detail for the first time about how much interest a year the money was making.

"So, you'd be getting about a quarter million a year from the bond fund?" She took a sip. "And the Swiss Bank is still waiting to put money back into some growth investments sometime soon?"

"Exactly. The plan was that if the growth or risk side completely failed, and we lost about three hundred thousand in a little over a year, the income side of about two hundred and forty thousand would almost replace it."

She shook her head. "You've gotta be kidding me."

"Nope. That's why I went into the laundromat business with Ken. I was trying get some of the money from over there into my account here without raising a bunch of eyebrows or questions."

"Now, it makes more sense."

"And the other guys, almost all of them did the same

except Pog. He put twenty percent into the growth. We all took the profits out and put it with the bond fund a few months ago, and now they're getting ready to put another ten percent into gold and silver futures."

"That's crazy." She shook her head.

"I don't understand it all," Dan said, "but when the oil crisis hit, oil went sky high. Every investor they'd put into the oil speculation made huge money off of it."

"I know. You've told me before, but I can't even imagine that much money." Christy puckered her lips and whistled.

"That's why none of us want to dicker around about giving the original money back. Tell Steve, once he's got the paperwork and convinced it's good, we'll have the monies wired to whatever he wants."

"So, all this time I figured you were counting pennies flying for Ken, in the Reserves, but you were a gazillionaire." Christy seemed to be putting it all together, at last.

"No, Honey, we're the gazillionaires." He reached over and took her face in both hands and kissed her.

The rest of the afternoon they spent going over the real estate plans. Christy showed him the office she'd picked out for the real estate end of the plan, the architect's plans for the eight model homes, and the club house for the first quarter section of the development.

They both avoided talking about the raid on Montoyo's drug operation coming up on Sunday.

A couple of days of being together helped them get ready for Dan's surrender. The plan was for Dan to turn himself in by the middle of the next week. With the FBI agreement in place, Dan and Christy were ready.

Steve's offer to the FBI was to return the stolen monies from Okinawa, have Dan tell them who had taken the payroll on Okinawa last fall, and co-operate with them. The

FBI's end of the deal was no jail time for any of the original four. And nobody was going to implicate Dennis or Ludwig in that caper.

Dennis Lee, and John Ludwig, picked up the money east of Okinawa on Luds' sailboat from St. Thomas and then had met with the other four in Hawaii.

From Hawaii, Jack, Dan, Roadhawg, and Pogy had taken their share of the money and flew to Switzerland. The two sailors, once they'd reached St. Thomas, took their share and flew to the same bank in Switzerland.

* * *

At midnight, Riley and Thomason were on watch at Montoyo's storage operation in Spanaway. "I still think Clements doesn't have enough firepower." Riley muttered without looking toward his partner.

Both Riley and Thomason knew the FBI tail had the semi-truck up north of Mount Vernon. And the semi-truck was about another hour to an hour and a half after that. They both feared for the guys Clements had assigned to lead the raid. Riley had told Clements, "You don't take a knife to a gunfight."

Both agents knew they'd tried. Riley assured Thomason he had the tape of Clements telling them to leak the information about Christy to the media, and Clements telling Riley and Thomason about the deal she'd made with Steve Mitchell. They both knew Clements had no intention on keeping the deal with Dan and Steve Mitchell.

"Well, we tried, and we're on the record," Riley said.

"That's why I'm glad you've got the tape."

Riley rolled his head.

At eight minutes after two, the semi slowed then turned into the storage facility. Everything appeared normal and quiet.

"Get ready. It's about to hit the fan," Riley said.

The driver eased up to a loading dock at the back of the facility. Instead of getting out of the big rig, he stayed in the cab. The doors from inside the facility opened and the bright lights shown on the rear of the shipment.

"Well, let's see how her plan is going to work out." Riley gripped the steering wheel as they viewed the scene now in action at the facility.

Two fork lifts and several men approached the rear of the trailer behind the semi. They opened the rear doors and began assisting the first forklift.

"There's Montoyo. He isn't here at this hour to help out with normal business. God, I hope that slime ball goes down tonight." Thomason muttered with the binoculars still pressed against his forehead.

At that moment, the first of the three Armored Personnel Vehicles's approached the front gate of Montoyo's business which had just closed. The APV's crashed through unnoticed by the crew unloading at the rear of Montoyo's building.

"What in the hell are they doing?" Thomason lowered the binoculars as dozens of vehicles, and patrol cars approached with their lights flashing. "Jesus, those idiots. Why don't they make it a bit more obvious." He dropped his binoculars.

Over the chatter on the radio frequency, Clements could be heard shouting, "Go. Go. All units go."

From a side access door, two of Montoyo's men came out with Rocket Propelled Grenades. They fired two direct hits on the APV's, disabling both. Several men followed with automatic weapons. From the roof, several more men appeared and numerous patrol cars and FBI units came under heavy fire. The last APV rounded the corner and opened fire on Montoyo's men shooting from the loading dock. Heavy smoke shrouded the entire area.

Thomason jumped out of the car, placed his rifle on the roof of the car and sighted in on the shooters at the top of the building. Riley joined him with his rifle. Thomason saw Montoyo between the cross hairs, pulled the trigger and watched Montoyo fall.

Thomason saw the RPG as it spiraled toward their vehicle. He grabbed Riley as he dove for a drainage ditch. Their car took a direct hit. Thomason stayed on top of Riley.

"Holy shit, buddy, that was close. Riles, Riley? Oh, shit, no," Thomason yelled.

By seven that morning, every Seattle news source carried the carnage at the drug bust. Juan Montoyo was dead along with fifteen employees. The FBI and local law enforcement officers had lost several vehicles. Seven agents were hospitalized, five of the seven in serious or critical condition.

Dan and Christy listened to the news from Westport. Jack and Ellen watched from their motel room. Roadhawg, Pog, Jones, and Ken watched from the storage building in the Tacoma dock area.

"Well, shit howdy. There you have it, girls." Roadhawg rubbed his hands together as the others sighed with relief.

"I guess that does it for Montoyo." Jones poured another cup of coffee from the fresh brewed pot.

The mood was celebratory as the four began to make plans for leaving the storage unit, because now the fear and threat of reprisal was a thing of the past.

Clements walked into Riley's room at the hospital. Thomason stayed seated with his eyes fixed on his unconscious partner. "How is he?" Clements said.

"The doctor's looking at the x-rays and should be back

any moment."

"What happened?"

"I grabbed him before the RPG hit our unit. I was on top of him. The car took a direct hit. Afterwards, I asked him how he was, and he was breathing but unconscious," Thomason said as the doctor walked in with the x-rays.

CHAPTER THIRTY

Monday morning took on different venues for everyone.

From his office Steve Mitchell finalized the agreement for Dan's surrender with the FBI legal types.

Christy called Steve's office, and made arrangements to have Steve meet with Dan that afternoon prior to his surrender.

Jack and Ellen sipped Bloody Mary's during their room service breakfast.

Jones and Ken made their way to their respective homes.

Thomason sat talking to a dazed Riley beside his hospital bed.

"I don't remember a thing. Honest," Riley mumbled.

"Man, it's probably for the best. But, ah…you do remember where you stashed the tape?"

With a thousand-yard stare, Riley shook his head.

"Don't worry. It'll come back or hell, we might stumble on a memory. Come on, Buddy, I know you. You're not that good at hiding stuff.".

Christy and Dan hurried cleaning out the mobile home.

"Well, Honey, this time tomorrow, I'll most likely be incarcerated."

"Don't talk like that." She looked away and wiped a tear.

"It'll only be a couple of days at the most, and then it'll be all over. Then, we can get on with our life."

"I just don't have a good feeling about the whole deal."

Dan came over and held her. He could feel the beating of her heart as his eyes began to water.

"You've got to be kidding," Clements spoke on the phone to Washington, D. C.

Her superiors were on a conference call with her. They'd just informed her the deal was off.

"But he didn't steal the money, and they've agreed to our deal," she argued. She listened then, spoke again. "And no crime was ever reported. What about it never happened on U.S. territory, or a military base?"

The powers that be, her boss informed her, were filing racketeering charges for money laundering. And also charging Ken, but wouldn't file charges if he collaborated. She argued that Ken's amnesty paperwork had already been delivered to Steve Mitchell. Then she blurted out, "But, you'll never get the money back."

"We don't care," her boss said.

"What do you mean you don't care?" she shouted.

"Listen…"

"What about the guys that really took it? Don't you want them?"

"This is coming from way above your pay grade," he said.

"The word is from above my pay grade? Are you nuts? Who's this coming from?"

"Shut the hell up. If you know what's good for you, get on board, or else. Do you understand me?"

"Yes, sir. Yes, sir…I understand. Yes, sir. I understand loud and clear. Yes, sir. I'm on board." She looked at the receiver and hung up the phone.

Clements buzzed her secretary and told her to send Thomason in. When he walked into his old office, she remained seated and motioned him to sit down.

"I just got off the phone with D. C."

"And?"

"And Dan Burton will be charged with racketeering. Ken Anderson will be let off for testifying against Burton."

Thompson jumped out of his chair. "Anderson has a deal?"

Clements nodded her head, "I was told in no uncertain terms, the Burton deal is off."

"But..."

"Call the President, or anyone you want and you'll find yourself terminated. That's what they said to me if I didn't like it."

"This isn't right," Thomason said.

"Right or wrong, those are our marching orders." She handed him the phone. "Go on, call anyone you want. You have my blessing. This is from the top."

"You're unbelievable."

"Listen, I'm screwed and I'm trying to not let it go to you or Riley," she said.

"Like I believe that."

They both sat in silence.

"I was just told that after Burton's in custody, I'm to immediately report back to D.C. for another assignment. Want to guess how far they'll bury me? My career is...gone. Over. Finished. I think they'll want Burton for the payroll heist."

Thomason got up to leave when Clements said, "I'll have your desk cleared out in a couple of minutes. More important, I haven't even asked how your partner is doing."

"He's awake, but groggy. He's going to be fine."

Clements got up and walked to the door. "I've got my stuff." She motioned to him that the office was his as she stood in the doorway.

"We're meeting Burton and his attorney at two in one of the conference rooms. I'm going to my hotel, change, go to the meeting, find a bar, and get drunk. Tell Riley I hope he recovers."

"Wait." Thomason stood in front of the door. "All of this over the bust last night?"

"No, the loss of agents. And somehow they found out about the leaks to the press came from this office. They know it came from me. I don't suppose you or Riley had anything to do with that, did you?"

"For what happened to Burton's mother-in-law? I have a hard time with my roll. And Riley feels the same about his. When you told us to do it, we should've told you to go to hell." He glared at her.

She nodded her head and walked around Thomason. Then, she turned to face him. "For the record, if I'm going down, you boys are, too."

"Like hell we are."

"What I'm trying to tell you... Oh forget it. It's not coming from me. We both know they'll be cleaning house."

At two that afternoon, Dan and Steve walked into the FBI's main office in Seattle. They were shown into a conference room.

"Steve, why are there so many armed guards at the door?"

"They'd best be trying to intimidate us." Steve took a chair, the gunfighter's seat, with his back to the wall, unbuttoned his coat, placed his clasped hands in front of his chest and tilted his head back. "Who's in charge of this meeting?" Steve said to an empty room.

At that moment, Clements walked in with three suits behind her.

"Gentlemen, let me introduce Mr. Walker from Justice." She motioned to the first suit behind her.

"Mr. Burton, please rise," Walker said.

Dan stood. Steve did also, and whispered to Dan not to say a word. Handing Walker his card, Steve took over. "My name is Steve Mitchell. I represent Mr. Burton, and we've come here voluntary to resolve this matter."

Clements was ushered out. Walker took Steve's card and set it aside. "Mr. Burton, you are being charged with racketeering." And then one of Walker's assistants began to read the Miranda rights to Dan.

The armed guards, as pre-briefed, came and hand cuffed Dan.

"This is not what we agreed to." Steve got into Walkers face.

"You can talk with your client after we process him." Walker turned and walked out behind Dan and the armed guards.

"What in the hell is going on here? We had a deal," Steve yelled at Walker's back.

An assistant to Walker said, "And D.C. just broke it. For what it's worth, you're right, and I'm on my way back there. It's all out of my hands."

"Tell you're "whomevers" in D.C. this isn't over. They'll have to answer to U.S. Senators. I've got paperwork and recordings. This isn't over by a long shot."

"Well, good luck," the assistant echoed as he marched out.

That evening, Christy was able to talk to Dan on a phone behind thick glass in the federal detention center. He wore an orange set of coveralls and a contented smile.

After the questions about the boys and Grace, Dan sat back. Christy brought him up to date on the charges against Ken and that he didn't want to cooperate with the Feds. Dan nodded in agreement.

"You act like you don't have a care in the world," Christy said.

"Tell Ken to work with Steve and Jones, and tell them to give the Feds enough to get him a deal or whatever."

"Really?"

Dan kept nodding. "Yep, and tell Jack, Roadhawg and Pog, plan B is in full effect. I'm going to expedite the process, and then let the games begin."

"I can't believe the Federal bureaucracy. I agree we don't have a whole lot of choices, but what are they trying to do?"

"I don't have enough pieces of the puzzle to have a clear picture of this whole mess, but it's dang sure they don't want the money or the thief. And that's clear as hell."

"None of it makes sense." Christy had to look away as her eyes grew misty.

"Our project, the land development? We'll go full steam ahead with that."

"And us?"

"They'll never catch on. I know that I love you, and that's all that matters right now. I just feel like such a screw up."

"Would you stop it? Baby, I love you with all my heart. Okay? And oh, this'll make you feel better," Christy said. "Momma and the boys said to tell you they miss you."

"That's the hardest part in this whole mess. I miss them more than you know. And, now, they'll have a crook for a stepdad."

"I'm going to ignore that. Anyway, they're doing fine, and can't wait to move in to our new place. They don't care about the move. They'll make new friends who don't associate any of this with us."

"I hope for their sake you're right."

"About the old house. George is almost finished and the landscapers have started. Plus, Grace can't wait to get out of the rental and into the new house."

"How're things between Steve and her?"

"They're planning a week in England." She giggled.

"I'm happy for them. He never left the hospital when it all came down. He's for real."

"Wait, if he and Mom...he'd be you're father-in-law."

"What? Are they talking?"

Christy nodded her head.

"Ask him if we get a family discount on his rates. Hey, wait, any chance of me getting a brother or sister-in-law?"

When the laughter stopped, Christy looked at her watch.

"Well, they sure can't keep us from laughing," Dan said.

"That's for sure, Honey. I've got to get, but remember I love you so much."

Dan placed his hand on the separation glass, agreeing. "That's my anchor. I love you, too. Now, we're on Plan B. Okay? And, I fully understand about you not being able to leave the boys."

"We'll still have our time together."

CHAPTER THIRTY-ONE

A couple of days later, Christy walked with George, to do a final inspection walk through of the finished house on Vashon Island. She and Dan had designed the four thousand square foot, four-bedroom house, with a separate mother-in-law unit. Dan's 1957 Corvette was the only thing in the separate 2,000 square foot shop for Dan's car restorations, otherwise it appeared abandoned.

Christy and Dan had picked out five secluded acres on a small rise with an unrestricted view of Puget Sound to the west. The location was convenient for Christy because it was northeast of Gig Harbor, a few minutes from her new office near the toll ferry to Tacoma.

"Are the plans still on for construction of the new housing development?" George shuffled his feet while he gazed at a container ship heading toward Tacoma.

"Yes, the permits for the club house were approved yesterday," Christy said. "And the same for the four model homes. Are you still on board and good to go?"

"I've been nervous and waiting." George unrolled the plans and placed them on the counter in the kitchen. "You know, with Dan's situation and all. But I've got three crews lined up, top notch foreman and at least two journeymen vets on each crew."

"I've been swamped with everything," Christy said. "Mom's out of the hospital, getting the boys settled again. Not to mention the insurance hassle with the house after the fire."

"Don't worry about that. I'd be glad to honcho that one for you. I'll be the general contractor and negotiate with the insurance company for you."

"That'd be great. One huge hassle less that I've got to handle. You know, with Dan's situation and all, I've put this project on the back burner."

George said, "Don't sweat it. I've worked with the insurance adjuster before. I'll contact him and see where we are, if that's okay."

"That'd be great. Thanks."

"Tell Dan I know that all this BS with the FBI is… well, you know. It's been proven he had nothing to do with the drugs, and nobody knows really why the FBI is even holding him."

Christy said, "We're on the same page there, George. Anyway, you've got the reconstruction of my old place and the insurance adjuster. The permitted building plans for the new development should be to you in a day or so, and the funds will be in the account to get the next project started," Christy said as she locked the door on their way out. "And I love the house, but now I've got to get moving. I'm supposed to meet with Dan in a bit." She checked her watch.

Steve Mitchell waited for Christy on a shaded bench by the parking lot outside the detention center.

"Hey, there you are," he said.

"Steve, good to see you." She sat down beside him.

"I've been trying to catch a minute with you. I just

spoke with Dan, and am on my way to have lunch with your mother."

By now, Christy was getting used to his cocky smile and manners. It was Steve just being Steve.

"Anything new?"

"Yes," he whispered. "I know you aren't supposed to be in touch with the other three of them...ah-h-h, you know?"

"Okay." Christy nodded her head.

"But my secretary got a call from a Quint Holland in Washington, D. C. and he said it was urgent to speak with one of the other three if at all possible. He said he flew with them in Vietnam, and they'd know what it's about. Here's his phone number." Steve slipped the folded phone number to Christy. "The D.C. area code is missing and the last two digits are reversed," he said.

"Got it." She grinned.

"Technically, the Feds can't search you and keep it, but if they do, let me know. I'm itching for a confrontation with them."

"Steve, thanks. Wanna know something?"

"What?" He cocked his head sideways.

"You're the best medicine that Mom's had in a long time."

"Now, do you want to know something?" Steve set his brief case down, took a small jewelry box out and opened it.

"Oh, my goodness. Is that what I think it is?" Christy admired the expensive looking diamond engagement and wedding ring set.

"Yes, it is and I haven't asked her, yet." Steve beamed.

Christy hugged him. They said their goodbyes and she made her way in to see Dan. She brought him up to date on George and the two projects.

"That's good. He'll handle the insurance company," Dan said.

"Yes, as long as they hurry up and get it going. I've already got two potential renters if we can get it finished before school starts this fall," Christy said.

"How'd the house look?"

"It's everything we wanted, and it's beautiful. But the Corvette looks lonely."

"Well, with what I've got looking at me...I wonder when, if ever I'll get to see any of it."

"Honey, I love your attitude. Can you at least be positive? And you know it'll all work out one way or the other."

They finished talking about the development project and how the boys and Grace were doing. She wanted to tell him about the info Quint passed on to her, but she knew they were most likely being monitored.

Christy took two days before the contact time, to and from the pre-arranged phone booths, to contact Quint Holland. When Ellen and Christy spoke they never mentioned names. The code for passing phone numbers was simple. The first three numbers for the area code was add one to the first number, two to the second and three to the third. Then reverse the next three numbers, and finish by using a date. So, January, 5, 1949, would be 1549.

Even though Quint and Christy were in phone booths, she didn't feel safe passing on the name. So, she said a guy they knew from Vietnam called.

After the phone call with the information passed on, Ellen drove back to the mobile home park.

Relaying the information, she and Jack decided Roadhawg would fly to San Diego and make the call to Quint. Air California and PSA flew ten to twelve flights a day from Oakland to San Diego.

The next morning, Roadhawg flew to San Diego from Oakland. From a pay phone he called Quint in D.C.

Quint gave him a pay phone number and a time to call back. Roadhawg had four hours to kill. He rented a car and drove to check out Ellen and Jack's rentals on Balboa Island, and his places in El Toro. He stopped at Oceanside to place the call to Quint.

After a few minutes of details, Roadhawg repeated the information. "So, Bedford has taken an unexpected leave of absence?"

Quint continued. "Scuttlebutt is that something's going on. He just took off. I mean disappeared. And nobody knows anything. I'm close to a guy who works with him. The guy says Bedford had had a couple of strange phone calls from some guy in the CIA. My friend said he was all nervous and quick to leave. I mean he's gone to dust. The phone number he left is bogus."

"Hey, man, thanks for the heads up," Roadhawg said. "Now some of the pieces to the puzzle are a little bit clearer." Roadhawg began talking about the baseball season. They small-talked about nothing, so if the call were monitored, they'd be safe. Roadhawg left the phone booth for the San Diego Airport to fly back to the Oakland airport.

When Roadhawg arrived in Pleasanton, he walked into the mobile home well past dinner time. He placed a bucket of Kentucky fried finger lickers with all the trimmings on the table. "Lord, I'm starvin'. I've been on the move all day," he said as he began eating while bringing Jack and Ellen up to date.

"Well, I would imagine Bedford's unknown accomplice from last year's heist is the nervous guy at the CIA," Jack said.

"Yep." Roadhawg wiped grease off his hands with a napkin and swallowed half of his bottle of Coors.

Ellen spoke first. "So, let me get this straight. The CIA guy was probably Bedford's mystery man on the heist. I'd love to know who he is."

"No kidding. He's probably given ol' Freddie boy the ultimatum. Get the truck outta Dodge," Jack said.

"Now, it makes a little more sense why somebody higher up screwed with the agreement we had with the FBI." Roadhawg picked up this fourth piece of chicken.

Jack grumbled, "They need to know this in Seattle."

"Well," Ellen said. "I'm calling Steve Mitchell tomorrow and giving him the information."

"I don't know if it'll help. I mean, they have the trumped up racketeering thing. So, screw 'em. They're still after Pog, and us." Roadhawg assaulted the biscuits and mashed potatoes.

"As far as I'm concerned, plan B is still front and center." Jack turned to face Ellen. She nodded in agreement.

Roadhawg related all the information about their property in Balboa and his in El Toro. Then he started a new subject about plan B.

"Let's see, today's Friday and I've got my first solo tomorrow. I'll fly the hills between the Bay and here in Pleasanton looking for a landing site."

"I think heading south would be the best." Jack motioned with his head. "Make them think we're heading that way or back to the Bay Area. And then we'll haul ass north."

Ellen said. "Are we still looking at around the first of October? That'll give us about three months."

"I think so. But we might move it up to Labor Day weekend. Anyway, we've still got a few things to get done before we set a date. Alright then, while you're flying tomorrow, Ellen and I'll be picking up another disposable," Jack said.

"The instructor has way fewer hours than me. And he's clueless about my experience."

"Honey," Ellen said. "Are you pretty sure they'll send Dan down here to the Pleasanton detention center?"

"I looked up all the sentencing from Seattle, and the non-violent types are sent here to Pleasanton," Jack said.

"I still think we're going to have a problem with picking him up out of the joint." Roadhawg frowned. "I hope you're right. I want to get Dan out ASAP."

CHAPTER THIRTY-TWO

The next day, Jack and Ellen bought a clean, beige, four-door 1964 Pontiac Star Chief. The seller emphasized that his dad owned it and could no longer drive. The car only had twenty-two thousand miles.

"This is so nice," Ellen said after she had driven it to Pleasanton. "I swear some of these cars you all are picking up are keepers. I mean everything works perfectly. The air conditioning is ice cold."

"Well, you can't be driving it around. It needs to be kept out of sight. When we leave, if they trace us back to here, we don't need them to know what we're driving," he said after they parked the Pontiac in a storage lot they'd rented in Pleasanton.

"Once we get Dan to the pickup point and head out, I think we'll be fine," Ellen said.

They parked the Pontiac, and headed back to the mobile home park. "What do you make of the information the guy in D.C. gave us?"

Jack grimaced. "Well, I think we can finally figure out who the mystery guy was. Also, he's probably running around in a panic. Dan's said he'll tell the Feds the whole story. No wonder Bedford's so worried."

"Yeah, but they've flushed Dan's willingness to give them information down the toilet," Ellen said. "And now, I can see why someone above the pay grade of Bedford has put the kibosh on making that deal."

"And, screwed Dan. But, now it's starting to make some sense." Jack banged the steering wheel as he drove.

"Finally."

"Well, the bottom line is, we'll disappear, and be three million better off." Jack grumbled. "We really need to figure out where Bedford's hiding. And more important, who's the mystery guy."

"I'm with you on those two items. Hell, I'd rather have given it back and get on with our life," Ellen said. "What if they offered a deal and a little jail time? How would you feel about that?"

"Well, we've got enough money to not worry about me having to find a job with a prison record. You know?"

"Yeah."

Jack said, "I'd consider it if it was a year or less, but I don't think that's anywhere in the cards."

Ellen nodded her head in agreement. "How about the other guys? Have you talked with them?"

"Yep. Pogy would buy into that deal. Shoot, he's sitting on close to ten in the bank. And Roadhawg's too goofy to get a straight answer."

For days, Steve tried to get Dan to change his mind and not plead out. They sat in the room provided for attorneys and clients at the detention center.

"Listen, Steve. Talking in here is like talking in a corn patch. There ain't nothing but ears."

"If they so much as eves drop, we'd get you out of here Scot free."

"Sure thing. Like the deal they promised us to get me to turn myself in? Anyway, you need to talk to Christy in private. She'll tell you the plan. I'm sick and tired of the government lying, changing their promises, and stuff like leaking the info that got the house blown up."

"Listen…"

"No more listening. If chicken shit's the name of the game, well, we're going to show them how to play. This isn't the only place to live in peace. All they've got on me is bringing money into the country through the laundromat. That's nothing. I declared the income and paid the taxes."

Steve held up his hand. "Stop it. We all know that. The charges are trumped up and we all know that, too. And now, you want to plead out and serve time and be done? Right?"

Dan nodded his head and broke out in a toothy grin.

"Okay, I get the picture. I'll talk to Christy tonight when I'm over there," Steve said.

"New subject, counselor. Are you going to be calling me son in the future? And don't tell me I've gotta call you dad."

They both began to chuckle and then broke out in laughter.

"Okay, Son. I'm out of here." Steve continued to laugh.

CHAPTER THIRTY-THREE

Steve sat beside Dan at the sentencing. The judge asked if they were still pleading guilty. Steve answered and the judge read his "decision."

After a couple minutes, Dan stood. He was sentenced to thirty months. He smiled as the judge announced the sentence to be served in the Federal Detention Facility in Pleasanton, California.

Jack had always been an artist at planning.

"Okay, Steve, when will they get me out of here?" Dan broke out in a grin.

"This is tax day, the fifteenth. So, they should have you there by the first of May."

"That'd be mighty fine." Dan held his arms out as the deputy placed the cuffs on him. Christy stood behind the rail back of Dan. She leaned forward, hugged him, and whispered in his ear. Then he was led out of the room.

Steve closed his brief case and turned to face Christy and Grace. "Christy, I don't suppose you're going to tell me anything?"

"As an officer of the court, you don't need to know everything." Christy winked and wagged her head from side to side, imitating one of Steve's moves.

"I can't wait to see how all of this unfolds." Steve took Grace's hand as they walked out the court room.

Steve and Grace left the next morning for London. Christy met with George and went over all the building details. The new house would be furnished with new furniture, courtesy of the settlement. The movers placed the furniture as it was delivered. Christy's mood improved as the house began to take on a personality.

At the new real estate development site, Ken and Bob Jones were overseeing the crews surveying and laying out the new development. The veterans were working out better than expected. They were getting along and making significant and helpful decisions.

Dennis kept a low profile at Grand Lake in Oklahoma, still drawing his pension and disability from the military. Luds followed suit in St. Thomas.

Christy visited Dan. She hadn't been informed when they would be transferring him to Pleasanton.

"Dan, Honey, you've got to stop worrying about everyone and everything." She puckered a kiss even though the glass was between them.

"I know. I know, but I still worry about all of the things going on."

"Honey, I just told you everything about everything and it's all good. And do you want to know something else?"

"Sure."

"Steve showed me the wedding ring set he'd bought for Mom. I think they'll come back from London as Mister and Missus."

A grin covered his face.

"See, there you go. That smile wasn't so hard, was it?"

"Naw, I'm just happy for them." Dan's expression

changed to one of joy, then one of seriousness. "We need to know where that bastard Bedford is. There's no telling what he could do. And we really need to know who the mystery man is."

"They're working on it. Roadhawg said Quint thinks he's got it narrowed down."

Roadhawg made the phone call from San Diego again. Quint was at the same phone on a break from his FBI duties.

"That's right. I've got the name."

"Are you sure?"

"I've got a copy of the recommendation for Bedford's hire."

"Still doesn't prove anything."

"It gets better, Roadhawg, I've got his leave request. Plus, I checked out his airline travel for the days in question."

"Wow. That outta be enough to do it."

"But, I'd feel better if I handed it to you in person. You need to come back here. Can you?"

"Sure as hell, buddy. I'll catch the red eye and be there in the morning. I'll call you at work. I won't say anything on the phone except three numbers, like six, three, four. That'll be my arrival time at Washington National."

"I'll meet you there," Quint said.

"How long from National to your office?"

"Forty-five to an hour."

"Got it."

Roadhawg was calling from the airport's bank of phone booths. He made his way to an airline ticket counter. Pan Am had the earliest arrival at 5:52 a.m. His return left at 8:00 a.m.

Upon arrival at Washington National, Roadhawg made his call to Quint. His dilemma was calling Ellen and Jack. He had the mobile home phone number. If he had to call it, the new plan was to move immediately if they sensed any trouble. Ellen and Jack had rented a two-bedroom apartment in Castro Valley, located between Pleasanton and Oakland, for just such an emergency.

Roadhawg made the call. "Hey, there, change of plans. I'll be an extra two days."

"Okay." Ellen responded. "I don't think that will change anything."

"Tell Spudnut I'll have the icing on the cake when I get back."

"Okay, see ya there." Ellen had let him know they'd be at the apartment.

Jack was listening only to her side of the conversation.

"Okay, he's worried that something's screwed up?"

"No, Honey, he just said he'd have the icing on the cake when he got back. And I take it that he's going to have something substantial to have to be delayed."

"The icing and the cake are two things. I wonder if he's got the location of Bedford and the mystery man?"

"Sure sounds like it. God that'd be nice," Ellen said.

They lived with the suitcases open and ready to leave. Ellen grabbed her toiletries as Jack closed his suitcase. They walked out to the station wagon. Ellen got behind the wheel. Jack placed the two suitcases and one small one in the back, and got in the front seat.

In less than two minutes, they were on their way. She drove them to the storage lot, parked the station wagon, Jack transferred the luggage to the Pontiac and they drove away in that car..

It took about thirty minutes to make sure there were no tails and to get to the apartment located beside the freeway in Castro Valley.

"Well, I think we're still okay, but I'm a bit worried," Jack said as Ellen parked in the carport of their unit.

"Yes, it's got me a bit worried, too. Come on, let's take

in the suitcases and go buy groceries. And then you can buy me dinner."

Jack kept looking around as they walked in. Damn, the Feds couldn't have got to the mobile home that quick. We outta be okay, but still...

CHAPTER THIRTY-FOUR

Roadhawg checked his watch for the gazillionth time. The flight was fifteen minutes late when they touched down. At 6:20 a.m. he got off the aircraft, almost 25 minutes late.

He traveled under the name of Grant Geeting, but he still hurried as much as he could to get off the aircraft. That was no time for a screw up. *What will I do if Quint's not here?* Roadhawg checked his watch, then he spotted Quint leaning against a column off to the left of the deplaning passengers.

Roadhawg got it. *Ignore Quint.*

Quint searched for Roadhawg. At first, he didn't recognize Roadhawg's disguise as Grant Geeting. Roadhawg's attire passed for casual business with his suit jacket over his arm. And he sported a cover of facial hair. Roadhawg stopped with his back to Quint, to look at the departure board.

"Hey, Gooser." Roadhawg said only loud enough for Quint to hear. Quint's pilot handle was Goose. "I recognized you with that cheap-ass government issued briefcase."

Quint cleared his throat, turned and walked away from the briefcase like he was late for a date.

The Roadhawg walked over as casual as possible, and took a position beside the briefcase. After a couple of minutes, when he felt certain no one was watching him, he picked up the inexpensive, plastic briefcase. He didn't dare risk flying back to Oakland, so he checked the departures for the flight back to San Diego.

That morning, a U.S. Marshall came for Dan to transport him to Oakland. The powers to be informed Dan he could wear his own clothes at the minimum-risk facility. Dan was embarrassed to wear handcuffs as they walked to the boarding gate.

The flight took a little over an hour, gate-to-gate. The ride to Pleasanton took about forty minutes.

Grant Getting landed in San Diego. With his carry-on, he headed to the nearest men's room. He'd emptied the brief case in the Washington National terminal men's room. In San Diego he changed into shorts, tee shirt, topsiders, and Ray Ban shades. Buying a ticket one way to Oakland required only cash or a credit card in the name Mr. Garrett Chavez. Roadhawg appreciated the fact that travel in 1972 boarded on casual.

Roadhawg landed mid-afternoon. He didn't see any tails as he made two circuits with the courtesy van to the long term parking. He drove through downtown Hayward insuring he wasn't being followed, then he checked out the visitor's parking spaces at the Castro Valley apartment complex. Nothing. So, he picked out a parking spot.

"I saw the Pontiac out front and figured you all were here." Roadhawg hurried into the apartment and closed the door.

"What happened?" Jack said.

Roadhawg told him about the phone call and his in-and-out of D.C. When Roadhawg showed him what Goose gave him in his briefcase, they all were amazed at the paper trail one Thomas James Peterson had left.

"Jeez, he arrived a week before Bedford, and Tanner took the payroll." Ellen looked at several of the stapled pages.

"I'm sure," Jack said, "some slick attorney could 'reasonable doubt' the whole thing."

"Well, it's good enough for me to fry his ass," Roadhawg said.

Ellen left to make copies of the paperwork while Roadhawg and Jack decided how they would check out the mobile home to see if it were safe.

Jack went in the Pontiac. Ellen and Roadhawg went in the car Roadhawg had taken to the airport. There they waited in a shopping center parking lot, because if one of them had to be caught, it'd be Jack. Roadhawg had a new pilot's license and they needed Ellen for their escape, if needed.

"Okay, Roadhawg. We said forty-five minutes and then we'd go back to the apartment." Ellen checked her watch.

"Jeez, Louise, Ellen. You worry more than Danny. And I thought he was the biggest worry wart in the entire universe. It's only been forty minutes." Roadhawg looked out his window. "And looky here. There'is the ace-of-the-base in person."

Jack drove into the spot next to the wagon, and said to Ellen and Roadhawg, "It's cool. I went in the mobile home after staking it out. If the Feds were waiting, they would've already busted me. Let's go hide the Pontiac. I'm ready for happy hour."

"Now you're talking," Roadhawg said.

"You had me worried." Ellen got out and slugged his arm.

"No, you just love to hit me," Jack teased as Ellen got in

the Pontiac with him.

Later that evening, Ellen left to take the check-in call from Christy at a phone booth in Pleasanton where they were to bring each other up-to-date.

Ellen had hurried back to the mobile home park to tell them, "Hey, guys. Dan's sitting over at the Camp Parks joint as I speak."

"So, I guess we're still scheduled for a Fourth of July date?" Jack said.

"Well, here's to keeping a low profile and getting everything ready." Roadhawg lifted his beer in a toast.

Near the end of June, Dan's routine became comfortable for him. The air conditioned room at Club Fed made reading more than relaxing for him. The guard walked in and said, "Hey, Burton, you've got a visitor."

"Really? Who would be visiting me?" Dan sat up on the side of his bed.

"An FBI attorney or something. Name is Toscas."

"Tell him I don't talk to them anymore."

From behind the guard, Greg Toscas spoke as he walked around the guard. "Don't blame you. But you might want to hear what I've got to offer."

"No, no, no. I don't make any deals with your type ever again. You all lie straight to my face and expect me to listen. Ha. Once, shame on you...twice, shame on me."

"Guard, can you leave now?" Toscas said more than asked.

"Well, seein' as how I'm here in yawl's Federal pen, I guess I don't have much choice. But, I ain't interested in any of your so called offers."

Toscas introduced himself and took the only chair in the room. Dan stayed seated on the bed.

"I've looked into your ordeal here. You were lied to, your family assaulted and injured...all of those things were wrong."

"Ah-h-h, and you have a Presidential pardon in that briefcase and I'm free to go now?" Dan began to laugh.

"Not yet, but we do need to talk. And you can call me Greg. Can I call you Dan?"

Dan shrugged his shoulder and picked up his book.

Rambling, Toscas talked for almost an hour about the original deal. Tell the Feds who originally took the payroll and testify to that in court. Plus, give back the money, and they'd let him go. Free and clear.

"So, what assurances do I get this time? Another bullshit dance up to the alter and I get screwed again?"

"No, this time the deal will come from the Attorney General, in person."

"You mean like, the Attorney General of the United States?"

"That's correct."

"Not good enough. I want a Presidential pardon for all of us, and my sentence commuted."

"That's not going to happen. President Nixon is in the middle of an election campaign. But, he'll give the AG the authorization."

"So, you say it's not going to happen. I agree, Greg. Without the Presidential Pardon …it ain't gonna happen."

Greg tried to talk around it, but Dan told him he was wasting his time. Dan suggested to Greg that he do most of the talking with Steve Mitchell. Dan's father-in-law.

That evening Dan called Christy and told her about the visit. She said she'd contact Steve and have him call Dan after Steve contacted Greg. Greg told Dan the FBI had assigned him to the Seattle office to work out a deal.

"Hey, Honey," Dan said, "for the Fourth, let's not celebrate this year. Maybe we'll do the fireworks later."

Christy called Ellen two days later at the appointed check-in time and brought her up to date. The best news,

Christy told Ellen, was that Steve was super encouraged after he'd talked to Toscas.

Christy had got the message. Get a hold of Roadhawg and Jack and bring them up-to-date. Christy knew Dan thought if there was a chance all of them could get a pardon or whatever, then it was worth waiting.

CHAPTER THIRTY-FIVE

Dan's phone privileges were unrestricted, but he didn't trust his privacy on the phone. He called Christy's new office in Gig Harbor and got the secretary. He asked her to have Christy call him because he was worried about the Vette. The code, if he asked or left a message about the Corvette, meant top priority.

In his room, Dan continued to read a John D. McDonald novel. He thought he'd like to live the simple life-style of Travis McGee. By six in the evening, he began to worry because he hadn't heard from Christy since his early afternoon call.

The guard came in and gave Dan a message. Dan tried not to show his anger after he read the time of the message -- a little after two. He made his way to the phone room and called the new house number.

Christy answered on the second ring. "I was getting worried when I didn't hear back," she said.

"I just got the message." Dan wadded up the note and threw it in the trash.

"How's everything going?"

"I got a very strange visit today from an FBI guy named

Greg Toscas. He seems honest enough. But I don't trust the Feds as far as you can throw them."

"What did he want?"

Dan sighed. "He's confused and thinks he's Monty Hall and wants to play Let's Make A Deal."

"You've gotta be kidding," Christy said. "What's the deal?"

"He's being very vague but he said they screwed up and he wants to try to make it right with all parties involved. We need to get Steve talking to him, Christy."

"Ah-h-h, I'll get a hold of Steve and have him call you tomorrow." She wanted to know how he felt about delaying the escape plans for the Fourth of July. "I think I'll have to put off the boys' celebration for the fireworks."

When she mentioned the "boys" it was Jack and Roadhawg. If it were Jason and Allen, she would have mentioned them by name.

"Yes, yes." Dan was silent for a couple of beats. "I know they were really planning on a big show, but they'll get over it." He just let her know that he agreed.

She went on to tell him about the real estate development. The water, sewer, and electricity were going in. The grading and roads were finished, and George had the foundation poured for the club house and two more of the model homes. All in all, they were ahead of schedule. Jones and Ken were getting involved and were a big help.

"Well, maybe we've helped those two turn a corner," Dan said.

"George and his three crews are making really good progress on the model homes, too. The first one is framed, the roof is on, and the electricians were pulling wire today."

"Fantastic. How're Jason and Allen adapting to the new house?"

"They've met three or four boys their ages and they're anxious to help with the construction. Get this. Steve and Momma took them over there and they're helping out by picking up the wood scraps and trash."

"Steve's actually pitching in?"

"You mean, Grandpa? Yes, he's walking around supervising and keeping the time cards. Get this. He's paying the kids fifty cents an hour. If you listened to Jason and Allen, you'd think they struck gold."

Dan began laughing, then said, "I'm really glad they're learning the value of a dollar."

"Well, they miss you, tremendously. I promised they could talk to you. Is there anything else?"

"Nope, Honey, I think we covered it all."

The boys couldn't stop talking to Dan about all the things going on. They loved being out of school, helping build the new houses, playing with their new friends, and getting to go sailing with their grandparents.

Dan wiped the tears as he listened to the boys. He made sure they couldn't tell he was upset, because he wasn't happy and missed everyone in spades.

Dan got back on the phone with Christy. They said their goodbyes. He made sure the guards didn't see him wipe the last few tears from his cheeks.

Damn it, if that Greg Toscas is for real, I'd make the Feds a hell of a deal to get out of here. But I can't let my hopes get up too much. I could've been outta here in less than two weeks, and now who knows what those lying bastards have to offer.

Greg met with Steve and a discussion began in earnest. Steve and Greg agreed to begin on a first name basis.

"Here's the deal. You've got my client on money laundering. And that's a weak deal. He paid taxes on the money. It's money from a foreign trust account. I don't see the crime." Steve slammed his papers down on the table in disgust.

"Okay, okay. We both know they have the money from the payroll."

"And your point is?"

"That's possession of stolen goods."

"No crime was ever reported to the authorities on Okinawa. What's the crime?" Steve leaned back in his leather chair and put on his best now-I've-got-you smirk.

"Okay, so, there's a lot of gray area. But, the fact is the income from those funds is what Mr. Burton most likely was bringing back into the country. Why else the laundromat ruse?"

"Greg, let's quit pissing around. What do you want? And then I'll tell you Mr. Burton's position."

Greg indicated they wanted the money back, some time spent in custody, and maybe parole.

When Greg tossed out, "Maybe parole," Steve showed no emotion, though, he was pleased to hear it. He wanted to know how they were supposed to trust the Fed's deal, if one were hammered out?

"The Attorney General, John Mitchell, will personally sign off on it. You'll have it before any funds are received, etcetera."

"Well, I'm afraid I have to see a Presidential Pardon for all the parties concerned. I mean these guys are combat heroes. They've been screwed, lied to, and treated like scum."

"Listen, I'm with you on that, but it's straight from J. Edgar. He's adamant."

"Well, as Dan would say, J. Edgar can kiss his ass. Dan won't put his combat brothers in harm's way. Nor will he accept anything at this point, less than those pardons."

"The director will not go to the President on this one. We're in a tough re-election campaign. The Democrats will have a field day with a bunch of Presidential pardons."

"Well, you go back to J. Edgar. Hell, let me meet with Nixon and I'll bet you dollars to donuts, I'll get a deal."

"Steve, that will never happen. But I'll put that suggestion in my report. As you know, I'm reporting directly to the Assistant Director."

"I take it the AD or words to that effect."

Greg began to laugh. "Words to that effect."

Later that evening, Dan got the call from Christy. She brought him up to speed with Greg Toscas and Steve's meeting.

"Well, Honey, you know I'll not give up on any of the issues. Things are going just fine. Mighty fine, as a matter of fact." Dan let her know he was ready to pull off the escape of the decade, in his opinion.

"Well, I'm encouraged that the Feds are wanting to talk."

"Me, too. But, I don't care, really and truly." They said their goodbyes.

Christy told Dan three days later on the check-in date, she'd brought Ellen up to date with the entire situation. Ellen in code had told Christy, she couldn't wait to get back to tell Jack and Roadhawg.

"Well, Piss." Roadhawg exhaled after Ellen told the guys about the progress between Steve and Greg Toscas.

"No kidding. That means we'll have to wait until Labor Day. Two damned months from now?" Jack shook his head.

"Do we really have to wait until a holiday?" Ellen said.

"Yes, because the holiday routine will be extra lax. The last thing we want is some guard at the prison opening up on us with their M-16 as we fly over the concertina wire fence."

Sensing Ellen's concerns and worries, Roadhawg said, "But, Ellen, with our plan there's no way they'll open fire. I promise."

After some conversation about the change, Ellen looked at Jack and then Roadhawg. "Well, we need to change our plans. I need to extend the rental. I don't see that as a problem. And we'll need to stock up on groceries and what not."

They all agreed and planned the strategy for the next two months. Roadhawg would do another stay in Southern California checking on all their property down there, and a few days to get away for a bit. His helicopter lessons were completed, but he had the license in the name of Garrett Chavez. Garrett turned out to be a very good student and made an excellent pilot.

Jack told Ellen and Roadhawg that the extension to Labor Day worried him. He didn't want to stay anywhere too long. And another two months seemed like an eternity.

CHAPTER THIRTY-SIX

The negotiations between Greg Toscas, a new man from the Justice Department, named Bob Watson, and Steve escalated and ebbed. The government wanted two main things.

First, they wanted the names of the original thieves. This would include testifying in court against them. Roadhawg had taken pictures of the aircraft being unloaded by Bedford's cohorts during the original heist. So that item was easy to prove.

The thieves all wore flight helmets and were unidentifiable, but three of them on board the helicopter helped unload the payroll boxes. The flight manifest listed only three crew members plus the two armed guards that were blindfolded and tied together. The pictures would prove the crew members were part of the heist.

Second, the government wanted the money back. Steve, with Dan's approval, agreed to both of those terms. The other issue the government still pushed was time behind bars. But, Steve negotiated with the government side to agree to drop the time behind bars in exchange for Dan, Jack, and Roadhawg's testimony. And, after the election,

Dan would receive a Presidential pardon.

Just before Labor Day weekend, the deal was hammered out in the Seattle FBI field office.

"Okay, Greg, just to be clear. After the election, we'll get the pardon." Steve left no doubt about that point.

"Yes, very much over J. Edgar's objections. The Oval Office wants this over, and the Presidential advisors have weighed in on this and have Nixon's approval." Toscas frowned.

"Now, we just sit and wait? Can't you do something to get my client out of jail?"

"No. Politically, it could be very damaging, and we're only talking eight weeks." Greg rubbed his chin.

"No, we're actually talking ten plus weeks. Greg, I want my client out. Free and clear...yesterday. You know beyond a shadow of a doubt, he didn't take the money. He was never out of the squadron area the entire morning in question. Come on."

"The rest of them are getting a free walk. They took close to eighteen million dollars." Toscas held up his index finger. "And they knew it was the military payroll." He held up two fingers. Then he held up three fingers. "And finally they buried it in a damn Swiss Bank. You know all this." He still held up three fingers.

The Justice Department guy listened and then reiterated that the White House had instructed John Mitchell to have the pardon ready for President Nixon's signature. Toscas would personally present it to Dan as soon as it was signed and delivered to the Seattle office.

The negotiations had lingered over the last nine weeks, and all three men let their frustrations show. Greg blurted out, "Steve, you and I both know, they're getting off easy. Very easy. And J. Edgar is still trying to nix the deal. But, the White House holds all the cards. So Steve, let me be very clear on this. I'm not spending what little credit I still have with the powers-that-be trying to get your client out earlier than after the election. They said it will be the day before Thanksgiving. They think they're doing a huge amount of good will to a well decorated veteran." Greg made quote signs with his hands, and scooted his chair away from their table.

"Okay, but…it would be a nice conciliatory gesture."
Steve glanced at Greg, and the Justice Department man. He shook his head and rolled his eyes. "Then we have a deal?" he said.

Greg nodded his head and the three men shook hands. Plans were made to fly down to Pleasanton for Dan's release. Steve, along with Greg, would present Dan with the pardon before Thanksgiving.

CHAPTER THIRTY-SEVEN

The planning for the breakout simmered down. Jack, Ellen, and Roadhawg only had a few items to cover. The cars were in storage. Roadhawg would rent a helicopter from the flight school once or twice a week. For all intents and purposes, the negotiated settlement was over, but the three of them wanted to be ready to go on a twenty-hour notice. Jack insisted on not abandoning the plan until they could drive to the Pleasanton Federal Penitentiary and leave with Dan.

The last item was the landing zone where they'd rendezvous after they picked up Dan. They decided to take one more look-see. No, really it was Jack who wanted the last look-see. The two-lane, winding road is called Niles Canyon Road. The landing spot they'd picked was to the eastern exit of the rolling costal hills and cattle grazing land. The spot sat behind a hill obscure from the main road. The gate didn't have a Keep Out sign let alone a lock. The three drove there and each agreed it was a good spot to land, shut down the helicopter, and drive off.

"Yeah, I could land it right here easy enough," Roadhawg said.

Ellen pointed toward the gate. "And I'd be waiting down the road, and come in once I saw you approaching."

"I think," Jack hesitated, "the best part is we depart the detention facility and fly off to the south. We're all familiar with Southern California, and it'd be the logical direction for them to start looking for us."

"Hopefully, we'd have a good three hours head start heading north." Roadhawg thought out loud.

"We can't count on it, but that's the plan," Jack said as they walked back to where they'd parked the station wagon by the road in Niles Canyon.

At that same time in Gig Harbor, Christy walked through what had been her fire destroyed house that George had rebuilt. She and George talked as the clean-up crew put on the finishing touches.

"Well," Christy said, "the house is technically finished. The crews have done a fantastic job, but the renters are ticked off because they wanted in by the middle of the month."

"The building department," George moaned, "held up several of the inspections. Now that the landscaping is finally finished, I've got an idea as a band aid for the renters. Why don't you give them half a month's rent as a peace offering?"

"That's what I've offered them." Christy nodded her head. "I know they wanted to be in before school started but it starts next Tuesday. That's a week away."

They finished their walk-through inspection.

"I can't wait to show Mother and Steve and the boys the finished house. Absolutely amazing."

As they walked outside, Christy admired the landscaping truck. The sign on the door of the truck read, "Veteran's Landscaping. We're putting it back together. "

Steve called Christy to bring her up to date on the deal

SEE DAN RUN

with Greg Toscas and the Justice Department. She, in turn, placed two phone calls from different phone booths to Dennis in Oklahoma and John in St. Thomas. Her purse was very heavy from the rolls of quarters. Dennis and John were both relieved and excited about her news. She reminded both of them to remain guarded with their optimism.

The next day was the scheduled time to contact Ellen. When Christy called, Ellen didn't seem to be able to contain herself.

"Girl," Ellen giggled, "do you realize we can all get our lives back. Live as normal good friends, and see each other when ever in the hell we want?"

"I think we outta spend a month in St. Thomas with John and Diane drinking all those foo foo drinks at happy hour to celebrate," Christy said.

"And, I can only imagine how anxious you are to get Dan back home."

Christy relayed how well the real estate development was taking off. In the first two weeks, they'd already sold seven of the eighty plus lots. The club house was almost finished along with the indoor pool.

Christy used a roll and a half of her beloved quarters and the lighter purse felt so much better.

She called Dan from the office that evening before she went home. He was worried that the deal wouldn't go through even with all the assurances from Steve.

"They lied before and I don't trust them."

"Honey, I know you want out of there as much as I want you home with me. But, what do they have to gain if they're lying? Really, I have a good feeling about this."

"Well, we'll see. Hey, how're Jason and Allen doing? Are they excited about starting school?"

"Yes, and no. They want to start driving nails, but they also want to be with their friends from school. Oh, Mom asked me if I'd ever wanted a brother or sister."

She could hear Dan laughing, "What a dog. Steve is un-be-lieve-able."

"Steve? What about Mom? Ah-h-h, wait a minute. Mom's only forty-four and I'm barely twenty-seven. What do you think?"

"Fantastic is what I think. It's been so long. I think you'd better be careful once we're alone. I've got triplets stored up by now."

Dan ended the conversation elated that in less than twelve weeks it'd be over. But, in his mind it would be over one way or the other, because he still didn't trust the government. He'd been screwed over way too many times. He'd been screwed in the Marine Corps in Vietnam, and now all of this. And plan B was still a real possibility. In his mind, he needed to be worried.

CHAPTER THIRTY-EIGHT

Pogy had been hiding out in Ft. Meyers, Florida. He'd called Luds and then they called him back from a payphone. He'd been living on a houseboat under an assumed name.

Everyone and anyone looking at the payroll heist knew Pogy's aborted roll in the caper.

Jack, Dan, and Roadhawg all thought the time had come for Pogy to disappear at the time when they had to.

Pog kept in touch every week with Luds. But his call shocked everyone.

In the middle of October, Christy, got a disturbing phone call from Diane and Luds in St. Thomas. Luds asked Christy to call Dan.

She got Dan on the phone and said, "Pogy said a round went clean through the houseboat less than two inches from his head."

"Tell me what you can." She knew from Dan's tone, he didn't want her to say too much.

She told Dan about the attempt on Pogy's life. She let Dan know Pogy had disappeared to be safe.

"Christy, are we thinking it's the same guy?"

"Yes, and it has everyone on edge."

Dan hesitated. "Can you and the boys go visit someone, someplace away?"

"Yes. Steve and Mom have taken care of all the details. I'll still call you. You can call the real estate office, because I'll be checking for calls. Plus, you can call your father-in-law."

Pog told Luds he'd kept a thirty-six-foot sailboat for just such an emergency. Pog stocked it every week with fresh provisions, and lots of cash. He asked Luds to get a hold of the others and to tell them to be careful. Both Pogy and Luds worried they were all targets.

Pog also said, "If they come at me at sea, they're in for a big ass surprise, Buddy. I'll call in a few." Pog hung up, walked to his thirty-six Santana, untied the mooring lines, climbed aboard, started the marine engine and pulled away from the slip. All the while, he kept a low profile behind the boat's steering wheel. He had a .50 caliber that could be mounted on either side of the sailboat, several M-16s, plus two RPG launchers. He sighed in relief when he was several miles out in the Gulf.

For the long Halloween break, Roadhawg took off for Southern California. Jack and Ellen stayed in Pleasanton. They took an early morning drive to Helen's Breakfast Diner in Danville, then they drove to the Altamont Pass by neighboring Livermore, east of Pleasanton. The race track there was abandoned and Jack wanted to check it out.

"This would be a perfect place for us to meet Roadhawg. He could pick me up, and you could drive to the pickup spot over in Niles Canyon." Jack surveyed the huge asphalt parking lot. "Then Roadhawg and I could be off to pick up Danny."

"Okay. Get in and let's time the drive to the pickup spot," Ellen said.

On the way, they passed just south of where Dan was incarcerated. Jack looked north at the detention center. *I wonder what Danny's doing this morning?*

"Do you really think they'll make the deal?" Ellen said.

"I think they're seriously thinking about it, and I don't think they'd go to all this trouble if they weren't. But, I don't have a warm fuzzy about it."

A bit later, Ellen drove to the access road off Niles Canyon. Jack checked his watch. "Just under thirty-three minutes. Let's give it thirty-five."

"And the plan's for me to pull on down this dirt road and wait for you all to land?" Ellen sounded tense.

"Yep."

"And the flight time to the prison from the pickup is seven minutes, then three on the ground at the most, and then eight minutes to get from there to here." She said more than asked.

"We'll give you a fifteen-minute head start. It'd be way better for you to be a few minutes early. We're not contacting Livermore tower even though we'll fly right by them."

"What if they try to contact you?"

"We'll be up Livermore airport's tower frequency, and approaching from the east. If we're lucky, it'll be a clear day, and we'll be coming out of the sun."

Ellen sighed, "I worry that the guards will try to shoot you all."

"Come on El, we've got that covered." Jack knew she worried and in an attempt to take her mind off of it, he leaned over and kissed her. "Come on, let's go home and fool around. Roadhawg's gone and…"

"That's what you said yesterday afternoon, and after dinner, and again this morning."

"Well, it must be working." He squeezed her hand.

"Nobody's around here." She checked the rearview mirror then pulled Jack close as they embraced.

The following morning, Christy's secretary told her she had a phone call and the man wouldn't say who he was, just that it was important. The secretive man was Quint. She gave Quint Steve's phone number and instructions that he could talk to Steve or leave a message.

After Quint called Steve, Steve contacted Christy and she waited in Steve's office since Quint was going to call back at four o'clock. A couple of minutes before four, the phone rang. Steve answered and gave Christy the phone.

Quint didn't say his name. He just began. "Christy, I'd never call except I think this is really important. Listen, there's a good chance they could be listening. I'm calling from a payphone, if that's any good."

"Gotch ya."

"I pulled a few strings and checked the phone records for the guy who recommended Bedford for the FBI. And he's got several long distant phone calls at approximately the same time each day."

"Okay."

"First three calls were from your area code a week to ten days ago. Then last week, several more were to or from the Ft. Meyers area in Florida. Here's what's got my attention. The last couple of days they're all from the area where Dan's imprisoned."

"Wait. Let me get this straight. Here in Gig Harbor, then Florida, and now in California?"

"Exactly. I don't know what it all means except my antenna is up. First your area code and now out by Dan in California."

"No kidding."

"Listen, if they caught me pulling those phone records, I could be joining Dan. But take this down." He'd called in some favors, and the calls were placed to a Holiday Inn in Livermore, California, room 108, rented to a David Smith.

Christy wrote everything down. "I've got it all...Holiday Inn, Livermore, room one-oh-eight."

She didn't say Quint's name, but thanked him before they disconnected. She immediately called Luds and Diane. Luds repeated the information and how it coincided with the dates on the attempt on Pogy's life. After the phone call, Christy bit her lip. Her next call to Ellen wasn't until Thursday evening. "Damn it, I need to talk to them right now. I'll fly down there."

It took Christy four hours to fly to Oakland and rent a car. By eleven o'clock she drove into the mobile home lot. She knocked on the door.

"Christy. What the hell?" Roadhawg had arrived earlier that evening. He looked around as he pulled her inside. "Excuse, me." He pulled on his jean shorts. "What's the matter? I thought you were some dead beat complaining about something."

Jack and Ellen rushed out of their bedroom. "Christy, what's happened?" Jack rubbed his eyes.

After she told them, she and Ellen left to call St. Thomas.

Jack's mind began to spin, "We need to check out just who in the hell is staying in room one-oh-eight out at the Holiday Inn. And I don't think it's good news."

"Well, it's gotta be the same somebody who checked out Gig Harbor. Then tried to shoot Pog in Ft. Meyers, and now they're out here."

"I don't think it's us they're looking for. But I think we know who it is."

"He's gotta be checking out Danny." They both nodded their heads. Jack finished. "And it can't be good."

The women returned and relayed Luds' concerns. Christy needed to get back to Seattle. They decided to have Ellen drive Christy back rather than fly. Then Ellen could fly back to Oakland later the next morning. They checked flight times. She'd arrive around two in Oakland. Without a lot of fanfare, the women left to turn in Christy's car at the airport and then on to Seattle. They'd leave Ellen's car with Christy.

"I swear, they're running scared is the only way any of this makes sense," Roadhawg said the next morning as he and Jack drove to the Holiday Inn.

Jack opened the duffel and checked the hand guns—two Browning 9mm automatics and a .32 automatic with a silencer and no serial numbers.

Jack rode shotgun. He looked at Roadhawg. "Bedford and this Peterson guy have a lot to lose if Dan's deal goes through."

"Yes, sir. Any bets Bedford's in room one-oh-eight?" Roadhawg said.

"Here's what I think. We'll stake out the place. See if we can follow whoever it is and then we'll make a move at that time."

They arrived at a little past nine. The trees behind the motel gave them good cover. They parked the car and stayed out of sight. The door to room 108 was in clear view. A little before ten-thirty, Bedford left room 108 and walked over to an obvious rental car. He drove out of the lot as the two sleuths scrambled back to their station wagon.

Staying well behind Bedford, they took an exit east of the facility where Dan was held. Bedford pulled off the two lane country road into a gated pasture. Trees kept his car out of sight. Jack and Roadhawg drove past, unnoticed.

"Dirtbag has no clue we're here, let alone following him," Roadhawg said as he continued north. "I say let's go kill him. We know he's the one who shot at Pogy."

"And Bedford's probably got a rifle with a scope to take out Danny. His yard time starts in about fifteen minutes at eleven-thirty. But, see if you'll buy into this?"

Jack told Roadhawg his fast developing plan. Roadhawg broke out into a huge grin as he turned the car around, and headed back toward Bedford's parked car. Roadhawg eased their car a little past Bedford's car, then stopped out of sight. Jack checked both Browning's and shoved thirteen round clips into each one.

Jack handed one to Roadhawg. He took it along with the silenced .32 and said, "I like your plan a whole lot. Let's do it."

Jack took the other 9mm as Roadhawg eased the station wagon back near Bedford's parked rental.

CHAPTER THIRTY-NINE

The overcast from the San Francisco Bay extended well behind them to the east. The cool breeze from the west was in their face as they crept up to an unsuspecting Bedford. Roadhawg nudged Jack and pointed toward Bedford who stood by the open driver's door leaning on the roof of the car, looking through a large set of binoculars. Jack and Roadhawg recognized Bedford was scoping out the outdoor exercise compound of Camp Parks less than a quarter of a mile away.

Jack's mind raced. Holy shit. He's looking for a kill shot. Roadhawg pulled a gun out of his jacket as they closed in on the engrossed sniper-to-be.

Jack grabbed Bedford by the shoulder. "Well, looky here what we got. You scumbag."

"What the hell?" Bedford shouted.

"This is curtains for you." Roadhawg stuck his .32 silencer against Bedford's temple.

Jack jerked the binoculars out of Bedford's hand. Bedford kept silent.

Jack began. "What were you looking for? Dan? Well, your sniper days are over." Part of Jack's plan was to stay

215

cool, calm and collected. No profanity, just get down to business.

"I suppose if we look in the trunk, we won't find a rifle with a scope...would we?" Jack said.

"You idiots. Get that gun away from my head. This is a free country and you assholes are in deep shit, anyway." Bedford glanced at Roadhawg. "I said get that gun away from my head, Hegidio."

"You probably wonder how we just happened by." Roadhawg pressed the barrel harder against Bedford's head. "Move real slow and turn around. Put your hands behind your back. Please, do something stupid so I can do something that'll make me feel good. Now, turn around."

Bedford did as he was told. Jack looked for something to tie Bedford's hands. He tore the leather strap off Bedford's binocular case, and tied his hands in front.

"So you say we're in deep shit. Is that right? Well, want to know a few things Bed...ford?" Roadhawg got close to Bedford's face, while he pressed the automatic into Bedford's crotch.

Jack reached in Bedford's car, took the keys out of the ignition and walked to the trunk. He returned with a M-14 with a fitted scope. "Was that you and these binoculars looking at us at our memorial service last fall?"

"I have no clue what you're talking about." One corner of Bedford's mouth twitched. Jack nodded to Roadhawg as they both noticed it.

"Hey, Slick." Roadhawg pressed the issue. "You know when you lie your mouth twitches. Now here's something else."

Jack took over. "You stayed in Fort Meyers and made several calls from there."

"That's a lie."

"Before that, you spent last week in the Seattle area. Freddy, Freddy, you're getting into deep water here. And you're still lying." Jack slugged him in the stomach. Bedford bent over, gasping.

Roadhawg stepped in. "Lordy, Jack. That looked productive. And then you spent the last couple of days out at the Holiday Inn."

Bedford stood, still gasping.

"So, here's where you are. You're going to do what your partner in crime told you to do. Disappear. Vanish. Whatever. And if you ever put in to collect your pension, we're coming and I promise we'll send you to hell." Jack pointed his index finger like a gun and cocked it with his thumb.

"As for today," Roadhawg said, "you're not getting a free pass, you son of a bitch. Trying to kill Pogany. Huge, huge mistake. You do realize that, don't you?"

"I have no clue what you two idiots are talking about," Bedford managed to say.

Roadhawg looked at Jack who nodded. Roadhawg took the .32 and pointed it at Bedford's forehead. Bedford squeezed his eyes. Roadhawg pulled the trigger. But not before he pointed it straight in the air.

"I knew you were bluffing." Bedford's voice quivered. "I just knew it."

"Well, tell that to Mr. T. J. Peterson," Jack said as Roadhawg yanked Bedford's right arm clear of his torso. "As for what we want to emphasize is you can leave here dead, or otherwise."

"Right." Bedford began to laugh.

"I'd take it easy, Bedford, you bastard. You've got two choices," Jack indicated for Roadhawg to continue.

"You can leave here alive," Roadhawg said, grinning, "but if, you ever come close to any of us again...you'll be dead. Understand?"

Bedford turned toward Jack, "And?"

Jack began moving from side-to-side, flexing his hands, while he did his McQueen half smile.

"What's so funny?" Bedford tried to yank his arm from

Roadhawg.

"It's your choice, Freddy boy." Roadhawg pulled Bedford's arm even higher.

"You're hurting my arm," Bedford cried.

"You need to hurry up and give us an answer," Jack said.

"Or, what?" Bedford winced.

"Or Jack or I will toss a coin to see who gets to blow your brains out. Then put this gun in your dead hands, and pop off a round to get gunshot residue on your right hand to match the entry to your right temple. That's what...Freddy."

After a few moments of silence, Jack took over. "Well, silence is no answer, so Roadhawg tell him what that means."

"No answer is, duh, no. Got any last words, Bed...ford?"

"Are you two assholes crazy?"

"Jack, who gets to do the honors?" Roadhawg tilted his head.

"I'd love to," Jack said. "For all he's done. Hell, yes, I want to. Please, I really want to."

"So, do I." Roadhawg exhaled.

"Wanna toss a coin?"

"You flip it and I'll call." Roadhawg pulled a quarter from his pocket.

"You incompetent idiots." Bedford began to wiggle loose.

Jack looked at Roadhawg with a deer-lost-in-the-headlights expression. Roadhawg's lips curled, and he said, "This is for Herb."

"Herb, who?" Bedford said.

"Herb Schutt," Jack said. "The one you selectively scheduled, and bragged about it to me when you sent Toddy and me to go fly Hueys."

Roadhawg cleared Bedford's right hand, placed the

silenced barrel in Bedford's palm and pulled the trigger.

Bedford screamed and fell to the ground, kicking. Roadhawg handed the automatic to Jack who reached down, jerked Bedford to his feet, untied the leather strap from Bedford's hands, and took the bleeding right hand.

"Just so you learn to write left handed…this one's for Todd, and for taking a shot at Pog, and for being in the Seattle area, and for trying to take a shot at Danny today." Jack placed the gun against Bedford's bleeding palm and shot a second round through it.

Bedford collapsed on the ground, this time against the car. Roadhawg took a rag out of the rifle's zippered case and bandaged the bleeding right hand.

"And Freddy, you can tell the hospital," Jack said, "you accidently shot yourself while playing with this little peashooter." He held up the weapon and ejected the clip.

Roadhawg laughed. "And you lost the clip after the incident. And, oh my goodness, the gun just started going off."

"Now, get in the car and get out of here. Oh, yeah, the nearest hospital is in Livermore. Any service station can give you directions." Jack flipped him off.

"I…I can't drive," Bedford cried.

"Then sit here and bleed to death," Roadhawg said.

Jack followed with, "And here's my last thought. If you or Peterson don't disappear, we'll be coming after you."

"Do we make ourselves clear? Answer me." Roadhawg growled in Bedford's face.

"Yes, I've got it."

Roadhawg yanked Bedford off the ground and leaned him against the car.

"It was you on that hill watching us last year? Wasn't it?" Jack said.

Bedford nodded.

P.R. STEELE

CHAPTER FORTY

Ellen had arrived from Seattle and paced in the mobile home waiting for Jack and Roadhawg to drive into the carport.

When they arrived they told her who they found and what they did. She remained silent and asked no questions.

Then Roadhawg said, "Well, is anyone up for something to eat? I'll buy. We could go to Helen's in Danville or grab something local."

"Why don't you guys go? I'm not very hungry." Ellen sighed.

"Honey, what's the matter?"

"I don't want to talk about it."

"Hey, you two, I feel like getting out for a while. Ahh, why don't I go grab a bite and let you have some time." Roadhawg moved toward the front door.

"Joe, you don't have to go," Ellen said.

"Naw, that's alright." He tilted his head as he opened the door. "Really, I'm starving. Okay?" He winked as he walked out.

Jack looked at her. "Ellen, what's going on?"

"Today, I just…" She explained how she felt, all kind of

screwed up.

Jack walked over to the chair at the dining room table and wrapped his arms around her.

Tears ran down her cheeks onto Jack's arm. He scooted a chair next to hers.

"At times, it's too much." Ellen went on and tried to explain how she wanted to live like normal people. When would she and Jack get to live in a real home, live in a real house, raise a family, go to a movie, take a vacation?

"I know, I know. I just don't know how to make it all end," Jack said with a worried look on his face. "But, Honey, I have to tell you today, I felt elated."

Ellen interrupted, "About shooting Bedford?"

"Baby, when we were in country we did a bunch of lousy stuff that made no sense. We weren't protecting any American lives, values or anything."

"What's that got to do with anything..."

Jack now interrupted Ellen, hugged her and said, "Today, it was like I finally got to do something to protect people...no my family. It was like I was finally doing something to make a difference."

Jack went on to tell how frustrated he was. No real future, being on the run, not being able to start a family, and living like they were.

Ellen agreed and held him tight, then said, "I keep wishing it could all come to an end. Then you come home today and you almost killed someone. I know he deserves it, but sometimes...it's just too much."

They talked about how Joe, the comical Roadhawg, was starting to show the effects, like walking out a while before. Then Ellen spoke about how hard it must be on Christy.

"Honey, I know you're close to Christy. How's she doing?"

"She doesn't mean to, but she shuts me out. I mean she keeps herself super busy with the boys, her work, and the real estate development. But, you know, Jack, I think she's frazzled."

Jack changed the subject. "It'll all be over in a couple of months and then we can go back to Balboa, birth a bunch of little shits, and get on with our lives." Jack held her close.

"What if I go visit Christy for a couple of days?"

"Sounds like an idea. You could fly and arrive unannounced. Screw the Feds. They won't know you're coming."

"Do you think it'd be okay?" Ellen wiped her eyes.

"Hell, yes. Fly up there on a fake ID. Or get a ticket under your name. Heck, it'd throw the Feds for a loop. And then you can fly out to somewhere else, and then fly back here. Hey, Honey." Jack began to grin.

"What?"

"Wanna try to start a family right now?" Jack gave her the old Groucho Marx up and down eyebrow routine.

"Thought you'd never take the hint."

Ellen flew to Seattle under an assumed name, but rented the car in her own name. She drove to Christy's real estate office in Gig Harbor.

When she walked in, Christy was at a huge table with a topographic model of the development project. Lots were numbered, many with sold markers on them.

Christy turned and recognized Ellen. "Oh, my God. What are you doing here?"

"Coming to pay you a visit. I've missed you and the boys, and I thought the trip would do me good. It's not a bad time, is it?"

Christy embraced Ellen. "No it's a good time." Then she broke into tears. The two women made their way into Christy's office. With the door closed they talked for almost an hour. Christy's receptionist held her calls.

"Do you really believe they'll make a deal before December?" Ellen said. "Dan and his attorney are at odds. Steve thinks they're legit this time. But you know Dan. He has very little faith in the Feds."

"Oh, my God. I forgot to tell you the latest. Do you remember Bedford, that bastard from Okinawa?"

Christy shook her head. "What about him?"

Ellen told her the whole story.

"You mean they caught him setting up to shoot Dan?" Christy gasped.

The shock in that turn of events pulled the conversation to the same place it took Ellen days before.

"Ellen, I swear, at times I want to throw it all away. Forget the whole mess. Then I realize how much I love Dan and...it's hard at times. I mean I've got the boys, and..." She broke down.

Ellen held her as they both wept.

Steve Mitchell met with Christy, Ellen, and Grace at Christy's new house. Steve went over the proposed plan from the government.

"Here's the deal. They've screwed around because of J. Edgar. The guy I'm dealing with, Greg Toscas, has been very candid and up front with their side of the deal." Steve shuffled some papers and handed one to each of the women.

He continued, "These are the preliminary settlement agreements."

The women looked over the main points highlighted in bold.

"We'll be meeting next Monday. Yes, yes, I know it's Thanksgiving week," Steve said.

"Any chance he'll be out before Thanksgiving?" Christy said.

"To be realistic, I'm afraid not. I think by December first for sure. But here's where the holdup has been. J. Edgar still won't sign off on it. Some assistant, whatever they call him, will."

"What a jerk." Ellen threw up her hands.

"Well, I'll be meeting next Monday with the bankers and we'll arrange for the money's to be returned. Justice signs off on it and then it's a done deal."

"Wait, how long will it take them to sign it once the money's been returned?" Grace said. "I'm sorry, I didn't mean to butt in."

"Mom, it's okay," Christy said, "But, Steve, what's to keep them from backing out on the whole deal?"

"This little piece of paper." Steve held it up. "Say's I keep the money in an escrow type of account until all paper work is signed, sealed, and delivered."

"Okay, what about the real crooks?" Ellen said.

"Remember the guy, Greg Toscas?" Steve saw all three women nod. "Well, he's told me, off the cuff, that there's some bullshit going on to keep that information off the table. It's like they want to let it go."

"I'll be damned if we'll let it go," Ellen said. "That bastard has taken pot shots at some of us. And, look at all the crap they've put us through. Something's still very screwed up with the deal."

Steve said, "Look, take the deal. So you can get on with your lives. I don't understand it, either, but that's my advice,"

After Grace and Steve left, Christy and Ellen sat in front of the fireplace in the living room.

"I guess I still have animosity for this Bedford clown." Christy took a sip of her wine.

"After what the boys did to him, I was strangely happy. But, I want to see him stripped of his retirement, put in jail or something. I just hate him," Ellen said.

"Yes but, if we can get on with life, let's do it. I'd say forget the past and that bastard."

"I don't know if it's in Bedford's demented mind to do that," Ellen said.

Christy took a deep breath. "Let's talk about something

fantastic. Dan'll be out in a week to ten days. I can't let myself believe it. It's too...you know."

"What if it gets screwed up? Would you disappear like we all talked about?" Ellen said.

"Jeez, it's scary just thinking about it. But, right now? I'd do it in a heartbeat. Have you regretted being on the run?"

"Not really, but there are times when it gets to me." Ellen had a hard time not breaking down. She took a sip of wine to hide from Christy's emotions.

Christy stared at the fire. "God, I know. Me, too."

CHAPTER FORTY-ONE

The Monday before Thanksgiving, Greg Toscas arrived at the correctional facility before Steve Mitchell. At 11:00, Dan joined them in a conference room. The negotiations began in earnest.

"First things first, Toscas." Steve handed Toscas some papers. "You have in your hand the escrow account, and you can see it's over fourteen million, three hundred thousand, and some change."

Toscas took the papers and nodded. "Yes, that's the agreed upon amount. We don't have to go over the names of the ones who actually took the payroll."

"Yes, we do." Steve handed Toscas the information about Peterson, his leave time, and travel to and from Okinawa which coincided with the heist.

Toscas said, "I don't know who this person is, but I'm sure it will not go unnoticed."

Dan sat silent as he looked from Steve to Toscas. Steve caught the nuance.

"Greg, when do you think my client will actually get out of here?"

"These papers exonerate and pardon the other five

individuals, listed, and commute Dan's sentence to time served. The pardon from the president is too politically hot. But Justice has signed off on the terms we've agreed upon. I think with your escrow paperwork, we'll be able to sign off tomorrow." Toscas glanced at his watch. "Oh, wow. It's past three in D.C."

"And?" Steve raised his hands.

"They might not get to this until tomorrow".

The conversation became adversarial as Toscas explained what had to be done to get the Agency and Justice to sign off.

"Damn it, Greg, light a fire under those lazy asses and get this done before Wednesday. Because, after that it'll be next week and that's unacceptable."

"Look, guys, you've got my word. Let's meet tomorrow after lunch and I'll have the signed documents. Okay?"

Steve glared at Toscas.

"You've got my word. I won't leave until we've got it finished. Okay?"

Dan spoke for the first time. "Greg, that's good with me. You've been a man of your word."

Steve blinked his eyes. "Obviously my client doesn't realize the layers of bureaucracy. He just wants the deal signed, sealed, and delivered."

"Deal?" Toscas put his hand out.

Dan shook it, followed by Steve.

After Toscas left, Dan said to Steve, "I think he's a straight shooter."

"Well, we've got until tomorrow to see, don't we? I'll contact the powers to be and let them know what's going on."

Jack and Roadhawg traveled to San Jose to make the call to Christy. When they got back to the mobile home park, Ellen couldn't believe the good news.

"Well, boys and girls," Roadhawg said between bites of

dinner. "I guess we can start closin' up shop here."

"God, I only hope so," Jack said.

However, Ellen cast a dark mood over the group. "I don't know, guys. We don't have any Thanksgiving plans. I'm going to go buy a turkey from Safeway. I think we'll be having Thanksgiving right here." She tapped the table with her index finger.

Tuesday, Steve and Toscas were working from a hotel in Oakland. The Justice Department had figured out a gazillion ways to keep changing the wording on the agreement. At one point, those in D.C. wanted Jack, Roadhawg, and Pog to plead guilty to possession of stolen goods and have their sentence commuted to thirty months on parole.

Steve and Toscas pitched a fit. Toscas argued with D.C. No eleventh hour crap as he put it. Later that evening, D.C. therma-faxed the agreement to the Oakland FBI office.

The next morning, Toscas and Steve picked up the paperwork and hustled out to Pleasanton where Dan and Steve went over the paperwork in detail.

"So, I'll have a record of racketeering, with the sentence commuted to time served?" Dan said.

"Yes, and before President Nixon leaves office, some sort of a pardon will be granted and the sentence will be removed from your record."

"I don't give a damn about that. I just want out and start living life.

"Well," Steve looked at his watch. "It's about nine-thirty. I'll sign this, drop it off to Toscas at the FBI office in Oakland. And it's a done deal."

"And Monday morning I'm outta here." Dan began to grin.

"Grace and I are taking a few days off," Steve said.

"Well, Christy's driving down and has a place rented on the Oregon coast for a couple of three days."

P.R. STEELE

"I'd better be getting a move on." Steve placed the paperwork in his briefcase.

Dan began to laugh. "I've got a quick question."

"What?"

"Christy knows her momma is expecting. Are we really going to have a baby in the family?"

Steve joined in the snickering, "Well, yes. And you'll be expected to attend all the soccer or little league games."

Steve left to meet Toscas at the local FBI office. The two of them exchanged their signed copies. As they were leaving, Toscas mentioned he had to hustle to San Francisco to catch his flight to Portland where he had to change planes.

"Really? My office has me catching a Northwest flight out of Portland. Maybe I'll see you there."

At the Portland airport Steve noticed Toscas in line for Northwest flight 305. Passengers were boarding for the 2:50 departure.

"Hey there Greg, small world." Steve said as he approached Toscas from behind.

Toscas turned, sat his briefcase down and shook Steve's hand. "It sure is."

"I'm looking forward to getting home. I feel for Dan, but Monday this whole deal will be behind us."

Toscas looked around as though somebody might be listening. "I, for one, think Dan's guilty of something, but no crime was ever committed, at least in the U. S."

They took seats near the front of the aircraft. Take off was normal. As the plane neared Seattle, Steve noticed a flight attendant make a beeline to the cockpit with a piece of paper in her hand.

A few moments later, the pilot announced they needed to delay landing for a small mechanical issue. One hour turned into two hours of circling. Both Toscas and Steve watched the lights around Puget Sound appear as the sunset

230

passed.

When they landed at the SeaTac airport, FBI agents were waiting for Toscas. They took him away before the rest of the passengers deplaned. One lone passenger remained seated in row eighteen.

"How dare you detain me? I'm an attorney and I know my rights," Steve argued with an FBI agent. Toscas walked into the interrogation room and interceded.

"I know this gentleman. I've spent the last three days with him." Then looking at Steve, he said. "Do you remember the guy a few rows behind us, sitting by himself, wearing the sunglasses?"

"Yes. On my trip to the restroom I thought he was unusual to be wearing sunglass. I mean, it was already getting dark outside."

One of the agents butted in. "Could you work with our artist and give us a look at how you remember him?"

"Yes, but why? We're way late and I've family waiting for me. What's going on?"

"Steve, they just told me our plane was hi-jacked. Does the name D. B. Cooper mean anything to you?"

"No. Is that the hi-jacker?"

CHAPTER FORTY-TWO

Grace and Steve walked into Christy's house on Vashon Island the next morning. The boys were watching TV in the family room. The house abound with Thanksgiving aroma. Christy couldn't wait to ask Steve about Dan. She could tell Steve wanted to tell them about his delayed flight home. Christy wrung her hands.

"Greg Toscas and I were on a hi-jacked flight out of Portland."

"What?" Christy said.

"It seems like all hell has broken loose. J. Edgar called Greg Toscas at three this morning and told him our deal was off."

"How can they do that?" Christy dropped into a chair at the dining room table.

"Greg called me. He's been reassigned. He said every agent in the Bureau had been placed on this hi-jacking. And I'm quoting Greg, 'J. Edgar was not making any deals with any hi-jackers.' They're going to catch holy hell from us tomorrow as soon as I get in the office."

Christy cried out, "I can't believe this."

"Honey, it isn't fair." Grace scooted a chair next to her

daughter and wrapped her arms around her.

The boys came running in. "Hey, Grandpa Steve, come outside and see our new boat dock," Jason said.

Steve took the boys outside to explain that Dan wasn't coming home.

Christy went to the phone and did the one thing they said they'd never do. She called Ellen, then hung up remembering the call could be traced to the mobile home.

"Mom, could you watch the boys?"

"Sure. What are you thinking?"

"Don't say a word to Steve. He can't know, but I'm flying down to see Roadhawg, Jack, and Ellen. I'll be back this evening." She got her purse and car keys.

"Christy, wait. Don't go off like this. Let's wait and see what's really going on." Grace followed her into the garage.

"This is the proverbial straw, Mom. I'll be back tomorrow at the latest."

Six hell-bent-and–plenty-pissed-off hours later, Christy parked in front of Jack, Ellen, and Roadhawg's mobile home. She didn't knock. She slipped in.

"Christy?" Roadhawg said.

Jack and Ellen stumbled out of their bedroom still half asleep.

"Guys, I gotta make this quick. That bastard Hoover just cancelled the whole thing because of the hi-jacking yesterday." She brought the group up to date. They had packed and were ready to leave Monday.

"So, the question is how soon can you put the escape plan in action?" Ellen looked at each of them.

Roadhawg explained that the soonest would be Saturday. Tomorrow, he'd call and arrange for the rental flight of the helicopter out to the flying service in Walnut Creek.

"Christy, this is unbelievable. I guess we all kind of

suspected if it could go wrong it would," Jack said.

"Have you told Dan?" Ellen put her arm around Christy's shoulder.

"No, but I thought about it on the way down." She told them she'd call Dan in the morning and use the key words after she spoke with him.

Jack said, "Well, we'll be ready by Saturday morning. And then see you in Portland late Saturday night or early Sunday."

"Do you want anything to eat?" Ellen opened the refrigerator. "We've got tons of food."

"I'll take a little bit, if that's okay."

"You're not leaving now, are you?" Roadhawg turned around to face Christy. She explained she didn't want the Feds to know she'd ever left from up there. Her mom and Steve were keeping the boys. Her voice broke up and it took her a minute to recover. "I need to be back this evening. So, I'm on my way. I can't be missing from there."

"Okay, you've got all the plans where to meet and everything." Jack went over the fact Christy would be operating solo all the way back. "I wish one of us could go back with you. I worry about all this sudden stuff."

"I'll be fine," Christy said. "See you all Sunday. Ellen, I wish you could go with me. Oh, I gotta go pee and get moving."

Ellen packed sandwiches for her. Roadhawg went out and appeared to be checking the cars, while Jack went over the plans.

"Christy, Ellen will call tomorrow night and confirm it's a go for nine in the morning on Saturday. Dan knows that's the plan. Have him ready."

"Okay. You know he'll be more than ready."

Ellen hugged her. "I can't believe our damn bad luck. We were so close."

"Well, screw 'em. I was getting pissed off all the way

down here. Screw all of them." Christy said her goodbyes and left for the airport.

"I'll call the flying service in the morning and have the helo in the air by eight on Saturday," Roadhawg said.

"It's all kind of rushed, but I think we're good to go," Jack said.

Christy called Dan Friday morning. Steve had called him Thanksgiving Day and explained everything. Steve might've suspected their plans, but had no direct knowledge.

"This sucks, doesn't it?" Dan struggled to keep from laughing a bit. "Okay, then. I understand everything. Hurry and send me some new books to read." He just told her he understood the extraction was set for tomorrow morning at nine o'clock outside exercise time.

All the plans were about to be put into action. Roadhawg called Friday morning and reserved the Bell Jet Ranger helicopter for two hours with an eight o'clock take off time. Their bags were packed and ready to go.

Jack checked items off his list. "Okay, we've got the cars packed and filled up. The place here is wiped down and clean."

"My rental car will be left at the flying service." Roadhawg pointed to that item on the list.

Ellen nodded her head. "And, the car I'll use at the pick-up in Niles Canyon I'll abandon in the shopping center."

The list was complete. Now they waited for Saturday morning.

Jack and Roadhawg left the two getaway cars in a shopping center parking lot in Pleasanton early Saturday morning. One car was parked on one side of the plaza and one on the other side. Their plan was for Ellen to pick up the guys in Niles Canyon. She would leave her car in the shopping center, because if someone saw a helicopter landing and a station wagon leaving they would have a description of the get-a-way vehicle.

When they returned, Roadhawg left for the flying service in his legitimate rental car. Ellen tried to get Jack to eat some breakfast. "Honey, come on, have a bite."

The day would be strenuous and long, so she made ample lunches for the four of them, and added the lunches to the extras they'd packed in both cars.

Ellen more than recognized Jack's concern. He worried that something would come up that he hadn't planned on. So, she tried to ignore his worries. She said, "Honey, I've got faith everything will go like clockwork. Now, will you quit worrying?"

"I know. I know. It's just that I'll feel better once Danny and you are headed out with Roadhawg and me following."

"Are you worried they might start shooting at you all when you land to pick Dan up?"

"Naw. Really, it's minimum security and the Saturday following Thanksgiving. The prison guards will most likely be inside watching football. We couldn't have picked a better day. El, it's going to be a walk in the park."

They closed up the mobile home. The drive to the abandoned racetrack on the Altamont Pass, where Roadhawg would rendezvous to pick up Dan, took less than twenty minutes.

The sun rose behind low clouds, blocking the Sierra range in the distance.

"Damn it, I wish the sun would get on up there," Jack said.

They made small talk as Jack checked his watch every couple of minutes. He followed the time check, searching the horizon to the north looking for the inbound Jet Ranger. The sun broke out at twenty after eight, and sure enough, a helo approached from the north.

Roadhawg landed on time at eight-thirty. The plan called for them to land at nine-fifteen to nine-twenty in the prison workout yard. Jack kissed Ellen good bye, and she left once he'd climbed into the copilot's seat.

"Well, she's got a thirty-five minute drive. We can depart and goof off until time to head in," Jack said.

"Okay, Bud. Do you want to fly a bit?"

Jack took the controls, nodded, and then took off.

"You seem nervous? What's bugging you, Jack?"

"Just thinking. What if she has car trouble or something?"

"Jack, Jack. You'd worry if they hung you with a new rope. We'll do just like we planned. We'll stop a motorist and get a ride to the shopping center. We know Ellen's route. Dan and I'll depart and you'll back track and pick her up."

"I know, but I just worry that something will go wrong."

"Come on, we've got all the contingencies covered. Let's go have some fun. You know this'd make a hell of a movie." Roadhawg chuckled.

"My gut sez be on the alert."

"Get a grip, Jackson. It's probably gas."

CHAPTER FORTY-THREE

They flew around the rolling hills east of the Pleasanton Detention Center. At five after nine, Roadhawg took the controls and flew parallel to the freeway on the north side heading due east.

"Okay, there's Livermore Tower, and I don't see anything in the pattern. I've got their frequency on the radio and we've heard nada," Jack said.

"Roger that. And up ahead is the facility." Roadhawg scooted low level toward the facility. An overcast ceiling and not much sunrise would have to do.

"Okay, the landing check list is complete," Jack said from the left seat. The cabin doors on both sides behind them were open, ready for Dan.

"I think I see him waving." Roadhawg pointed as he transitioned to a hover approaching the exercise yard area.

Jack took out the plastic Colt model 1911 .45. "When we get in close, you know the drill."

"Yeah, you're going to hold it to my head and hope they think I'm flying against my will. They won't shoot because they might injure me."

"Once we get him in, we're gone."

Roadhawg flew the approach until he was three feet off the ground. Jack saw the dust blew sand everywhere as Dan ran toward the helo. One of the guards shielded his eyes as the other held his hand over his eyebrow trying to see what was going on.

"Alright," Jack shouted over the intercom, "nobody's pointing anything at us."

Before he could finish, Dan jumped aboard. Roadhawg took off without hesitation. Dan closed the door next to him and then the one on the other side. He strapped on the seatbelt, and put on a headset in the back compartment. "Well, girls, let's haul ass."

Roadhawg executed a perfect high-speed take off.

The intercom was busy with all of them talking. Roadhawg kept the helo low level until they were at the junction of the 580 and 680 freeways, about five miles to the west. Roadhawg turned south staying on the west side of the 680 freeway heading toward Niles Canyon Road. They increased their altitude to about five hundred feet to avoid any eyes.

"There's the sign down below for the Niles Canyon exit." Jack pointed for Dan to see.

"Yes, sir, the LZ's about a couple of miles. Up there around the hills." Roadhawg pointed.

"Well, boys, I'm glad as hell, to be out of there. And now, you're both guilty of assisting in my escape."

"Hah. Let 'em add it to everything else." Roadhawg kept his eyes on the road to Niles Canyon.

As they followed the road, Roadhawg slowed the airspeed to what seemed like a crawl. The dirt road appeared ahead and to their right. Ellen had left the gate open. They eased their way around the narrow dirt road hiding the helo from the main road. Ellen stood outside her car. Roadhawg sat the bird down and expedited the shutdown with the rotor brake. Once the rotor stopped, the three jumped out and trotted over to Ellen.

"I'm so relieved to see you guys," she said as everyone climbed in the station wagon. They started down the dirt road when a pickup truck approached them, blocking the road.

"What the hell?" Roadhawg said.

"Let me talk to him," Jack said. He got out of the car and approached the pickup.

"Could I help you, sir?" Jack said as he walked to the driver's side of the truck.

"Is everything alright?"

"I'm a realtor. We have a buyer who wanted to look over the property." Jack pointed to the soon to be abandoned wagon.

"Well, I flew as a crew chief on helo's in Vietnam and just wanted to make sure you weren't in any trouble," the driver said.

"Naw. We're fine and thanks for asking."

"Well, you all have a good day, then." The driver turned around and left.

Jack got back into the escape vehicle and repeated the story. As they approached the shopping center, they went over the radio procedures and contingencies. Ellen parked the car. After the four of them walked into the shopping center, they split up. Dan and Ellen exited out the other side of the mall. Jack and Roadhawg gave them five minutes and walked to their car.

In case the driver of the pickup gave the authorities a description of the wagon Ellen drove. She abandoned it in the parking lot, wiped clean.

Once in his car, Jack turned on the walkie-talkie. "Two, calling one. Check in, over."

"We have you five by," Ellen said as Dan drove north.

Every hour on the hour, Jack checked in. Three and a half hours later, at one in the afternoon, Dan drove into a filling station. Five minutes later, Jack and Roadhawg, passed them and pulled into the next row to get gas. Dan drove into a fast food restaurant. Both Ellen and Dan, she in an elderly woman's disguise and Dan in kind with a cane, went in and ordered their lunch to go. Jack and Roadhawg walked in the restaurant after they'd filled the gas tank, also in disguise, and ordered, never speaking a word to the couple. Dan and Ellen left with a little head start, Roadhawg and Jack followed.

By four that afternoon, the group closed in on Grant's Pass, Oregon. "Hey, one. This is two."

"Go," Ellen answered.

"Let's stop and top off."

"Will do. I'll call our filling station when we get there," Ellen said.

Jack double clicked. The plan was to keep moving, but night fall was approaching. Jack wanted to fill up while it was still light. The topping off went with precision. Back on the road, Jack picked up his walkie-talkie. "One, this is two."

"Go ahead," Ellen answered.

"We'll close up a couple hundred yards behind."

"Understand."

Nearing sunset, Jack and Roadhawg turned on their lights, and so did Dan.

Jack keyed the walkie-talkie, almost pulling it out of the cigar lighter.

"One, come in, over."

"We're up."

"You've got a driver's side tail light out, over."

"Wait one," Ellen said.

"Pull over. The spares are in the glove box." Jack closed his eyes and shook his head.

Dan pulled over, and armed with a Philips screw driver and a spare bulb, walked to the back of the car. Roadhawg pulled up behind him with the lights on. Jack got out so he could help Dan work on the tail light. Roadhawg grumbled as he stood by them because the repair job was taking longer than he liked.

Jack kicked the bumper and swore. "We'll have to switch cars. This piece of crap light is messed up. Both bulbs are good. Dan and Ellen will follow us. If it gets worse and goes downhill, they'll go on to Portland."

Well after sunset, nearing Eugene, Jack couldn't believe his eyes.

"Oh, shit," Roadhawg said.

"Yeah, I know." Jack watched a highway patrol car pull in behind them.

"Two, this is one. You've got trouble," Ellen said.

Jack double clicked as the trooper turned on the flashing lights. Roadhawg pulled over and stopped. The trooper did the same, and stepped out of his car. Jack and Roadhawg got out and the three of them met off to the side of the interstate.

"Sir, could I see your license?" The trooper glared straight at the Roadhawg.

About that time, Dan and Ellen passed them, as Roadhawg handed the officer a fake ID.

"The reason I stopped you is because this tail light is out." The officer pointed.

"Well, sir, we just happen to have a couple of spares. Let me go get one," Jack said knowing it wouldn't work.

After they tried the replacement, Jack began. "Sir, could you follow us to an auto parts store so we could fix it? Eugene is only a couple of miles away."

"Well, if you can't fix it, you'll have to leave it there until it's fixed." The trooper handed Roadhawg his license.

Once they were comfortable in the car heading toward town, Roadhawg said. "Man, what'll we do?"

"I can fix it with a five-foot piece of wire. We'll splice into the right-hand side, cut the wire coming out of the bad light and then wire them together."

"That'll work."

"Now, we've just gotta find a parts store or filling

station with a garage," Jack said.

Once off the interstate, Jack and Roadhawg pulled into the first station they hoped had a garage. The trooper slowed, waved, and drove on.

Roadhawg went in and bought a short piece of wire. Jack used the wire cutters and cut the dead line going into the bad tail light. He used the splicer fitting and tapped into the good left side tail light wire. Then he wired the jumper wire to the right side of the cut wire, and the light illuminated. The black tape finished the job. They were back on the road again.

Jack keyed the walkie-talkie. "One, this is two."

"Go ahead, two."

"We're back on the road. Let's keep moving."

The double click from Ellen ended the conversation.

Fifteen miles out of Portland, Ellen contacted Jack. "Two, this is one."

"Go."

"We've got a broken water hose. The temp is starting to climb."

"Pull over and we'll change cars again," Jack said.

"Jesus, we're almost there." Roadhawg banged his hand on the steering wheel.

After about five minutes, both Jack and Roadhawg saw the steaming car on the side of the road. Roadhawg pulled in front of it. Dan and Ellen got out, and with very little conversation, got in the good disposable car and left.

"Well, Jackson, let's see what we can do to get this piece of shit out of here."

Jack handed Roadhawg a flash light as he opened the hood. Hot water was everywhere. He searched with the light and found the ruptured radiator hose.

"Well, lady luck is on our side," Roadhawg laughed.

"Yeah. It's the top hose. Okay, let's get the duct tape, and a towel."

They dried the hose several times, and tightly wrapped duct tape around it. Then they filled the radiator and left the cap off. That way the water wouldn't be under normal pressure. Roadhawg started it up. A small leak dripped from the duct tape. Jack shut the hood.

"Let's haul ass. It's dripping water, but the temp is down." Both he and Roadhawg eyed the temp gauge as Jack pulled back into traffic.

Ellen and Dan arrived at the rendezvous rental without a problem. Christy was elated.

As soon as Roadhawg took the exit, the transmission began to slip. They were able to pull into a closed filling station, but the car wouldn't move. They got out and opened the hood. Roadhawg still held the walkie-talkie.

"You sure the walkie-talkie isn't working?" Jack asked as he pulled the transmission dipstick out.

"Yep. They're out of range." Roadhawg tossed the walkie-talkie on the front car seat.

"What tranny fluid we've got is burnt. When the radiator over heated, it must've cooked the transmission fluid. We're dead. And, just what we needed," Jack said as a patrol car drove up beside them.

"You boys from California?"

"Yes, sir." Jack answered.

"You wouldn't be those two that sprung that boy outta prison, would you?" The patrolman asked as he kept his spotlight on the pair.

P.R. STEELE

CHAPTER FORTY-FOUR

"What are you talking about?" Jack laughed as he walked to the patrol car.

"Some fellas down there flew into a prison and flew out with a convict." He went on to tell them all about it. Jack and Roadhawg said they'd been on the road all day and hadn't heard any news.

"Well, that ain't us," Roadhawg said. "for sure. We're on our way to see my sister, and this thing has been on its last legs for the last two days,"

"I think we'll push it over there." Jack pointed to a parking spot. "And see if we can get it fixed tomorrow."

"Is there a Motel Six anywhere close?" Roadhawg sounded so innocent.

The patrolman told them one was a couple of miles away, and then left.

"I about had a heart attack when he asked us if we'd sprung Dan," Jack said.

"I about shit." Roadhawg chuckled.

"I've got to get better glue. My mustache felt like it was about to fall off."

The payphone worked, so they called the rented house.

Christy answered. Ellen went back to pick them up.

The reunion lasted well into the night as everyone got caught up on what was going on. As the evening wore on, they began to talk strategy.

Jack yawned. "Hey, Christy, has Luds or Dennis heard anything from Pog?"

"He's somewhere in Mexico at some high altitude lake called Chapalla or something like that. But Ludwig said he's doing well."

"Did Luds tell Dennis it was Bedford who was shooting at him?"

Christy nodded her head.

"Okay, new subject. We're outta here day after tomorrow. Is everyone good on the travel?" Jack looked at each one. "We fly from here to Miami. Change names and fly out the next day to Australia, and then to New Zealand."

"And I drive out to Dillon, Montana," Roadhawg said.

"And we're off to Scotland." Ellen winked at Jack.

"Then in three weeks we rendezvous with Roadhawg in Butte. If all goes well, he'll have the place in Dillon all set up."

The plan was for Roadhawg to buy a desolate place they'd had on their radar. They'd own a well-kept dude ranch with a little over two thousand acres in the middle of a beautiful set of mountains, with a large lodge. Roadhawg had convinced the realtor they were setting up a hippie commune and wanted to be isolated and left alone.

The realtor hinted, more than once, that he'd like to join them. Roadhawg told him the people putting up the money didn't want any more people for the time being, but he'd be first on their list. Naomi, Roadhawg's girlfriend from Southern California, soon to be his bride, fell in love with the lodge when she visited it with him. Roadhawg said the place was so large, they could go days without bumping into each other.

Roadhawg would drive up there, close the deal, get

enough provisions to last the winter, and buy a couple of newer 4x4 vehicles for the winter snow. That place would be one of the gang's retreats.

Jack and Ellen had their sights set on a manor house in the Scottish Highlands. Total seclusion with all the modern conveniences, made it very appealing. The story for all three of the couples, for anyone asking, was a place for a new start for a family that had suffered a terrible fatal traffic accident. The large insurance settlement made it possible for them to get away from it all.

The working ranch in New Zealand drew Dan and Christy to make a decision on the third place they looked at. Christy had previewed all three properties over the phone. They both thought the working ranch would make a perfect hideout.

All three places made it easy to remain secluded without arousing local suspicion. The law offices of Taylor, Garrett and Hannah in Napa, California, would be their version of an answering service and message center. They agreed to check in twice a month. If any problems arose, they could keep in touch. The law office had never worked for any of the three couples and knew nothing as to why they were retained.

The next morning, Jack and Ellen drove to the station where the broken disposable car with the cooked transmission was abandoned. Jack, in full disguise, could've passed for a hippie.

"Good morning," he began. "I had to leave that Ford here last night." He pointed to the car. "Is the owner here?"

The well-dressed station attendant raised his hand and said, "That'd be me."

"I don't know what's wrong with it, but I think it's the transmission. I don't need the headaches. Do you know anybody who'd be interested in buying it, cheap?"

"What's your ideal of cheap?" the owner said.

"Make me a reasonable offer."

After a little dance of wanting to buy low and wanting to sell high, Jack took $175 for it. He signed the title, took the money, and walked out of the station.

"Okay, that little problem is solved. Honey, I'm ready to get out of here and have a couple of weeks of R & R in England."

"Jack, it's actually Scotland."

"You know what I mean."

"I've always wanted to go to England, take a train, and do the non-touristy thing," Ellen said.

"Well, we're outta here for Chicago and then to London in a little over three hours." Jack checked his watch as they drove to the rented hideout house.

"Dan, I can't believe we're getting to travel. I've never thought about visiting New Zealand, but I'm getting excited," Christy said as Roadhawg drove them to the airport.

"I'll take this car," Roadhawg pointed to the steering wheel, "And after I drop you all off, I'll take Jack and Ellen to the airport, and wal-la, start my sojourn to Montana."

"I think the three days delay in Hawaii will be way cool." Dan gave Christy a hug.

Christy kissed him on the cheek. "I've never been there."

"Hey, knock the huggy crap off. Christy, are you going to wear a grass skirt?" Roadhawg snickered.

She giggled. "I just might."

"Danny, did you pack your grass clippers?" Roadhawg said as he pulled up to the curb at the airport.

"Hell, no. I know how to untie those grass skirt strings."

"Hey you guys, have some fun," Roadhawg took off in the rental.

Roadhawg hurried back to the rental house, then

followed Jack in the last disposable car to a lot advertising automobiles for cash. Jack haggled a bit, signed the papers, and hurried out to Roadhawg's Ford.

"I'm all packed and ready to go. As soon as I drop you all off...I'm off," Roadhawg said as he drove Jack back to the rental to pick up Ellen.

Ellen had cleaned the rental and was waiting. Their plane left in a couple of hours. They packed the car and hurried to grab a bite of lunch. Roadhawg dropped them off and began, in no big hurry, to drive to Dillon, Montana.

The heather covered hills of Scotland waited for Ellen and Jack. The new frontier in New Zealand waited for Dan and Christy. As for Roadhawg, the Big Sky awaited him.

P.R. STEELE

CHAPTER FORTY-FIVE

Dan and Christy departed Miami after a three-night stay in Honolulu. Four days in the islands seemed too short, yet, the flight to Sydney seemed to last forever. They had a row to themselves. The row in front and back of them was vacant too. Christy asked Dan what started the animosity between the guys and Bedford.

"Well, we began to sense that a lot of the most dangerous missions were scheduled by Bedford with our names on them. I mean the lieutenants seemed to be getting an extraordinary amount of the worst flights. The missions we used to joke about as being 'suicide sandwiches' now had our names on them." Dan fidgeted with his drink.

"And what happened?"

"Well, it was back in '68 during the Tet Offensive. Jack started screwing with Bedford. You know, little stuff." Dan laughed. "We all were drinking and Jack thought it'd be a good thing to go piss in the gas tank of Bedford's Jeep."

"You mean, so it'd stall out and wouldn't run?"

"Yep." Dan laughed even harder. "But Bedford didn't know we were screwing with him. He was late for the All Officer Meeting in the ready room, which everyone called the AOM. He made the maintenance crew tow his Jeep to the hangar and told them to get it fixed." Dan continued to chuckle.

"So what happened then?"

"Jack went out and told the crew chiefs working on it to break the gas line to the carburetor and crank the engine until gas came out. That fixed it. The crew had a good laugh over it."

"But that isn't anything," Christy said. "And this was while you guys were in country?"

"Yeah, and a few days later, again after a lot of drinking, Jack thought it'd be a dandy idea to fill up Bedford's Jeep with a lot of the sandbags. The sand filled bags were used to build blast walls around the hootches.

Christy chuckled. "Now, that's funny."

Dan took a swallow of his drink and continued. He told her none of them were really feeling any pain. "All of us buried Bedford's Jeep under one big pile of sandbags. There wasn't a speck of Jeep to be seen."

Then Dan told Christy about Bedford's typical reaction as he made the maintenance crew uncover and dig out the Jeep. "The crew dawdled, so it took them until four in the afternoon."

Dan continued. "The next morning at the AOM, Bedford threatened if he found out who did it, he'd court martial them for destruction of government property, because two of the Jeeps tires were blown. The whole squadron broke out laughing."

"That's too funny. Why haven't I ever heard this before?"

"It seems so long ago, but anyway it escalated. A few nights later, Jack took a hack saw, after a few Jack Daniel's, and sawed the gearshift lever in Bedford's Jeep almost off. When the prick grabbed it to shift out of reverse...he held the broken off gearshift lever in his hand."

"So he was stuck in reverse?" Christy seemed to struggle

to keep from laughing.

"This only gets better." Dan coughed out of control from laughing. "A few nights later, Jack led the seven of us on the best mission. Remember the sandbags and the blast walls?"

"Yeah."

Dan told Christy how they began to put them in front of Bedford's door. He said they were so loaded that they stacked them to the roof of his Quonset hut all the way out to the street.

"Now, that's really funny."

"Then some dastardly bastard cut his phone lines. Only Majors and above had phones in their hootches. So, it took the maintenance crew most of the day to uncover Bedford's blocked door.

"The next morning at the AOM, Bedford got up and as he started to speak, Jack farted so loud it stopped Bedford before he said a word. Nobody knew who did it, and even though everyone was trying not to laugh, they did anyway."

Christy broke up laughing.

Dan continued telling her that Roadhawg must've had the same culinary delights that Jack had for breakfast, because when the laughter died, Bedford started to speak again, and Roadhawg let it loose. It was even louder than Jack's. This time everyone at the meeting broke out laughing. Bedford turned fifty shades of red. He glared at them like he was going to explode. Dan said, "If looks could kill, they were all dead Marines."

Christy started hitting his arm as she laughed.

"Then, when it quieted down, somebody let out a little squeaker. Bedford meant to shout out, 'stop that laughing,' but it came out. 'Stop that, men. Stop that farting.' Now everyone was out of control."

"This is hilarious." Christy wiped tears from her face.

"I know it sounds impossible, but it gets better.

Finally, old Freddie-boy Bedford got silence from the

group, and said, 'When I find out who cut my phone lines and sandbagged me in, I'm filing attempted murder charges.'"

Then Lieutenant Colonel Earp, the commanding officer, stood up and said, 'Fred...attempted murder charges?'"

Christy said. "You gotta be kidding. This is too funny."

"Lemme finish. Bedford shouts out, 'Yes, if my hootch had caught on fire and burned down...I could have died.' I mean immediately Colonel Earp laughed and said, 'God, Fred, don't give them any ideas. Men, I've lost control of the AOM. You're dismissed.'"

"Was that it?"

"Yes and no. The CO asked Jack if he could buy him a coke from the snack bar the squadron had set up."

"And that's it?"

"No. Bedford was the scheduling officer and the bias became obvious. The shit-sandwich missions, the most dangerous ones, were more and more often scheduled with the seven of us flying 'em. Then, the morning of May second, Herb led a flight of four. Dennis and Ludwig were dash two, Danny and I were in dash three, and Roadhawg and Toddy were tail end Charlie."

"Was that the day Ludwig and Dennis were injured?"

"Yes, and Herb was killed."

After a little bit. Christy squeezed Dan's hand and wiped her tears with a drink napkin. The silence was louder than the jet engine noise inside the planes cabin.

A few minutes later, Dan continued. "And then, on Jack and Roadhawg's second tour last year, the miserable son of a bitch admitted it to Jack and Todd just before he kicked them out of the squadron. Bedford wanted Jack to hit him so he could court martial him, but Jack just grinned at him. I swear, if I ever get the chance, I'll send him straight to hell." Dan stared ahead in a trance.

The conversation had changed, but the mood still lingered.

"I truly believe that sick bastard isn't through," Dan said.

"What do you mean?"

"Taking shots at Pog, coming out to Seattle, and then Jack and Roadhawg catching him scoping me out. They should've killed him."

Christy held his hand and said, "Honey, revenge and hate is a lot of baggage. A good life is the best revenge."

He turned to face her, and whispered, "Maybe so, but I don't think he's going to quit."

P.R. STEELE

CHAPTER FORTY-SIX

The flight to Sydney connected to Christchurch and then to Auckland, one of New Zealand's northern islands. Christy and Dan had read Friday's Wall Street Journal because that edition always listed the Real Estate ads, worldwide, no less.

The ad Dan had read about earlier was a working ranch for sale on the southern part of Auckland on the coast. He had Christy check it out, unbeknownst to the Feds, while he was still incarcerated in Pleasanton. She had all the information.

The ranch had a couple of snow-fed creeks, scenic level pastures, and a newer ranch house. She'd checked out the ad and made an offer on the ranch with a contingency dependant upon their visit. They'd already decided to build their version of a ranch house, if they felt that was the right place.

The stay overnight in Christchurch could've been better. Jet lag consumed both of them. The short flight to Auckland only built up the excitement of a new life for them.

"I can't believe how beautiful this place is," Christy said as they walked out of the terminal to the baggage claim area.

"I'm afraid it beats New Mexico all to pieces."

"It's so laid back. I mean, they just bring the luggage out to this staging area," she said as she spotted theirs.

Renting a car seemed easy enough, because they'd cleared customs in Christchurch. The credit card Dan carried in an assumed name, worked in Miami, Honolulu, and the night before in Christchurch.

They decided in Honolulu to change her passport to read Burton. The change for her passport would follow as soon as they submitted paperwork with a safe return address. They'd use their new real estate office in Gig Harbor as the mailing address for most everything else. Dan's current passport read Timothy Roberts and Christy's read Alice Elliott. But she would be Alice Roberts from now on in New Zealand. They practiced calling each other their new names.

The next day, the realtor met them and drove them out to the property.

"Oh, my, it's just beautiful," the new Alice said.

"Honey, it is for a fact." The new Tim used names, like 'Baby', 'Honey', and 'Sweetheart.'

The realtor showed them the vacant ranch house, and it was more than what they'd expected. The hot tub and sauna off the master bedroom captivated Christy. The shop included a car lift, air for power tools, and a welding machine. The work benches and shelves looked new.

The kitchen came with all new appliances. Looking out the living room the front vista covered over one hundred acres sloping down to the ocean. That sold both Tim and Alice.

"Alice, I love the place," Dan said to Christy.

"Honey, so do I."

Tim turned to the realtor, "What's their bottom line?"

After a considerable reduction in the asking price, the realtor said it'd be hard to ask the seller to come down any more. Yet, they agreed to offer about ten percent less than $700,000 U. S. dollars.

Christy's experience helped out. "We're offering to settle in two weeks after all inspections, and we're also offering them to carry fifty percent of the price for five years at eight percent interest. That's two percent higher than they'd asked."

"They might not want to finance any of the selling price since it's much lower," the agent said.

"If that's the case, this might help them. We can still settle in ten days. In other words, we don't need to find financing. But we'd like an answer in forty-eight hours."

After they signed the offer in the realtor's office, they got in their rental car and drove off to sightsee. Christy had tourist ads from the airport.

As Dan drove she began, "Dan…"

He interrupted her, "Tim."

They both grinned.

"Honey, is that better?"

"Yes, Honey." He winked at her.

"This is so perfect. I mean the climate is, according to the longitudes, identical to the Puget Sound area. Except the seasons are opposite."

"Amazing isn't it? I gotta tell you, I hope they take the offer. I only see upside potential."

He explained they could hire a couple of full-time hands and start the ranch operation again. And that it'd bring in income and pay for the hired help. "I mean the grass grows almost year round." Dan rubbed his chin.

"Wouldn't it be nice to winter down here?" She stopped. "I've got to quit that kind of thinking. I was thinking of spending time down here with the boys and Mom and Steve."

"And that reminds me, how's the new brother or sister-in-law coming along?"

She told him what little she knew. They'd set up a phone

contact with Grace at random phone booths with times set for Seattle. Christy hadn't changed her watch so she knew what time it was there.

The next morning, Dan drove her to a phone booth where she checked in with Grace. Grace gave her a new phone booth number before they hung up. The time difference was seven hours. Eleven in the morning for Christy turned out to be six in the evening for Grace.

"Mom said the boys are fine, and she's starting to show. Steve's ecstatic. He's somehow got Cuban cigars for either a boy or girl. Mom says he's hoping for twins."

"Now for the business," Christy said as Dan drove. "The Veteran's company is doing fantastic. She said Bob Jones and Ken Anderson are doing a gang buster job. They have three crew's working for George building custom homes on the development. And the taxi business is up to six full time cabs each with veteran drivers."

"Wow, imagine that? Ken and Bob Jones doing honest work? Amazing."

"No kidding. I have to admit I'm pleased the way they've turned out.

"Kind of makes you want to be there and help out, doesn't it?" Dan said.

"Not really. I'd rather be with you. Oh, Mom also said they're looking into renovating houses in depressed neighborhoods. George is putting together a crew and they're going to test the waters, so to speak."

"You know there's a ton of opportunities if people'd just use some imagination." Dan turned to face her.

She reminded Dan he was forgetting it depended on the seed money to make it happen, the deep pockets. She asked if he thought the development would've come together without the guys fronting the money for the land, utilities, and roads? Before he could answer, she finished by saying she didn't think so.

Dan said, "You're right. How many times have you

heard, one's gotta have money to make money?"

The next morning, the realtor called with the counter offer between the asking and their offer. Christy told the realtor to counter back at their original offer. Dan grinned listening to her negotiate.

"You're sharp as a tack. You smelled blood...didn't you?" Dan said.

She told him she could tell that the realtor wanted the sellers to take the offer and they, for whatever reason, had to have a little bit more. She told Dan it wasn't a deal breaker. She said she was wearing her realtor hat instead of being a motivated buyer.

Listening to her made Dan proud of her knowledge and intuition. "I think the place could breakeven for itself with hired help as a working ranch concept, and actually, come out money ahead. I was checking out the prices for lamb down here. I just never thought I'd be a sheep herder or a goat farmer."

"Honey, you could be the mutton king down under." She rested her head on his shoulder.

"I don't care if we raise sheep. But, I can tell you this...we're going to run a few head of cattle and some horses."

They continued to talk about the possibilities. Dan put a pencil to paper and worked out the numbers. But the fact the sellers were selling worried him. Yes, it could be profitable, but why didn't the sellers make a go of it?

"Hey, Alice," he teased. "We need to ask why the sellers pulled up stakes and quit ranching."

"Well, Timmy," she over emphasized. "I already asked. The wife left with someone else, and the distraught husband is now doing the selling. I guess it wouldn't hurt for us to meet his price. But, we'll wait and see."

Later that afternoon, the realtor called and informed them the seller would accept the deal at their counter offer and carry 50% of the selling price at 8% interest.

"That's fantastic. We'll still have plenty with the money I'm getting on interest from the Swiss bank," Dan said. "The payment would be less than three grand a month. So, we'd still be over twenty thousand a month to the good from the money we have on deposit there." Dan picked Christy up and swung her around.

"This is all unbelievable. It'd be perfect if all the crap stuff would just disappear."

Although Dan knew she was accepting the present situation, he felt Christy still longed to be back with the family in Gig Harbor.

CHAPTER FORTY-SEVEN

Escrow closed in less than two weeks. Tim and Alice drove to their new ranch. The excitement overtook the couple as Tim unlocked their front door.

"Honey, what would you think about having the Roadhawg and Naomi from Montana, and Jack and Ellen come here for a stay?" Dan said walking into the kitchen. They had the phone logistics to and from the States already well in place.

Dan had set up John Ludwig and Dennis as points of contact. Either one of them would call from a phone booth to the attorney's office because they didn't want to leave a trail from a home phone or any phone booth. They'd leave a phone number and time. Then Dan would call them from a phone booth in New Zealand to another phone booth in either Oklahoma or the Virgin Islands.

"Do you think it's safe having everyone in one place, now?"

"I checked with Steve. They don't have extradition down here for non-convicted criminals." Dan pointed to Christy, "Me, on the other hand, would provide the Feds with a questionable dilemma."

"Well, it sounds okay to me. What're you thinking?"

"Several things. I could use some more hands. It'd be good to see the Roadhawg and Jack, you know? Plus, it's winter in Montana and England. We've got summer coming down here. I mean, this weather is far out." He grinned at Christy and nodded.

"Well, hells bells, let's get them down here then. We've got more than enough room. I mean the guest house, and the second master bedroom. It'd be perfect."

"Okay, I'll make the call to Dennis or Luds. Today is the check-in day for us at the law offices."

Later in the morning, Dan returned to say he'd left the message for Dennis to contact him. He also left a message for Jack and Roadhawg with times and a phone booth number.

Christy asked again if there were any extradition problems for them? Dan admitted it was a stretch. Then she wanted to know why they needed to hide their locations. Dan told her it'd probably be okay for her to be the point of contact and start going through Steve Mitchell's law office in Seattle. After all, she hadn't broken any laws. But if the Feds were looking, it'd be an easy link to connect his location.

They discussed all the ranching possibilities. Then, they talked about getting new vehicles and an escape plan for Dan, if the authorities ever came to New Zealand. After all, the ranch was way off the beaten path, and Dan already had an early warning set up and a quick getaway, if needed.

"You know that creek we've got?" Dan changed the subject.

"Yeah." Christy was working in the kitchen putting things away and making a list of more things she needed. "What about the creek?"

"If I could get Jack and Roadhawg down here, I'd like to dam it up...make a water reservoir and a pond back up there." Dan walked to the kitchen window and pointed it out to her.

"But the creek runs year round. Why would we need to dam it up and make a pond?"

Dan put his arms around her. The sun was breaking over the mountains. The morning overcast left dew on the whole landscape.

"I'm thinking a fella could put in a water wheel, attach a generator to it and make all the electricity you'd need."

"Really?"

"Yep. Run a car-type of alternator into a DC battery bank. Then run lights to the shop, etcetera. Then hook up an inverter and we could run our house 'electricity."

"You could do all that?"

He told her he and Jack had talked a lot about it on their first tour back in '68. During the times in between drinking, they were sober and bored. He said he'd run all the wires underground in a new plastic conduit. He'd have a battery bank attached to the water wheel in the generator house. "It'd be a good project. Plus, we'd stock the pond with fish."

They both thought the boys would love it when Christy could bring them for a visit.

"Do you really think we could get them down here?" She stopped her shopping list and turned to face Dan.

"Basically, I'm an escaped criminal. The extradition process would be lengthy, if they could extradite me. Steve's kind of positive they can't."

"You mean as long as we're here, you might be safe?"

"Hope springs eternal, Honey," he said.

The next morning, Dan returned with good news. He'd talked to Dennis and everything was okay. Jack and Ellen were on their way via Delhi, and Roadhawg and Naomi would be a couple of days behind them.

After Dan told Christy, she ran over and hugged him. "Oh, it'll be a long overdue get together. I've never really met Naomi, but I'm sure we'll all love her."

"If she can put up with Roadhawg, we'll love her to pieces.

"But for now, I've got to go check out a front loader with a backhoe I saw advertised in the paper."

"Lemme guess. For the dam, for the pond, for the electricity?" she teased.

"You forgot the fish." Dan winked. He kissed her and grabbed the newspaper off the table.

The next morning, Jack and Ellen arrived at the Auckland airport. The party began. Two days later, Roadhawg and Naomi arrived. Dan and Christy had bought a GMC Suburban with four-wheel drive, because they needed room for six and for winter driving. Dan had a three-quarter ton pickup, too, with four-wheel drive.

By the time Roadhawg and Naomi arrived, the other four had decorated the bedroom in the guest house for a honeymoon room that looked like something straight out of the movies. Jack and Ellen had the second master bedroom. The long overdue party began.

Dan and Jack had already begun work on the pond. Roadhawg was ecstatic to get the project underway the next morning. In less than two weeks the pond was filled. The generator house was almost finished. The underground wiring just needed to be tested and covered up.

Dan rubbed his hands together surveying the project. "Well, we've got the lake filled and the water overflow turning the water wheel. It ought to start making electricity." Dan admired the earthen dam and generator house.

"I like it a whole lot. Hells fire, I love it. Just like we planned way back in Vietnam. I can't believe the opposite seasons down here," Jack said.

"I think we ought to move to Montana in the spring, England in the fall and down here for the winters. I mean to tell you girls, this place is kick ass," Roadhawg said looking out at the deep blue South Pacific.

"Danny boy," Roadhawg continued. "This place has it all. Year round running creek, grass that'll grow most all year long, and a spectacular view." He stood leaning on a shovel admiring the view of the emerald rolling hills behind them.

"Best of all," Dan said motioning with his arm, "the Feds will have a tough time getting us back if they ever find us. And that prick Bedford will never find us. The only drawback is not being able to spend time on our Veteran's Hiring Veterans project in Seattle. And, I know Christy is missing the boys and her mom."

"Could she go back and visit them from time to time?" Jack said.

"The Feds would most likely follow her travels, and that'd lead them back to you, Danny." Roadhawg sighed.

"Yeah, I know, I know. But, I'm getting to where if they do, I'm outta here slicker than owl shit on a limb."

They all laughed, then began to talk about the Seattle estate project.

Dan started the conversation. "Hey, Christy just heard that the real estate development has sold seven more lots and George is waiting for spring to start the construction. I mean the thing is going to be making money hand over fist."

"And you were telling me, what do you call it, the renovations of the older houses are making over fifty cents on every dollar? Amazing," Jack added.

"Hell, we'll be millionaires all over again. But, I like the part of putting most of the profits back into the retirement plans for the guys." Dan leaned on his shovel.

"Hey, girls. New subject." Roadhawg hesitated as he continued. "Has anyone heard anything lately outta Pog?"

Jack told them he'd heard from Luds, and he'd heard from Pogy once since he'd gotten settled in Mexico. But that was at least two or three months before. And Luds told Jack he was just a bit worried. Jack reminded him they all said they'd check in once a month. Dan scrunched his mouth, and narrowed his eyes. "We need to follow up."

"Well, with Christmas and New Year's, maybe he's gotten behind, knowing him." Roadhawg grinned.

Dan said. "I've been thinking about having Christy head on back home for a while."

"How would she travel? I mean under a fake ID or...?" Jack shuffled his feet and didn't look at Dan.

"I'd say fake a ID to fly home, or fly to Portland or to Vancouver and then drive home to Gig Harbor. The Feds could say whatever they wanted, but she could tell them to go to hell. It'd help if you guys wanted to hang around here," Dan looked at each of them.

"Well, hell yeah, I'd stick around. Naomi and I have fallen in love with the whole deal down here," Roadhawg said.

"Are you sure? We wouldn't be in your way, or what not?" Jack stared at Dan.

"Give me a break. That'd never happen."

Later that evening, Dan and Christy talked about her being home with the boys for Christmas. They worked out a little bit better contact system to use while she was back in Seattle before they'd left for New Zealand. But it still would be phone booths to phone booths. And if she really needed him, she could call him on the phone they had just installed.

Dan kept the encouragement up front, but he took her to the airport alone. He didn't need the boys seeing his eyes sweat.

On December 22nd, Christy boarded the plane for Sydney and then changed identity and airlines to Hawaii. Nobody in the Seattle area knew she was coming home.

CHAPTER FORTY-EIGHT

Christy arrived on Christmas Eve. The boys, Grace and Steve, were overjoyed. Late that evening Steve was able to get some time with just Grace and Christy.

"The Feds are all over the place with this D. B. Cooper fellow." Steve sipped a little merlot. "Toscas has been very candid and still hopes for Dan's sentence to be commuted. The Justice Department is a little miffed about the breakout, but Greg feels sure they're over it."

"Well, what would it take to make it right?" Christy said.

"It would take J. Edgar Hoover to get off his high horse. But right now, they're highly embarrassed about Mr. Cooper being able to make a clean getaway. And they, the guys pulling off a perfect escape, iced the proverbial cake for J. Edgar." Steve leaned his head back and shook it with his eyes closed.

Steve exhaled and continued. "I understand the guy who gave Joe Hegidio, ah-h-h Roadhawg, the flying lessons couldn't or wouldn't positively identify him. You can tell me. It was him who flew the getaway helicopter, wasn't it? Anyway, he's in the clear."

Their conversation continued on the progress the real

estate development made over the last month. But the next morning Christy called John Ludwig. She found out he hadn't heard from Pog in over a month.

Now Luds and Diane were concerned. It seemed Pog had run into a volunteer worker at an orphanage and Luds thought Pogy was awe struck. Luds had given Pog a couple of months and now he'd begun to worry. He said Pog was hanging out with the orphaned kids and a volunteer woman, and he'd seemed to be getting along very well. He used the word cozy.

Christy knew she needed to pass this on to Dan and the rest of them at the ranch.

The day after Christmas, Christy drove to the airport and used a phone booth there to call Dan at the ranch.

"Hey, baby, are you missing me, yet?"

"A ton. How's everything?"

She relayed the information from John Ludwig about Pog. The real estate development project was starting to shine, and the other new ventures were showing progress and growth. She told him Steve's thoughts on everyone's legal status, more important to the Auckland gang, because D. B. Cooper had pulled off the perfect aircraft hi-jacking and was still at large. Steve thought the Feds had no interest in pursuing Dan, Jack or Roadhawg.

She told Dan the two boys missed him a bunch, and he'd have a new brother or sister-in-law around the last of May. She could tell he was excited and happy.

"Christy," Dan said. "I can't believe they're taking a pass on the escape and everything."

"The word is that they are befuddled with your status, and the thinking is a deal might be in the mill. But for me," Christy said, "I think it's a bunch of bull. Thank goodness this phone system is working out just fine," Christy said. "If you take a letter to a post office, and mail it to me here, I think it'll be alright. Although, I think it'd be pushing the issue for me to write back."

"I agree," Dan said.

"Okay, Honey. It's good to be home and be with the boys, but I sure miss being there with you."

The New Year came and January rushed by. Even though it was the rainy season in the Pacific Northwest, four lots sold. And George had three contracts to build houses. Ken and Bob Jones did most of the showing and selling of property, and keeping business moving.

February came and Valentine's Day turned out to be a downer for Christy and Dan. Grace wound up spending a lot of time off her feet. Steve hired a RN to be in their house while he was at work. Christy debated disappearing back to Auckland but she kept close to Vashon Island.

Luds contacted the answering service at Steve's law office and left Dan an urgent message. When Dan got back to him, Luds hadn't been able to get in touch with Pog. The lapse of time had everyone concerned. Dan made the decision to fly to Mexico City, take the short flight to Guadalajara, rent a car, and drive to Chapala.

He arrived at the orphanage the first week in March, near dusk. Margaret, the person in charge, or as she preferred to be called, Peggy, was cute, charming, and charismatic.

"Well, Peggy, I'm a good friend of this guy." Dan showed her a picture of Pogy. He slipped up and called him Pogy.

"Oh, you mean, Roger Simpson."

"Yes. We're close and I haven't heard from him in quite a while. I was in the area and thought I'd stop by."

"That's what the other guy said."

Dan said, "What other guy?"

Peggy frowned and described Bedford.

Dan gathered all the information he could. It seemed Bedford had been there three or four days earlier.

The cool evening breeze off the lake stirred Peggy's blond hair. She took a loose strand and pushed it behind her ear. The sun had fallen below the mountain tops to the west and a brilliant pink sunset illuminated the courtyard. The kids were getting ready for dinner and the noise was heart-warming to Dan. But the Bedford news worried him sick.

Peggy took his arm and led him into the hacienda. "Well, there's a wonderful opportunity in the San Francisco area that Roger went to investigate." Peggy bubbled with excitement.

"Oh?" That was all Dan could say trying not to be concerned about Bedford knowing Pogy's whereabouts.

"There's an opportunity to buy a vineyard north of San Francisco, outside a town called Napa. The land is all in vines, and it would give Roger and me the opportunity to have fifteen families immigrate there to work the vineyard."

"Wow. How big a vineyard are you talking about?"

"Nearly one-hundred and sixty acres and the asking price is just under five-thousand an acre. It has two houses and a large bunk house."

"And Po, I mean Roger's looking at this for you all?"

"No, he's looking to buy it and let families from around Chapala move to Napa to take care of it. Isn't it just wonderful?" Her vivacious smile filled her face.

"Well, that sounds wonderful. Is there an address? I need to go to L. A. and I could catch a flight up to San Francisco to surprise him," Dan said, planning to go warn Pog.

He got the address for the winery, and the real estate agent's name and phone number. Dan dreaded crossing the border and re-entering the U. S. The next morning, he boarded a plane out of Guadalajara to San Francisco, non-stop.

When Dan landed in San Francisco, he let his anxiety get to him. A few months before, he'd been incarcerated only a few miles from where he was renting an automobile. He kept a sharp lookout everywhere.

Dan drove to the property in Napa arriving mid-afternoon. No Pogany. The Real Estate agent had a local phone number for him at a nearby Holiday Inn.

Dan knocked on the door. "Who is it?" Pog said through the door.

"Pog, it's the tooth fairy. Open up, you over-grown baboon."

Pog yanked open the door and stood with his mouth agape. "Well, I'll be damned. Get your ass out of the hall you over grown hippie." Pog grabbed Dan's arm and escorted him into the room.

"Dan, your attire would put Sonny Bono to shame." Pog said hugging Dan.

Dan said, "Do you know you've got everyone of us nervous as hell about what's going on with you? Can't you remember to call and check in?"

"For one, phones in Lake Chapala are non-existent, and I called and checked in with Luds when I arrived two days ago."

"Well, as you can see, they sent me to make sure you're okay. Bedford was at the Chapala orphanage four days ago. Buddy, he's here. And you need to disappear. Close the deal, or whatever, but you need to get the truck outta Dodge."

Pog told Dan he was going back the day after tomorrow. And he'd lay low at the orphanage.

Dan told him he had a red eye leaving at eleven out of SFO going back to New Zealand.

Their conversation turned operational. They talked at length about Bedford, the orphanage, and the vineyard.

"How'd he find out?" Pog began with an infinite list of questions. Dan told him about his conversation with Peggy.

"Well, Dan, I gotta tell you the Chapala orphanage is a life changer, but this vineyard has me really excited."

Pog couldn't quit talking about the vineyard. He told Dan the deal was a true steal, a bargain extraordinaire at a great price. He'd already signed the preliminary papers. The Mexican families would be green carded, legal, and all upstanding people. Their work ethic impressed him, which was the deciding factor for him. He wanted to funnel the majority of the proceeds to Peggy and the orphanage.

"Hey, Buddy, she's kind of cute, you know," Dan said.

"Yes, Peggy's the first one in a long time who doesn't want something like money out of me. And she likes me."

Pog told Dan he thought she was honest among other things. He hinted to Dan that they could be getting serious. Pog smiled. "I've bought an engagement ring."

Dan was elated.

Peggy knew the woman selling the property so Pog got a really good deal on it.

"The woman who owns the winery survived a car accident, but her husband died. She can't manage the place by herself anymore. She just wants out. I could've priced it down but I didn't want to. She liked the idea of financing part of it."

"That sounds cool," Dan said.

"She'll have a monthly cash flow giving her some extra money each month."

"I'm impressed with the whole deal. Man, I wish you could see the place we've got in New Zealand. Roadhawg and Jack are there as I speak."

They continued to catch up over dinner. The sun was setting as they walked to Dan's car. Dan noticed a car approaching them, then swerve across the center line in their direction. A sawed-off shotgun hung out the driver's window. He yanked Pog and spun him around as they fell to the sidewalk, Dan's back facing the shotgun. The blast sounded like all hell had broken loose. Dan felt buckshot hit his shoulder.

"Holy shit, Dan, are you okay?"

Dan rolled over and grabbed Pog as he got up and ran for cover. "I'm fine, but we've got to get out of here. Move it." They sprinted around the next corner and hurried to Dan's rental car.

Pog drove, but he could see the wound. "Dan, you're bleeding. We've got to get you some medical help."

"No, let's get to a drug store and get some bandages. It's only my shoulder." Dan winced as he tried to look at the bleeding.

Pog stopped and bought tweezers, scissors, bandages, gauze, rubbing alcohol, and a new ointment for scrapes and burns.

After they got to Pog's motel room, he dug the buckshot out of Dan's shoulder with the tweezers and flooded the wound with alcohol. The bleeding stopped.

"Dan, you're going to need some penicillin."

"It'll have to wait until I get back to my ranch," Dan said as he put on one of Pog's hippy-looking shirts.

Pog cleaned up the mess, put it in a paper bag to throw away, and walked with Dan to his car.

"Are you sure you need to go?"

"Absolutely. I'll be fine, but I need to get the hell out of here. And so do you. Hey, chicken lips, thanks for the patch job."

Dan dropped off the rental, called Christy from the airport and brought her up to date. He thought it'd be best to tell her about Bedford shooting at him when he got back to New Zealand. He asked her to call Luds and tell him Pog was okay.

His next call was to Steve. Dan told him what happened and that he was okay. He thought the information about the shooting coming from Steve would be easier for everyone to hear, rather from him. He wanted Steve to tell Christy and everyone to be extra observant.

Even though it was late in the evening, Dan was extra

observant in the San Francisco airport. It seemed like there were a thousand eyes looking at him as he boarded the flight to Hawaii, but once in the air, he was able to relax.

Even on the layover in Honolulu, it was still the USA. The military presence on the island made him nervous every time he saw a Marine in uniform waiting for a flight. He checked out the back of his shirt in the men's room at the airport. No bleeding had come through Pog's patch job. Then he left for his departure gate. But before departing for New Zealand, Dan needed to check in with Jack or Roadhawg at the ranch. He was almost to the phone booth in the airport when a sergeant in uniform stopped him. "Excuse me, sir."

"Yes," Dan said. Oh, shit. It's Ted Jones.

"You weren't ever in the Marine Corps, were you?" He was, in fact, one of their old crew chiefs from Vietnam.

No, no, no. Ted recognizes me. "No, I wasn't ever in the service." Dan blinked and avoided eye contact.

"Well, you look like a pilot I used to know." Ted wouldn't let it go. He kept talking. He was stationed at Kaneohe, and was on his way home. Ted told Dan he was getting out of the Marine Corps looking for a job, no less. And of all places, he was going back home to the Seattle area.

Dan wrote down the phone number for George. "I've got a friend there. What a co-incidence. They only hire veterans. Tell him Christy referred you. She's my wife and she'll explain it all. Hey, they're calling my flight to Tokyo. Nice meeting you, Ted. Thank you for your service." Dan turned and hurried down the corridor.

Shit, I can't believe I got made even wearing my Poncho Villa mustache. And I've been shot to boot.

His shoulder throbbed as he stepped into a phone booth.

CHAPTER FORTY-NINE

Dan listened as the phone rang. Jack answered.

"Hey, man," Jack didn't want to use Dan's name. "We've got some bad news. Ludwig called, and someone put a bomb aboard one of their boats."

"Is he okay?"

"It's Diane. She's in intensive care." Jack, shaken up, continued after a moment. "She's not expected to make it through the night. And I'm leaving in less than three hours to fly back there and be with John."

"An explosion? It's gotta be Bedford and his buddy Peterson." Dan choked up. "Now they've gone to explosives."

"I can't be a hundred percent sure," Jack said. "Everything's happening so fast, but I'm convinced it was Bedford."

"I'm convinced it's that Peterson guy." Dan went on to tell him about his trip to see Pog and the shotgun deal.

Dan's wound had stopped bleeding, but Dan felt heat and he couldn't move his right arm because it was no doubt infected.

When they got off the phone, Jack made plans to have Dan picked up when he arrived in Auckland. As soon as Dan arrived Roadhawg would take him to a local doctor's office. Jack had concocted a story to cover why Dan was so late in getting his wound attended to when they went to a doctor there in New Zealand.

The story would be they were out hunting pheasants, and Dan was in front of the other two and caught some pellets by accident. They thought they'd cleaned the wound, but now they were worried.

Dan's airplane landed on time. Roadhawg broke the tragic news that Diane had passed away. They rode in silence as Roadhawg took him straight to the doctor's office. When the doctor looked at it, the infection hadn't materialized as much as Dan had feared. The doctor dressed the wound, and laughed.

"Strangely enough, you're not the first one who's ever been shot by one of his mates." The Doctor told them about a couple of previous accidents he'd cared for.

As they were leaving, Dan said, "That does it. Bedford and his buddy have signed their death warrants."

"I knew we should've killed him that morning in Pleasanton," Roadhawg said.

Dan looked and couldn't remember if he'd ever seen Roadhawg that serious. "Has Jack arrived in Saint Thomas?"

"Yes. I talked with him shortly after he arrived."

They began forming plans to get Bedford and Peterson. When they got back to the ranch, Ellen said Christy had called and left word for Dan to call her.

The tension from the current situations dominated the conversation when Dan called.

Christy sobbed. "John shouldn't be alone right now."

"Honey, I think you outta go somewhere safe, take the boys and disappear. Let Dennis and Georgia go and be with

Luds. We'll try and get together with him real soon. But, right now, I worry about you and the boys' safety."

"Honey, I've talked to Dennis and Georgia. They thought it'd be best if the boys and I came to be with you in New Zealand. The consensus is it'd be safer there."

After a couple of moments, Dan said okay. Vashon Island was isolated, but that had disadvantages, also. They agreed to come to New Zealand in about a week or so with the boys. During the entire conversation Dan thought it'd be best not to mention to Christy that Bedford had shot him.

Six days later, John Ludwig and Dennis arrived. Georgia went back to Oklahoma to take their boys and disappear to her parent's farm. Everyone at the ranch was in a keep-out-of-sight mode.

In Seattle, the secretary in Steve Mitchell's office buzzed him. "Mr. Mitchell?"

"Yes," Steve said as he looked over some court documents.

"There's a Mr. Tom Earp to see you. He doesn't have an appointment and would like a minute. He says it's extremely important."

Steve shuffled the papers into a neat stack. "Extremely? My, my. I'll be there in a minute."

A tall, well-dressed gentleman with a briefcase stood waiting. When Steve approached, he noticed the man's wry smile and clear blue eyes. Lot's of salt and pepper. Tall and in good shape, he was no doubt in his mid-forties.

"Mr. Earp, is it?" Steve extended his hand and cocked his head to the side. He broke into one of his mischievous smiles.

"Yes, sir. And you must be Mister Mitchell."

Steve nodded and took his time. "I have a couple of minutes, if you'd like to step into my office."

"I think that'd be best," Mr. Earp said.

Steve showed him to a chair. Once seated, Mr. Earp began. "You represent one Daniel Burton, and I have some very important information for him."

"Well, first could you tell me who you represent, and then we'll go from there." Steve leaned back in his leather chair, not taking his eyes off the stranger.

"First, some background. I was Daniel Burton's, Jack Higgins', Joseph Hegidio's, Dennis Lee's, John Ludwig's, and Charles Pogany's commanding officer in Vietnam back in 1968. I've got an offer for them. I'd like you to relay it for me."

"I represent Mr. Burton, but I haven't been in contact with him for quite some time. I'm sure you know his current situation."

"I'm very aware of all of their current situations," Tom Earp said.

"That's nice. You mentioned some sort of an offer?"

"Yes, that's correct. It is similar to Special Agent Toscas' offer."

Steve leaned forward with his arms on his desk. "Really? For one, how do you know about Special Agent Toscas' offer? Second, just who do you work for, and what guarantees can you offer? It seems the government changes their offers whenever it suits them." Steve continued his intense stare of Tom Earp.

"First thing's first. I work directly with the President. I know about the offer. In my briefcase are not three, but six Presidential pardons. One for each of the Marines I mentioned."

"Really?"

"Would you like to see them?"

"That, I would. Yes, Mister Earp."

"I'd really rather go by Tom or Colonel Earp."

"Okay, Colonel Earp. If, you have the pardons, may I see them?"

Colonel Earp handed them to Steve, who inspected each of them, even holding them up to the light to verify the watermarks and seal. He laid them back on his desk.

Colonel Earp explained the deal—return the money, and no further consequences. But, he wanted the boys to come work for him again or as consultants with him, as he put it. Colonel Earp only wanted to talk with them about the job descriptions.

"How do I know, and how do they know just who you really are?" Steve said.

"Ask Dan what nickname I gave Jack in country. It was Big Fella. And I told him it was from the movie Little Big Man. Calling him Little Big Man, I thought, would most likely embarrass him. I told him as much. That was between Jack and me. Tell him that, and the boys will know it's Wyatt who's making the offer."

Steve blinked and smiled. "Who's Wyatt?"

"My call sign, nickname, or whatever. Get it? Wyatt...Earp. I was their commanding officer."

Steve nodded his head and grinned. "Yes, if you say so. I can't promise to get a hold of them, legally, you know."

"That, I know. Legally." Colonel Earp grinned. "I'd like it if you could arrange to meet with them and go over the offer. But the pardons are for real. Whether they accept my proposal or not, the pardons stand."

"I see you have executive pull, Colonel Earp. Or should I call you Wyatt, Or Tom?"

"I'm okay with whatever makes you comfortable."

"If Colonel Earp is okay, I go by Steve."

They worked out some of the logistics and made plans to meet the next day for lunch. Steve made sure Colonel Earp didn't know Steve knew how to contact the boys. The Colonel told Steve about John Ludwig losing Diane. It was important for Steve to warn the boys ASAP, because Colonel Earp feared they might be in danger and Steve figured Colonel Earp knew more than he was letting on.

But Steve didn't tell him they already knew of Diane's death. Steve still didn't want to trust Colonel Earp one hundred percent until Dan confirmed everything Colonel. Earp had told him.

After Colonel Earp left, Steve cancelled his next appointment. He called Christy and told her everything he'd just learned. She said she'd call New Zealand as soon as Steve hung up.

Dan called Steve and verified everything about Colonel Earp. When he got off the phone, Jack, Roadhawg, Luds and Dennis sat waiting for Dan to relate the news.

"Well, I'll be damned," Jack said.

Dennis agreed. "It's gotta be Colonel Earp."

They made plans to give Steve's office a call the next morning at ten o'clock Seattle time. They stayed up most of the night. To Dan, it felt like old times back in '68 before they lost Herb and Toddy, but the idea they and their families were being targeted kept all of them focused. Revenge dominated their conversation and the atmosphere. Being pardoned seemed to take the fore front. It seemed too good to be true.

Steve began speaking while the boys gathered around the phone. "Dan, I'm holding a legitimate Presidential pardon for you and the rest of the guys. You all can come home anytime you want."

"You've got to be kidding, Steve. For real? It's over?"

"I've still got the funds in the office account, and I assume you are all willing, at the appropriate time, to have me turn them over to the appropriate government folks?"

"Yes, that was our intent months ago, if you're certain the legal quagmire is over?" Dan nodded as the others listened and agreed. "Then transfer the money or whatever."

"Okay, I'll take care of that. And, Dan it's over."

The celebration was relative subdued considering John Ludwig's loss. Steve told them Colonel Earp wanted to meet with them as soon as possible.

"Where does the Colonel want to meet, and when?" Dan said.

"Where ever you all would like. He'll set it up and he emphasized the sooner the better."

They started making plans. Dan called Steve back who said he had to put Dan on hold, because he had Colonel Earp on another line. The jist of the three-way conversation was that Colonel Earp suggested they meet in Hawaii. Where upon Dan and the guys wondered if Colonel Earp knew where they were. Somehow it seemed very convenient to meet in Hawaii—in the middle. Dan told Steve Hawaii would be okay. Steve put them on hold, and came back.

"Dan, are you still there?"

"Yes."

"Can you be at a place Colonel Earp told me you all knew. It's called Bellows, and he suggested, get this, tomorrow."

"I guess, but hold on a sec." Dan checked with everyone. They all nodded their heads in agreement. "Yes, we'll try to be there."

"This guy seems to be able to pull a lot of strings. He said he'd have individual accommodations for each of you starting tomorrow. Is that good for you all?"

"Yes," Dan said, "and Steve could you attend? We'd like you to be there if you can. We want to see the pardons. For my part, just keep mine in a safe place."

Steve had them hold while he talked with Colonel Earp. Then Steve spoke with Dan telling him, "This guy was amazing." Steve relayed that the plan was for Christy and the boys, and he and even Grace to fly to Hawaii on a military aircraft with Colonel Earp. Then Steve said, "A C-141 is waiting at the Auckland airport to take the five of them to Hawaii.

Dan was shocked. "Okay, Steve, that sounds good, but hold on. The guys are all excited and want to say something." Dan held the phone while the others agreed to have Steve keep their original pardons, too, and bring copies for them to Hawaii. Dan didn't want to ask, but wondered about the C-141 pre-positioned in Auckland. Steve ended by saying they were free to call anyone they wanted, anytime they wanted.

After the phone call ended, the guy's conversation centered around what did Colonel Earp want from them? They also wondered how he knew where they were, and that they'd be agreeable to meet in Hawaii. That worried all of them. But, the truth of the matter was, they trusted Colonel Earp to hell and back. If Wyatt said, "Frog," they'd ask how far.

CHAPTER FIFTY

The excitement and disbelief continued well into the next evening for the gang down under. Back in the Seattle area, Christy, Grace, Steve, and the boys celebrated, but at an undisclosed location. The physical threat was for real, and they took it serious.

"Mom, are you sure you're okay to travel?" Christy said.

"Honey, a free trip to Hawaii?"

Steve had already introduced Grace to Tom Earp. "Are you kidding? And Tom said the aircraft has beds if we needed them on the flight. This is too much."

The undisclosed location was McChord Air Force Base just south of Tacoma. They spent the night secure in the general's visiting quarters on the base. Guards were posted outside their suites. Steve wanted to clarify some issues with the pardons, so he spent some time in Tom Earp's suite.

Their C-141 departed for Hickam Air Force Base in Hawaii early the next morning. Allen and Jason couldn't believe they got to sit in the cockpit with the pilots. Christy kept thinking it was too good to be true, but in fact, Steve assured her it was all on the up and up. At last, they could get on with their lives. That is, after Bedford and his buddy were taken care of. Christy was fine with what ever taking care of him might turn out to be.

Several hours earlier, the New Zealand contingency departed for Hickam. The mood was somber because Diane wasn't there. Dan could feel Ludwig's level of sorrow and need for revenge. Ludwig's loss had turned to anger and he couldn't fully engage in the festive atmosphere.

Dan smiled at Roadhawg. He carried three bottles of booze aboard. He and Naomi were celebrating. Roadhawg's first question to the fight-suited flight attendant revolved around mixers and ice.

The plane took on a couple of standby military family passengers after the aircraft commander asked if that would be okay with them.

Roadhawg answered for the group. "We don't mind. That is, if they don't mind a little liquid libation enroute."

The flight plan for them from Auckland was direct to Hickam. The flight crew marveled at the party atmosphere. When they landed at Hickam, government sedans waited for them.

"Damn, I can't believe the VIP treatment," Jack said.

Dan asked one of the sedan drivers after they landed, "How long are you all going to provide transportation for us?"

The airman said, "Our orders are for as long as you need transportation."

"Do you know where Bellows Air Force Recreation Station is?" Jack said.

"Yes, sir," another driver said, holding the door open for Ellen.

"Jack, I know what you all did, but I never thought it'd get you this kind of attention." Ellen giggled.

The convoy of sedans departed Hickam after the luggage was loaded. In the lead sedan, Ellen, Georgia, and

Naomi sat in the back seat. In the second sedan, Luds rode up front with Dan on the bench seat, and Dennis, Jack, and Roadhawg sat in the back.

When they arrived at Bellows, the gate guard waved them through with no ID checks. Dan looked back at Dennis as Luds spun around. "That's a first," Dan said. And then to the driver, he said, "I assume that we were expected?"

"Yes, sir."

Dan asked his name. The driver gave him name and rank.

"Come on, lighten up," Jack said. "What's your momma call you?"

The driver glanced at Jack in the rearview mirror. Jack's grin seemed to relieve the driver, "I go by Larry, sir."

"Okay, Larry, if you're attached to drive for us, here's the deal. That clown in the front seat next to you goes by Dan and the other one by Luds. I'm Jack, and my sidekick back here in the middle goes by Dennis, and Roadhawg's on the far side. Can the "sir" stuff. Okay?"

"Yes, sir."

"No, an okay, Larry, is all we wanted." Dan saw Larry check the rearview mirror again.

"Okay...Dan," Larry said.

The biggest surprise wasn't driving past the regular places where they stayed before, even when they passed the senior officer's quarters, but when they parked in front of the VIP/General's units.

Dan was in awe as Allen and Jason shot out of the front door, followed by Steve and Grace. Christy strolled out holding a tray of Mai Tai's followed by Colonel Earp with a huge tray of hors d'oeuvres.

Allen and Jason almost tackled Dan as he scooted out of the front seat. Colonel Earp placed the tray on a table and went to greet the newly pardoned gang.

After a half-hour or so, Steve suggested the adults

adjourn to Colonel Earp's suite. Grace took the boys ten yards or so down to the beach to play.

Colonel Earp began by explaining Presidential pardons were signed by President Nixon in Colonel Earp's presence, and were delivered by the Justice Department to the Oval Office.

He fielded all sorts of questions from the wives and the guys. Steve also added his legal opinions. It seemed obvious Colonel Earp wanted to talk to the guys alone. Almost on key, Colonel Earp nodded to Steve. Steve patted his heart and said, "Ladies, how about we go join my bride and the boys on the beach?" He smiled the typical Steve smirk, with his head leaning a bit to one side and his arm extended toward the door.

The conversation began with their disbelief in getting to see their favorite commanding officer.

"Well, Colonel, what's up?" Dan started the questioning.

"Okay, men. Here's the deal. I answer only to the President and then to the Secretary of Defense. We've been commissioned to form a combined force of active and former military men to work on, ah-h-h, this must stay with us, whether or not you chose to participate. Understood? Have I got your word on that?"

"Yes, sir," they answered in unison.

"We'll be doing some special military ops that will never be known either in the public eye or anywhere else. Borders will be crossed, and yes, actions taken against those who pose threats to the United States. There will be times of engagement and then months of inactivity. You'll be on call, so to speak."

"Will we be engaging unfriendly armed forces?" Jack said.

"Sometimes, yes," Colonel Earp said.

"Will we be used only as helicopter pilots," Dan asked.

"Yes and no. Some of the planning will be coordinated with you. You'll also be communicating with pilots during some of the operations."

"So, Luds and I will be filling that function?" Dennis said as he turned toward Luds who nodded his head.

Roadhawg looked at Colonel Earp. "What will our status be as far as rank, or whatever?"

"You'll all start out with GS ratings equal to Lieutenant Colonels. You'll also be paid full time, even when you're home and not on assignment. Regardless, you'll receive full benefits like retirement, medical, etcetera."

"How about commitment? What if we change our minds?"

Colonel Earp explained in detail that they could leave anytime, anywhere. And that he would be their reporting senior. In other words, if they needed horsepower, so to speak, Colonel Earp was next in line to the Commander-in-Chief.

"So, if we have a conflict with any active duty types, you'll intercede?" Dennis said.

"Exactly. Did you notice how flawlessly the evolution to getting you boys here went?" Colonel Earp glanced at each of them.

He related to them how the Dan's extraction from Pleasanton caught some positive attention from the Joint Chiefs of Staff. Colonel Earp quoted them. "We didn't. No, they didn't think you guys could pull it off that well."

"Well, Colonel, as you know…"

Colonel Earp interrupted Jack. "Men, I'd prefer to go by Tom, Wyatt or something like that."

"Sir, with all due respect, you'll always be Skipper or Skip or Sir to us." Jack said.

"Okay, I'm fine with that. And boys, I'll always be on first name basis with you. But Jack, go ahead before I interrupted you."

"Anyway, Skip, I promised Bedford I'd kill him if he ever came near us again. And he just shot Dan. And his buddy, Peterson, most likely blew up one of Lud's boats and killed Diane." Jack looked at Luds.

"Well, here's what I can offer on that. We'd rather see the two of them in Leavenworth for life. Stripped of all retirement, military standing, and whatever else we can do."

"But, I want to kill 'em," Luds said.

"Can't blame you, but could you work with me on putting them away for life?"

Luds said, "If they're put away without the possibility of ever, and I mean ever getting out...maybe. But if, they put up a fight, I want to pull the trigger."

"Is that fair enough with all of you boys?" Colonel Earp looked from one to the other. Each one nodded his head in agreement.

"So, we work on standby, planning operations and actually participating in some of them?" Roadhawg said.

Colonel Earp smiled. "And draw full pay and allowances. Starting yesterday, if you boys agree."

"For my part, I'm in if they're in," Luds said.

They all agreed. Colonel Earp said he had the paperwork for them to sign whenever they were ready.

"Will we always get this type of red carpet treatment?" Dan grinned.

"As long as I'm in charge."

"Well, when you're not, I'm out," Jack said.

"That goes double for me," Dan said. The rest followed suit.

"Now, boys, what do you need to track down Bedford?"

In ten minutes they'd given Colonel Earp a list of everything they could think of that they needed. Dan noticed the Colonel smiling as he went over their list.

"Bedford," Dan said, "this time your ass is grass."

The hunt had begun.

ABOUT THE AUTHOR

P.R. Steele flew as a pilot in the CH 53 helicopter for the
Marine Corps in Vietnam, and also the money run on
Okinawa. He is retired from the military with 27 years of
service on active duty and the reserves. He lives in
Northern California and enjoys tinkering on his old cars,
writing, avoiding work and honey dos.